Quick as a Cricket

by Audrey Wood

illustrated by Don Wood

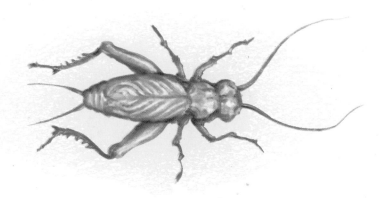

Published by Child's Play (International) Ltd

ISBN 0-85953-151-1 (h/c) ISBN 0-85953-306-9 (s/c) ISBN 0-85953-331-X (big book)
© M Twinn 1982 This impression 2006/3 Printed in China
Library of Congress Catalogue Number 90-46413 www.childs-play.com
A cotalogue reference for this book is available from the British Library

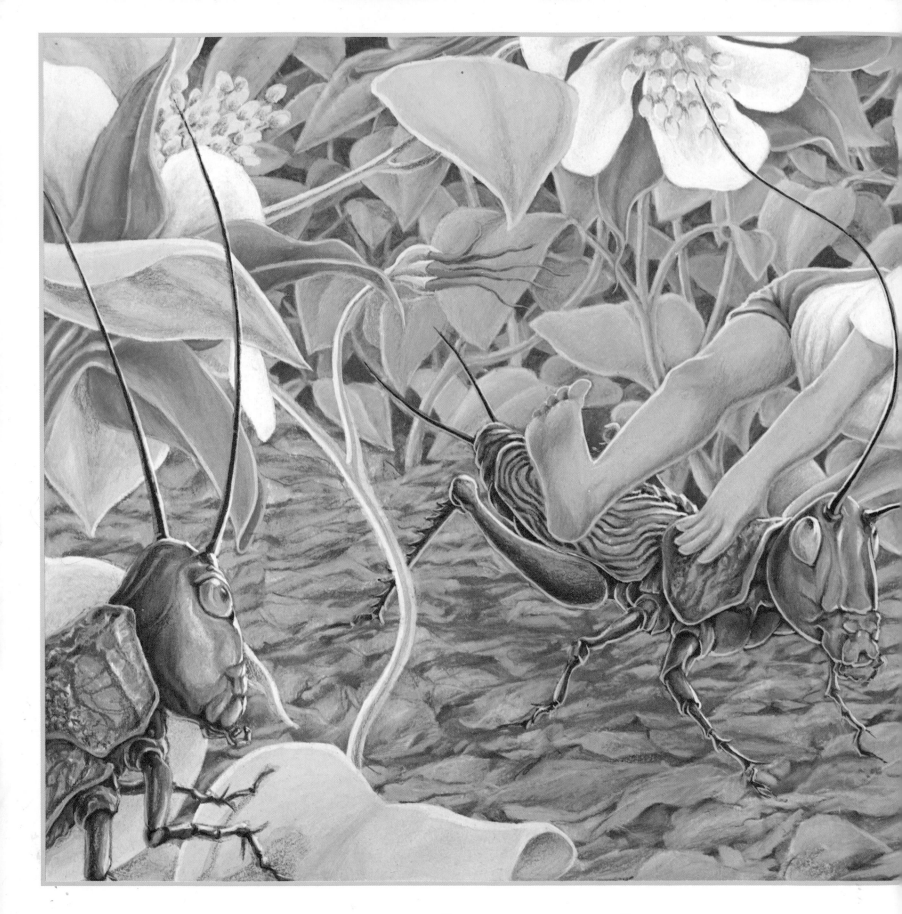

I'm as quick as a cricket,

I'm as slow as a snail,

I'm as small as an ant,

I'm as large as a whale.

I'm as sad as a basset,

I'm as happy as a lark,

I'm as nice as a bunny,

I'm as mean as a shark.

I'm as cold as a toad,

I'm as hot as a fox,

I'm as weak as a kitten,

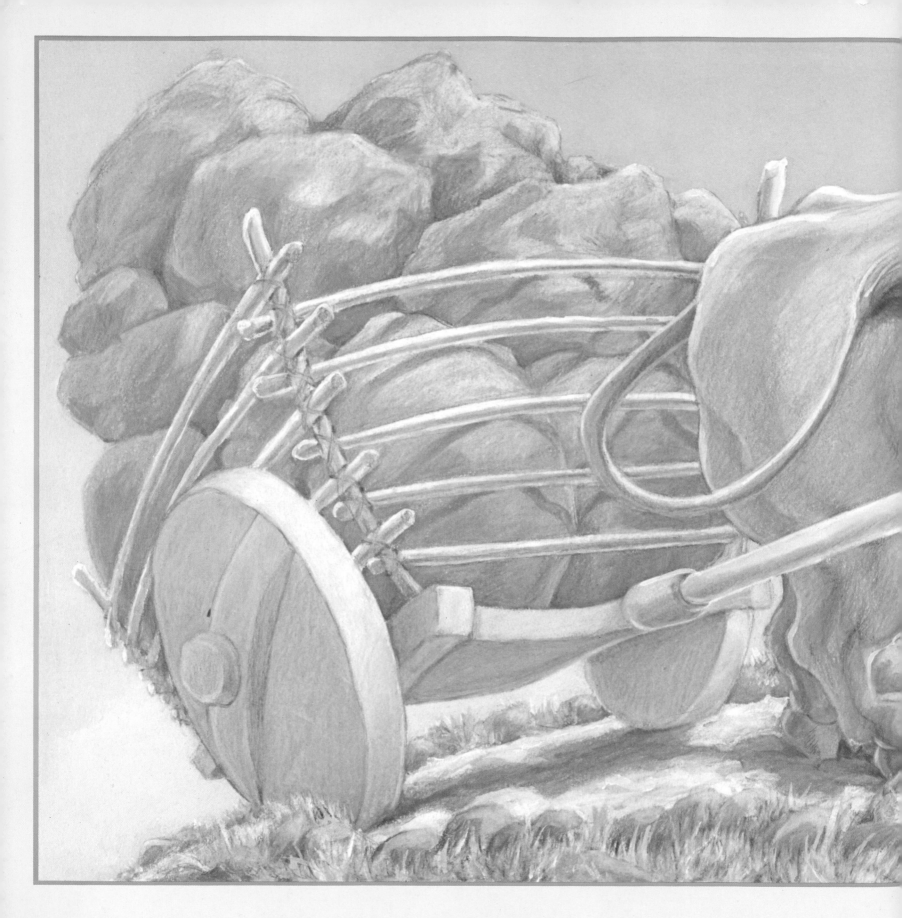

I'm as strong as an ox.

I'm as loud as a lion,

I'm as quiet as a clam,

I'm as tough as a rhino,

I'm as gentle as a lamb.

I'm as brave as a tiger,

I'm as shy as a shrimp,

I'm as tame as a poodle,

I'm as wild as a chimp.

I'm as lazy as a lizard,

I'm as busy as a bee,

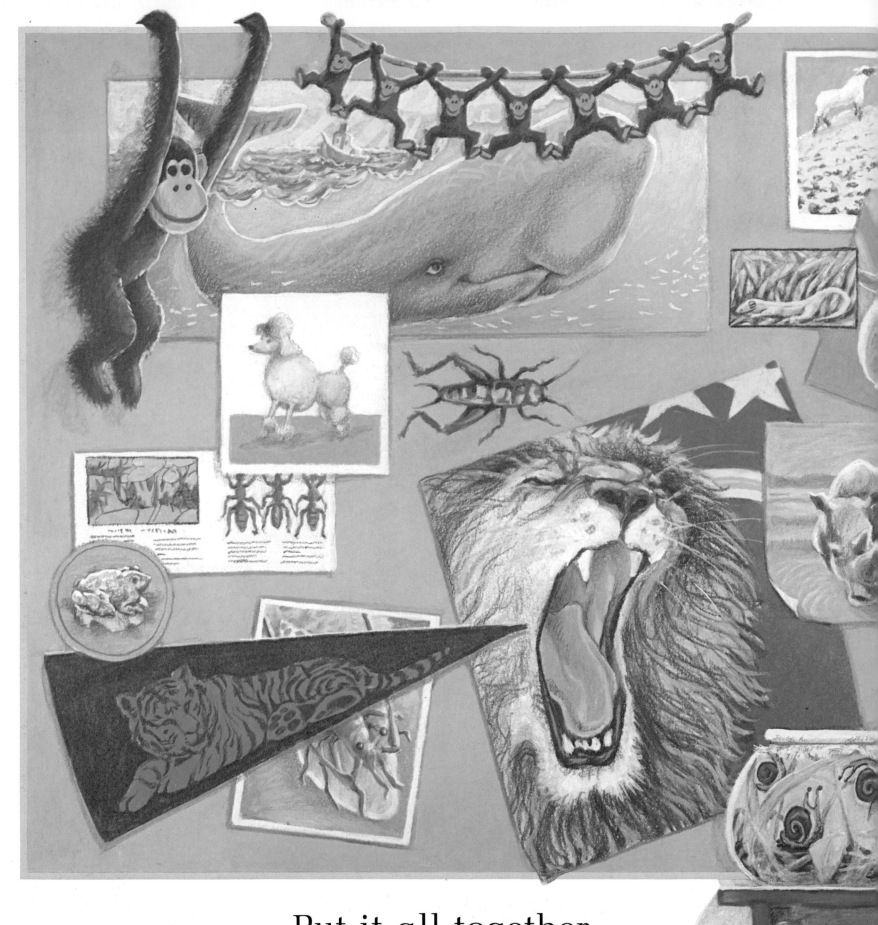

Put it all together,

And you've got ME!

How to
Find a Job on
LinkedIn
Facebook
MySpace
Twitter

AND OTHER SOCIAL NETWORKS

How to Find a Job on
LinkedIn
Facebook
MySpace
Twitter

AND OTHER SOCIAL NETWORKS

Brad and Debra Schepp

New York   Chicago   San Francisco   Lisbon
London   Madrid   Mexico City   Milan   New Delhi
San Juan   Seoul   Singapore   Sydney   Toronto

2 3 4 5 6 7 8 9 0   WFR/WFR   0 1 0

ISBN: 978-0-07-162133-5
MHID: 0-07-162133-4

Readers should know that online businesses have risks. Readers who participate in online business do so at their own risk. The author and publisher of this book cannot guarantee financial success and therefore disclaim any liability, loss, or risk sustained, either directly or indirectly, as a result of using the information given in this book.

McGraw-Hill books are available at special quantity discounts to use as premiums and sales promotions, or for use in corporate training programs. To contact a representative please e-mail us at bulksales@mcgraw-hill.com.

This book is printed on acid-free paper.

To my coauthor, husband, and best friend, Brad.

You've always been the center of my every network.

DS

To Deb, what you said. You've always been better with words.

BS

CONTENTS

ACKNOWLEDGMENTS

I t's always a challenge to thank every person who has helped us turn a manuscript into a book. Under any circumstance, that represents a pretty big crowd. Open that up to the 35 million people currently on LinkedIn, and Hercules would begin to get nervous. Beyond that, the entire world of social networking could conceivably deserve a nod because the number of people who were willing to connect with us and share their experiences includes folks from half a dozen other social networks in addition to LinkedIn. All we can do is our best and hope that anyone who doesn't see his or her name here will understand that at some point "thank-yous" have to stop and the book begin. We appreciate every e-mail you sent, every question you answered, and every bit of wisdom you provided to us. So here goes; our best shot.

First of all, we'd like to thank our agent, Bill Gladstone, of Waterside, Inc., for once again being a true advocate for our work. You've never let us down, Bill, and we appreciate that. Knox Huston at McGraw-Hill has rightfully earned a place among our favored editors. He's smart, savvy, kind, and agreeable. What else is there for writers to ask for? On the McGraw-Hill production team, we'd also like to thank Daina Penikas, Jim Madru, and Penny Linskey. We hope our manuscript wasn't a headache-producer!

So many people were kind enough to respond to our requests for information about how they used social networking sites: Dwight Robinson, Patty and Doug Gale, Sharon DeLay, Kristen Kouk, David Becker, Steven Burda, Virginia Backaitis, Elizabeth Garazelli, Dave Stevens, Scott Bradley, Laurier Tiernan, Rayanne Langdon, Kama Linden, Sarah Caron, Miriam Salpeter, Tracy Gosson, Lorne Epstein, Ben Thompson, Jason Alba, Megan Owen, Ruth-Ann Cooper, Eric Kiker, Simon Stapleton, Jocelyn Wang, Tim McMahan, Tracy Bagatelle-Black, Kenny Golde, Gary Dale, Kellie Schroeder, Robb Hecht, Dr. Scott Testa, Bob Wilson, Matt Batt, Jay Zipursky, Evo Terra, Kim Woodbridge, Susan Schwartz, Marina S. Martin, Gordon Whyte, John S. Rajeski, Leslie Carothers, Josh Chernin, Jeff Ragovin, Jacqueline Wolven,

Anne Pryor, Priss Benbow, Karen Jashinsky, Chuck Hester, Mike O'Neil, Pinny Cohen, Todd Herschberg, Terrence Seamon, Stephen Weinstein, Gary Unger, and Ralph Lagnado.

We tapped public relations and press representatives often, and they were always responsive to our requests and supportive of our research. Thanks go out to John McCrea (Plaxo), Athena von Oech (Ning), Michael Weiss (Robert Half International), Peter Shankman (and his invaluable "Help A Reporter Out" Web site), Jeremy Downs (whose Peek e-mail device made life so much easier every day), Yee Wah (Xing), and Andrew Lipsman (Comscore), and a big tip of the hat goes to Krista Canfield, the public relations manager at LinkedIn. This book simply would still be in the making were it not for your competencies at your jobs.

On a smaller scale, we'd like, as always, to thank our family, who listened to endless conversations about social networking. We can easily grant our kids and their significant others the discovery of this amazing phenomenon and thank them for first sharing it with us. We hope to have paid you back with a book that you can use as you launch your own careers, which are bound to dazzle us, as your achievements always have. So Ethan, Stephanie, Andrew, and Laurel, thanks for listening and sharing too! To relatives and friends far and near, we're now open to accepting invitations to dinner and weekend getaways, so please invite us again.

And last of all, a little thank you goes to Mollie and Max for warming our desks and protecting us from all terrors real and imagined. It was in the waning days of this project, in the dreary, gray, endless winter of economic bad news, that Mollie first alerted us to the return of spring's first robin. She'll never catch it, but strange as it may seem, just seeing it helped a lot!

INTRODUCTION

It was noon in Manhattan, circa 1980, and we were in one of those delis with heaping sandwiches named for Milton Berle, Jack Benny, or some other comedian, lots of colorful people and waiters all talking at once, and no elbow room. If you've ever seen a Woody Allen movie, you know just what we mean. Across from us was Uncle Nat, a much revered but little known relative who had "made it big" in Manhattan. He was there to help us start our careers.

Frankly, Uncle Nat scared the heck out of us. He was everything we were not. He was rich, successful, polished, and part of the exciting world of New York advertising. To us, as brand-new college graduates, this was a world that looked fantastic and impossible to fathom at the same time, certainly no relation to any life we'd yet experienced. No wonder we were scared! Uncle Nat could be our meal ticket into that world. A shortcut! We couldn't disappoint him.

That lunch did lead to an "information interview" with someone very much like Uncle Nat, another master of Manhattan. And that led to . . . nothing. You can understand. When the spotlight was on us, all we could say was, "Yes, we wanted our first job, and here is our résumé, and didn't we take all the right college courses? Isn't it clear how hard we worked and how smart we are?"

With the shadows of encounters like these still lingering, no wonder "networking" still intimidates us to this day! And thank goodness our kids will never have to go through that. And neither will you, thanks to social networking sites like LinkedIn.

Are you looking for a job or more work for your own business? If you're not now, chances are that you soon will be. These are scary economic times for anyone who needs that next paycheck, which includes almost all of us. And even when this deep recession of 2007 to "whoknowswhen?" passes, all of us who lived through it will carry the memories and feelings it engendered forever.

You've probably heard since you first starting looking for a job that the best way to find work is by "networking." You need to connect with others in a position to help you. That's good advice, but it freezes many people in their tracks. (You may have made it to Manhattan, as we did, but no further.) And what if you're too young to have developed much of a network? What if you've lost track of your coworkers? What if you're shy and picking up the phone intimidates you?

We understand. And for all these reasons, social networking sites finally make it possible for us all to do what we should have been doing all along—connecting with others, staying connected, sharing resources, and networking.

LinkedIn, Facebook, MySpace, Twitter, and Plaxo—they're all known as social networking sites. But LinkedIn is actually more about business networking than being social, and even those other sites can be host to what could be called "business." The point is that all these sites can be key tools that should be a part of every job search. And at least one or two of them should be part of your Internet routine, whether you're actively searching for work or not.

Absolutely, your top network should be LinkedIn, which we'll go on the record here as calling the most important tool for business communications since e-mail. We devote Part 1 of this book to that site, and by the time you reach the end, you'll know how to create a standout profile, connect with others, gain expertise through answering questions, and find work.

In Part 2 we show you around MySpace, Facebook, Twitter, and Plaxo and explain how they can help you to get a new job or more business. You'll find real examples of people who have done just that. We'll also describe less well-known sites such as Xing and Ryze. You may not yet have heard of these, but they are also valuable to anyone who wants to connect with the right people and land that new job or assignment, wherever it may be.

We will step you through creating an online profile that most effectively highlights your strengths and experience. Then we'll help you tailor it for each network you decide to join. Your MySpace profile should be different from your LinkedIn profile, even though it will include much of the same information. You simply don't have to start from scratch each time.

As for LinkedIn, once you join, you'll see that it's important to use the site often. As with all tools, there's a learning curve before you've really mastered them. Before too long, you'll be using the site's resources not just to find work but also to accomplish some of the tasks you face on the job, day in and day out.

To give you a head start, here are just a few tips for using social networking sites:

- Update your status often.

- Keep your information fresh and current.

- Connect to others.

- Comment on what you see.

- Use the medium: Post pictures, videos, music, whatever is appropriate to the site and your situation.

- Be respectful of others' time.

Before you give the clerk your cash or credit card for this book, you deserve to know a little about us and what makes us qualified to write such a book. We've written about technology, and specifically the Internet, for many years. It never stops amazing us, and that well of wonder we have hopefully shows in this book. At the same time, we've also written career books, so between our Internet and business book background, we're confident that we're well qualified to explain how to use social networking sites for business purposes.

What can you expect from this book? Well, what does a plumber expect from a wrench, an accountant from a calculator, or a writer from a computer? You can expect to come away from this book with the knowledge of how to use arguably the most important tools job hunters now have at their disposal: social networking sites. You will never have to hunt for work in the same way again. We think Uncle Nat probably would be proud of us after all.

How to
Find a Job on
LinkedIn
Facebook
MySpace
Twitter

AND OTHER SOCIAL NETWORKS

PART 1

Getting LinkedIn

CHAPTER 1

Putting the Work in Social Networking

As we write this book, the world has passed an amazing milestone, almost without recognition: There are now 1 billion global Internet users. Social networking is just the latest Internet phenomenon. At one point, the fact that your thoughts and information could be passed from person to person was the big step forward, but e-mail was easily adapted to, and most of us did so without much difficulty. Internet shopping was the next innovation to surmount. Once, only the brave ventured onto eBay and Amazon, and then only because they couldn't resist the temptation of good prices or rare collectibles. Most of us, at first, considered that a little too risky. Now a galaxy of safe and reliable Web shopping destinations has supplanted the original e-commerce models. Sure, you may still find a few holdouts who don't trust Internet shopping , but you're much more likely to talk to people who research, locate, and purchase all kinds of commodities on the Web. It's simply no big deal.

Social networking, however, is a little bit different. It began largely as a phenomenon of the young. In 2002, programmer Jonathan Abrams created a Web site where like-minded people could gather in virtual communities, exchange profiles, and greatly broaden their scope of friends. His site was called Friendster. A year later, MySpace sprang from Friendster, and within months, Facebook came along, too.

When Facebook was just starting out, it was strictly for college students. Those of us watching students pour hours into the site began to wonder what all the hype was about. If you were fortunate enough to share your life with members of this demographic group, you could see pretty quickly what kept them glued to the site. Here was a chance for newly minted high school graduates to go off to their separate college campuses but take along with them all their best friends from high school. Having written about online technology since the 1980s, this seemingly sudden blossoming of social networking comes as absolutely no surprise to us. Almost from the very moments people began to dial out from their computers over their telephone lines and log on to "online services" such as CompuServe, Prodigy, and America Online, they did so with, more than any other purpose, the hope of connecting with people sharing their thoughts, goals, and philosophies.

Once people began to understand the power of the Internet, they also began to understand the value of networking with people across time zones and without regard to geography. Consequently, it didn't take Facebook very long to branch out and invite parents and other grownups to join their social network (even if the students redoubled their efforts to bar them at the door!). But, with the phenomenon of social networking growing at dizzying rates, it was only to be expected that the grownups, the professionals, the people with so much work to do, ultimately would need their own place to network. Today, LinkedIn can serve as a combination Chamber of Commerce, where folks come together to enhance their professional connections, and office water cooler, where like-minded people swap advice and expertise. The difference is that you are no longer limited to networking just with the people who live within your sphere or belong to your own organizations. LinkedIn literally brings the whole professional world into your life and invites you to join.

WHAT EXACTLY IS LINKEDIN?

Simply put, LinkedIn (see Figure 1-1) is a professional's dream come true. It's also the Promised Land for job hunters. Short of calling it a magic job machine, which, of course, is only hype, LinkedIn is a professional social network that allows you to connect with millions of potential colleagues who

Home | What is LinkedIn? | Join Today | Sign In   Language

Over 35 million professionals use LinkedIn to exchange information, ideas and opportunities

Stay informed about your contacts and industry

Find the people & knowledge you need to achieve your goals

Control your professional identity online

Join LinkedIn Today

First Name:

Last Name:

Email:

[Continue]

Already on LinkedIn? Sign in.

Search for someone by name: First Name   Last Name   [Go]

People directory: A B C D E F G H I J K L M N O P Q R S T U V W X Y Z more

Company   **Customer Service** | About LinkedIn | Learning Center | Blog | Advertising | Press | Partners | Career

Tools   Overview | Outlook Toolbar | Browser Toolbar | JobsInsider | Developers | Polls

Products   LinkedIn Answers | LinkedIn Jobs | LinkedIn Updates | Company Directory

LinkedIn Corporation © 2009 | User Agreement | Privacy Policy | Copyright Policy

Use of this site is subject to express terms of use, which prohibit commercial use of this site. By continuing past this page, you agree to abide by these terms.

Figure 1-1: The main LinkedIn screen, which you'll see only until you set up an account.

come together to share their career expertise, their experience, and their passion for their work. There is no magic job-hunting machine. LinkedIn won't simply throw out the perfect job after you enter the right combination of data into the site. But LinkedIn will allow you to build a strong and vibrant network of professional connections that will allow you not only to job hunt more efficiently but also to enhance your job performance and career goals, no matter what phase of your career you happen to be working on.

Just out of school? LinkedIn can help you to find mentors, stay in touch with your favorite professors, and locate the hiring managers within your chosen career. Have you been in the workforce for a while? Well, LinkedIn will allow you to move throughout your career never losing touch with colleagues you respect and admire, no matter where your paths may diverge and cross. Throughout your career you can stay up to the minute with the latest developments in your industry. You'll use LinkedIn to find vendors, contractors, and maybe someday new hires for the business you currently dream of building.

LinkedIn: An Internet Phenomenon

Since its founding in 2003, LinkedIn has grown dramatically and changed forever the way professionals interact. Consider some statistics culled from the site:

- LinkedIn now has more than 35 million members from 200 countries.

- New members sign up to LinkedIn at the rate of *one per second*.

- Google employees have an average of 47 LinkedIn connections.

- Harvard Business School grads have an average of 58 connections.

- There are 5 million unique visitors to LinkedIn each month.

- Around 600,000 small-business owners are on LinkedIn

- Every one of the Fortune 500 has employees on LinkedIn; 499 have employees at the director level or above.

- The average LinkedIn user is 41 years old and earns more than $110,000 per year.

- LinkedIn members are 64 percent male and 36 percent female.

LinkedIn has become a must-have tool for ambitious professionals, whether they're currently looking for a job or not. In just a few years it's grown into the largest and strongest business network in the world.

Based in Mountain View, California, LinkedIn was spawned in 2002 in prototypical Silicon Valley fashion, from the garage of Reid Hoffman and co-founders Allen Blue, Jean-Luc Vaillant, Eric Ly, and Konstantin Guericke. The group formally launched LinkedIn in 2003 when they asked 300 of their most important business contacts to become part of the network they were building. Today, LinkedIn can safely boast that its 35 million members live all across the globe, and the service is available in English, Spanish, French, and German.

In terms of popularity and necessity, think of Facebook or MySpace, but for serious professionals, LinkedIn members are more interested in serious networking than in learning about the music their friends now like or who their old high school flames are hooking up with. LinkedIn is *the* way to recruit top business partners, get that dream job, find venture capital, recruit that corporate superstar, or find that college roommate from long ago whom you had given up ever finding again. Is your desk drawer cluttered with old business cards? Is your Rolodex gathering dust? Do you still spend way too much time hunting down old references or forging new contacts? LinkedIn is for you.

TIP

One of the driving forces behind the LinkedIn phenomenon is the concept of *pay it forward.* We heard this term itself and the idea behind it from countless active members of the LinkedIn community. In essence, it means that when you come to LinkedIn, be prepared to offer more than you ask for. You'll find countless ways to do this throughout the coming chapters, but it's important that you understand the philosophy before you even approach someone on the site.

The Inspiration behind LinkedIn

In the March 2009 issue of *Saturday Night Magazine,* LinkedIn cofounder Allen Blue explained how the concept for LinkedIn came about:

> When you're an entrepreneur, you do almost everything with the people you know. The founders of LinkedIn knew this first-hand, because we had all been doing it for years. With LinkedIn, we were looking to build a system that would let professionals not only stay in touch with friends, co-workers and college classmates, but also let them search their network for people that had expertise in certain areas. Every professional is more successful when they can get answers to tough work-related questions like "How do I begin a career in advertising?" or "What vendor should I be looking at to help me solve 'X' problem?" from people they know and trust.

Why You Must Use LinkedIn

Your professional life exists on the Internet, whether you realize it or not. Just do a Google search for your name, and you're likely to find all types of references you may or may not have known even existed. You can use

LinkedIn as the dashboard that drives your Internet presence. Carefully crafted (and don't worry, we'll explain all this in Chapter 2), your LinkedIn profile will be among their first search results whenever someone prowls Google to find out more about you. Since you create that LinkedIn profile, and you can link it to more of your own good work, you gain control over what people are most likely to learn about you from searching the Web.

LinkedIn should be one of your regular online homes, where you spend time every day or at least every week. Here are just some of the things you can accomplish through the site, all of which we'll explore in detail throughout this book:

Market your business

Gain free access to top experts

Do unique company research

Create and maintain your online Rolodex

Find professional peers you may have lost contact with

Control your online business identity

 ## Anne Pryor
Coaches Careers and Builds Wellness

Anne Pryor helps her clients as a career consultant and a coach for living an enriched life.

Anne Pryor describes herself as a "master connector." Anne has spent much of her career in coaching and consulting with others who seek to find their best career paths and lead fulfilling lives. One of her first jobs was at a theme park called Berry Fair. "I spent 10 years creating memories for families," she told us. "I sold packages to companies for their employees." Anne's personality leads her to seek out people and find ways to help them. In her current role as career consultant and life coach, she's found LinkedIn to be the perfect place for a people person such as herself to thrive. Based in Minnesota, Anne has found abundant work. "We lost 30,000 jobs last month, just in Minnesota alone," she told us. "LinkedIn is a tool I'm teaching now at our company to help people connect." Anne was kind enough to share a story with us of one young woman who came seeking help.

"Jennifer" was looking for a job as a marketing director for a law firm when she came to Anne. "Her LinkedIn profile was about 75 percent complete," Anne told us. "First, we enhanced her profile. Her profile URL wasn't completed with her name . . . , so we fixed that to ensure that she would be picked up in Google searches. We plugged in where she graduated from, and we uploaded her classmates from the small college she'd attended in Minnesota. We saw that some of her classmates were marketing directors in the law firms she wanted to connect with. She sent them invitations to connect through her network. They responded back, and she followed up with a phone call. She accomplished this in four minutes!"

Anne Pryor looks at LinkedIn a little more broadly than many of the other career professionals you'll meet throughout this book. "My mission in life is to promote wellness—mental, spiritual, physical, and emotional—and to be well, people need to be connected. As someone with a background and interest in wellness and spirituality, I know we are all connected. LinkedIn offers a way that we can connect here on this earth. It's more than just business. People appreciate it when they see the value in connecting with people they haven't seen in years," she continued. "Their eyes just light up! People go behind closed doors of the companies, and they close themselves off from people beyond those doors. I do my job by serving others and helping them succeed by reconnecting them with themselves and then connecting them with others so they can easily and effortlessly manifest their desires. LinkedIn is the tool where we can connect and not be isolated," she said. "I'm grateful for this invention."

JOB HUNTING THROUGH LINKEDIN

Although by now it's clear that LinkedIn is more than just a job-hunting portal, that doesn't mean the arrival of this site hasn't changed a great deal about what job hunting is like in the twenty-first century. Still, some aspects of the task will simply never be easy. Job hunting ranks right up there with a root canal for so many of us. Maybe that's because you never know what you're going to have to contend with. You probably have your own share of horror stories. They're hard to avoid. Whether you're after your very first professional job or looking to break out into the next level of your career, job hunting is just plain difficult. Sure, sometimes interviews do go swimmingly.

The planets align for you just so. You click perfectly with the manager interviewing you, you get an offer that suits you, and you're ready to start your new job. More common than those golden moments, though, are the times you're likely to realize before the interview is over that the job's a poor fit. Or, even more discouraging, you feel like you did a fabulous job only to have the interviewer disappear without a trace, not even a word. Then you know you'll have to pick yourself up, brush off your battered ego, and face the same ordeal another day.

It's been said that job hunting requires that you endure a steady stream of "Nos" before you can get to that one final "Yes." So your challenge is to turn on the flow of interviews that will let you swim past the "Nos" and achieve that golden "Yes," meaning that you've landed a job that suits you. We admit this has never been easy, even in the best of economies. But before you put this book down and go back to bed, let's remind you that you are much more empowered than job seekers have ever been before, even those people who were job hunting as recently as six years ago.

The job of finding a new job has always been better with loads of opportunities and companies to choose from and mentors to turn to. Just think how wonderful it would have been in years past to have been able to talk to people who actually work at the company you're interested in joining or to be able to search for others who have the exact job you're dreaming of and then follow their career histories to see how they got where they are today. What about joining a group that permits you to approach the very people who are working at the career you're building? What if this group allowed you to see what these successful people are reading, discussing, sharing, and working on? Too bad we've all had to wait this long to have LinkedIn! No matter what the current state of the economy is, you're so fortunate that LinkedIn is here for you to use right now.

Steven Burda
a LinkedIn Giant

Steven Burda is a LinkedIn LION. By that, we mean that he is a LinkedIn Open Networker, accepting invitations from anyone who wishes to connect with him. At the time we spoke, he already had 36,500 connections in his network. "I get 50 to 100 invitations every day," he said. He also happened to have more than 1,300 recommendations! At the age of 27, this MBA is busy on all levels. He works

LinkedIn LION Steven Burda has many tens of thousands of LinkedIn connections.

in the financial industry for a Fortune 50 company based in Philadelphia. He maintains his broad connections on LinkedIn, helping others to find good jobs and interesting opportunities through the site. It also happens that when we spoke, his son was just five days old!

Clearly, Steven brings the energy of youth to the world of social networking. He refers to himself as the "Mother Teresa of social networking." "I get a lot of personal satisfaction in helping people," he said. "A lot of people now contact me asking for people they can hire, or I hear from people who are looking for a job. I have a Google mail account just for LinkedIn." When we asked him how he manages all these connections, he explained his methods. "I have a device like a BlackBerry, but it just does e-mail. I am a speed-reader, so at night I devote about an hour to my network, and in the process, I may help from three to seven different people." On his LinkedIn profile, Steven leaves us with a little bit of philosophy and wisdom gathered from the writer Alvin Toffler. "The illiterate of the twenty-first century will not be those who cannot read and write, but those who cannot learn, unlearn, and relearn." No wonder Steven includes this quote in the Specialties part of his LinkedIn profile. It reflects the goals he holds for himself.

A QUICK GUIDED TOUR OF THE LINKEDIN SITE

Maybe you've already joined LinkedIn and you're hoping to use this book for improving your social networking skills and land a new job. In that case, you already know at least a little about navigating the site. If you haven't yet joined, LinkedIn's home page doesn't offer much for you to explore. You can use the links there to learn more about the site and the benefits about becoming a member, but beyond those basics, you'll need to become a LinkedIn member. So, by all means, if you haven't yet joined LinkedIn, now's the time to do so. It's fast and free, and once you're signed up, the whole site opens for your exploration. Of course, you'll want to create your profile (see Chapter 2) and build your network (see Chapter 3), but that's getting a little ahead of ourselves. If you've already begun these two steps, you'll see in the upcoming chapters lots of great advice for enhancing your LinkedIn image and building a powerful network. For this tour, we're going to show you the site through one of our own profiles. That way, you can get a feel for the whole site and begin to better understand the benefits of joining and using LinkedIn.

The LinkedIn homepage that you see once you've created a profile and connected with some people will resemble Figure 1-2. Through the navigation column along the left, you can get to all your customized content (all of which you'll learn more about in subsequent chapters), including your groups, your profile, contacts, your inbox, and so on.

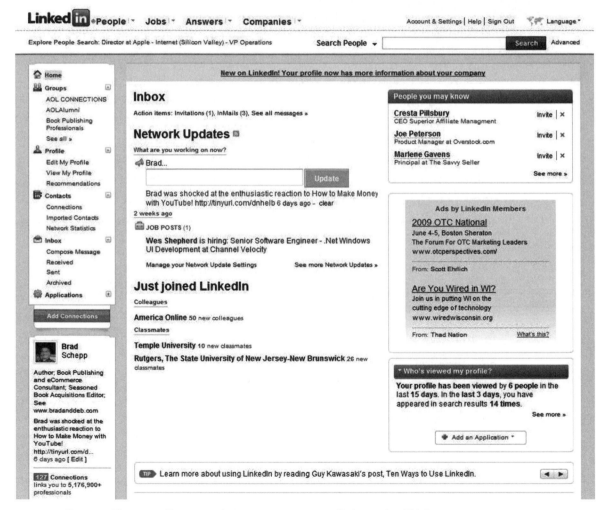

Figure 1-2: The personal homepage that appears once your profile is complete. This becomes your own LinkedIn homepage.

Next to the LinkedIn logo at the top of the page are hyperlinks from which you can quickly get to the main public areas of LinkedIn. These include People, Jobs, Answers, and Companies. Drop-down menus next to the hyperlinks will take you to specific content within those areas.

 Settings

Profile Settings

My Profile
Update career and education, add associations and awards, and list specialties and interests.

My Profile Photo
Your profile photo is visible to **everyone.**

Public Profile
Your public profile displays **full** profile information.
http://www.linkedin.com/in/bradschepp

Manage Recommendations
You have received 11 recommendations
1 manager, 3 co-workers, 1 client, 6 partners

Status Visibility
Your current status is visible to **everyone.**

Member Feed Visibility
Your member feed is visible to **your connections**.

Email Notifications

Contact Settings
You are receiving **Introductions, InMails, and OpenLink Messages.**

Receiving Messages
Control how you receive emails and notifications.

Invitation Filtering
You are receiving **all invitations**.

Home Page Settings

Network Updates
Settings for the display of Network Updates on your home page.

RSS Settings

Your Private RSS Feeds
Enable or disable your private RSS feeds.

Groups

Group Invitation Filtering
You **are receiving** Groups Invitations.

Personal Information

Name & Location
Control your name, location, display name, and account holder icon display settings.

Email Addresses
Your primary email address is currently:
bschepp@gmail.com

Change Password
Change your LinkedIn account password.

Close Your Account
Disable your account and remove your profile.

Privacy Settings

Research Surveys
Settings for receiving requests to participate in market research surveys related to your professional expertise.

Connections Browse
Your connections are **allowed** to view your connections list.

Profile Views
Control what (if anything) is shown to LinkedIn users whose profile you have viewed.

Viewing Profile Photos
You can view **everyone's** profile photos.

Profile and Status Updates
Control whether your connections are notified when you update your status or make significant changes to your profile and whether those changes appear on your company's profile.

Service Provider Directory
If you are recommended as a service provider, you **will** be listed.

Partner Advertising
Settings for LinkedIn partner websites.

Authorized Applications
See a list of websites or applications you have granted access to your account and control that access.

Figure 1-3: The Account & Settings screen allows you to customize and control the information you receive and the views allowed to others interested in your profile.

At the top of the page along the right are the Account & Settings hyperlink, the Help hyperlink, and a Sign Out link. There are also links along the bottom of the page in the categories Companies, LinkedIn Tools, and Premium Services, although they are not visible on the figure.

You will want to click that Account & Settings hyperlink as soon as you're up and running on the site. When you do, the screen in Figure 1-3 appears. From this, you can update your profile, change your profile picture, and set the many privacy settings that control what content relating to you others can view, as well as the content that's posted on your homepage for you and others to see when reviewing your profile.

The Network Updates setting is especially important because more than anything it determines the content you view on your homepage. By default, LinkedIn will show you every kind of update from your network. You may want a less cluttered look, preferring, for example, not to know every time someone in your network has changed his or her profile photo, received a new recommendation, or joined a new group. However, if you're job hunting, you will want to be certain to receive new job postings and perhaps even notices of new discussions happening in your groups. Another way to control the amount of information you receive is by setting the number of updates shown to you.

Now your homepage will include your network updates, but someone else who is just viewing your profile, of course, will not see all that information. It's your network, after all, not a public one. Instead, they will see just the main facts about your background, including your summary, experience, education, and any links to sites such as your Web site and blog that you've added. However, even what's shown to others can be changed through the Account & Settings area.

Most of what you'll be reviewing when you go to your LinkedIn homepage is in the middle area that you can view by looking back at Figure 1-2. This includes messages in your in-box, network updates, group updates, and information on the number of people from your employers and schools who have just joined LinkedIn. To the right of this area is additional information for you to review and possibly act on. This includes people you may know that LinkedIn has found for you, details about how many people have viewed your profile recently, events you may be interested in from the groups you belong to, answers from your network, and also job postings.

🔲🔲 Using Social Networking Sites Securely

As with every other part of the Internet, there are people who use social networking sites to trick others into revealing sensitive information such as passwords, personal identification numbers (PINs), Social Security numbers, and the like. It seems to be a truism that wherever humans come together, some of them arrive with larceny as their goal. Don't let that happen to you! We want to encourage you to use social networking, but we also want to help you learn to use these sites securely. We spoke with Jose Nazario of Arbor Networks (www.arbornetworks.com), a leading global network security company, who shared some very good advice.

1. An article in *eWeek Security Watch* noted that "social networking is a powerful tool for good purposes, and clearly, for some bad ones as well. And the fun has only just begun." What are you seeing?

   Employees will be drawn to social networks, and employer policies might lag. They may not keep up with all the latest sites. This means you have to work to protect yourself. I'm seeing hijacking [diverting your Web browser to fake sites], phishing [tricking you into revealing personal data], malware spreading and more, especially with Facebook and Twitter accounts being hijacked. Accounts are stolen through phishing. It's also possible to have all of your passwords stolen.

   Facebook is a new brand site for targeting; people set up fake Facebook accounts to get in other people's networks and "get the message out there to buy cell phone equipment, Viagra, whatever." These people realize that these accounts have content and value. I'm seeing this with Facebook and Twitter, not so much with LinkedIn. But on LinkedIn there are a bunch of poisoned profiles set up. You're directed to a [fake] profile, with malicious file links in it. For example, there are fake profiles for Hulk Hogan that entice people to go to them with the promise of seeing Hulk Hogan nude. People are coming across these profiles just through innocuous keyword searches.

2. What steps can users take to protect themselves?

   It's challenging because Facebook and Twitter accounts especially have value to spammers and attackers. So you really want to use a very good password, change it now and then, and not fall for phishing attacks. Be careful when you see suspicious links.

   Good virus programs go a long way to preventing these common attacks. You need to consider their performance impact when choosing them (for example, how much they may slow your computer when running), and also their coverage and ease of use. Commercial products I recommend include NOD32 (www.eset.com/), ESET Smart Security 4 (www.eset.com/), and Kaspersky antivirus (www.kaspersky.com/). Also, some free virus programs are okay. The AVG program (www.avg.com/), for example, provides decent coverage of possible threats.

You need an antivirus program that works in the background while your computer is running. People get impatient with these programs, because they slow their computers down, but they should be patient!

Also, Windows update operates in the background on many computers with newer versions of Windows. Don't stop it from running. Allow it to download things . . . just go take a coffee break and let the updates download. Also, update your antivirus program.

Finally, Internet browsers will now scan links you are about to click on to warn you about threats. I recommend Firefox over Internet Explorer.

3. So would you advise people to use social networking sites less or even to avoid them given these risks?

No, they offer a lot of value. But as these sites get more popular, they become even more attractive to spammers and attackers. A lot of all this is common sense. The topic has an air of mystery about it because we're talking about websites. Yet, if a shady character came to the door offering you $1,000 for $600, you would be suspicious.

All the social networking sites are aware of the potential security risks that come with using their sites. We can tell you from personal experience that Facebook notified us when one of our profiles had been hijacked before we even realized that this had happened. A friend posted a note on our wall saying that something may be wrong. As we logged into e-mail, we already had a message from Facebook security that explained what happened and gave us ample steps to take to secure our profile. Help was just that swift and simple.

The LinkedIn Learning Center

You'll find a wealth of information about using LinkedIn through the Learning Center shown in Figure 1-4. Find the Learning Center by clicking the

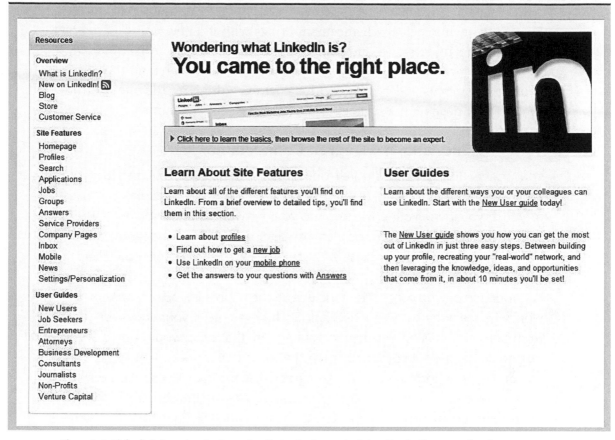

Figure 1-4: LinkedIn's Learning Center makes it easy to stay up to date with what's new on the site.

link for it at the bottom of your homepage and many other LinkedIn pages, too. The Learning Center provides an excellent guide to everything on the site, with plenty of hyperlinks so that you can easily locate the areas you have questions about. Note there is a section of the Learning Center just for job hunters at http://learn.linkedin.com/job-seekers/.

Right next to the Learning Center link is a link for LinkedIn's blog, which will keep you up to the minute on all the new features the company rolls out.

LINKEDIN COMMUNICATIONS METHODS AND NETWORKING DETAILS

Every new technological advancement brings with it a new vocabulary and new ideas to understand and digest. Communicating on LinkedIn is the same. In order to be well versed, you simply have to understand the words you'll come across and have a feel for how everything on the site is structured. Don't despair. It's simple, intuitive, and relatively painless.

Your 1st, 2nd, and 3rd Degree Connections

Your connections on LinkedIn are made up of the people you invite to join your network and, by degrees, all the people in the networks of those directly linked to you. If you invite your coworker into your network, that coworker becomes your 1st degree connection. You also may share some other 1st degree connections with this individual because you may both have invited other coworkers to also join your networks.

Your 2nd degree connections include all the people in your coworker's network who are not also in your network. So, for example, if your coworker's boss from her last job is her 1st degree connection, that boss would be your 2nd degree connection. In order to reach that boss directly, you would ask your coworker for an Introduction. If she agrees that the two of you would share commonalities, she'd most likely be happy to make the introduction, at which point you'd be able to invite her former boss to join your network and therefore become a 1st degree connection for you, too.

Your 3rd degree connection may be the boss of your coworker's friend. Suppose that your coworker has linked with the person at her old job who has your exact title. That's her 1st degree connection, of course. But she may not even know who her friend's boss currently is. Of course, if you have some reason to want to meet the equivalent of your supervisor at this other company, you can still work your way through your network and your coworker's network to get in touch.

You would simply ask your coworker to ask her friend about making the introduction between you and his new boss. You'd have to supply some reason why you think that boss would be interested in your work or background, and that may or may not have to do with a request for a job interview. Suppose that you're working on a presentation that you believe this manager at another company would be interested in. That could be a perfectly valid reason to want the introduction. Provide your coworker with the details, and ask if she'd speak on your behalf.

In most cases, your 1st degree connection should be happy to help you reach out. In the end, after some communication, that 3rd degree connection could easily become a 1st degree member of your network, and you'll gain an ally and colleague at yet another company. If the day comes when you're ready to make a move, you'll have a 1st degree connection who also may be looking for someone just like you. Of course, by then, you'll know each other well enough to avoid a lot of the stress that comes from job hunting.

Communications Methods

Throughout the chapters of this book, you'll learn a great deal about how you can identify and approach other LinkedIn members. To put you one step ahead, let's look at the different forms of reaching out to others and the structure of the network you'll begin to build.

INVITATIONS These can be sent to anyone you have an e-mail address for, whether or not they happen to already be on LinkedIn. Once the parties you invite accept your Invitations, they become your 1st degree connections, and you can send messages directly to them through LinkedIn.

MESSAGES These are used to communicate directly with the people already in your network. One of the biggest advantages of using Messages is that once you've made a connection on LinkedIn, you never have to track that person's e-mail address again. You will always be able to reach the person directly through the site.

INTRODUCTIONS You just saw how you'd use Introductions to get in touch with people who are connected to your 1st degree connections but not directly to you. With the basic free membership on LinkedIn, you'll be able to request five Introductions per month. If you find that you need more, you'll know you're ready to upgrade to a paid LinkedIn subscription. You'll learn more about that in Chapter 6.

INMAILS These are private messages that allow you to directly contact any LinkedIn user while protecting the recipient's privacy. If the person you send an InMail to is not in your network, you'll only be able to view his or her name and e-mail address, and then only if he or she accepts the InMail. With a free account, InMails are only available when purchased individually at the cost of $10 each. You will gain access to InMails with the premium LinkedIn accounts.

Best Jobs Table

The 10 Best Jobs to Get through Social Networking Sites

We think you can get just about any kind of contract work or new job with the help of one or more social networking sites. Now you wouldn't necessarily turn to MySpace to get your next job as an actuary. Then again, LinkedIn may not be as helpful to you if you were a musician looking for new gigs. But by using a combination of these sites, we're convinced that you can land that next job faster. If that job happens to be one of the following, your task is even simpler. We present these in no particular order.

1. *Public relations (PR) manager.* Whatever you want to call it—communications manager or PR director—as a professional communicator, you really should be able to make your online profile sing. Just about any company has someone in a PR role and may be looking for someone just like you. Even if a company isn't currently in the market for someone with your skills, you can keep your name in front of the right people by careful and frequent networking through the sites we discuss in this book.

2. *Social media strategist.* Of course, you can demonstrate how well you know this new field by skillfully using the tools that comprise it. Executives are just starting to realize how essential it is that they have someone on board who can use sites like Twitter to provide customer service, seed the market with news about their companies, dispel rumors, and much more.

3. *Musician.* MySpace alone justifies including musicians in this list. Thankfully for this group, MySpace came along when it did. CD sales were dropping steadily, making life as a musician even more challenging than ever. Thanks to MySpace, musicians (especially smaller independent artists) can find new work and contacts and promote themselves in ways they never could have even imagined before.

4. *Blogger.* Everyone's attention span is shrinking to that of a fly's, and sites like Twitter don't help. But we all make time to read the words of someone

who can help us to do our jobs better or maybe just better understand the world we inhabit. Whether your goal is to be an independent blogger or blog for a Web site or corporation, social networking sites can help you to promote your work to millions of people.

5. *Copywriter.* With so many sites offering you the chance to let everyone know your current status or to microblog about what's got your gears going, writers of all types have powerful new showcases for their talents. Copywriters are just one type, but a good representative example.

6. *Consultant/freelancer.* If you're in business for yourself, you should be spending a good part of each workday marketing yourself and your skills. An excellent way to do this is through LinkedIn's Answers section, where you can demonstrate your expertise in a worldwide forum and unobtrusively include your background information just in case you've inspired someone to hire you.

7. *Information technology (IT) worker.* Many programmers, software engineers, and their managers use social networking sites; they've always been early adopters of new forms of electronic communications. These sites should be one of the first places you turn to when you're looking for that next IT job, but you probably already knew that!

8. *Comedian.* We're going to thank MySpace again, this time on behalf of comedians, for making it easier for them to promote themselves and get new gigs. And we're not kidding around, either.

9. *Web designer.* Businesses of all sizes need Web designers to help them get their sites up and running and then Webmasters to keep them going. You can demonstrate your skills in this area in many ways while using social networking sites. These include the design of your MySpace or Facebook page, the portfolio you include as part of your LinkedIn profile, or the questions you answer on those ubiquitous discussion boards.

10. *Marketing manager.* Prove that you can sell yourself, and you may have an easier time convincing someone that you can move products for them as well. Social networking sites make it much easier for you to sell yourself to a worldwide audience through your words and accomplishments and reach people who would care.

Now, if you haven't found your own profession on this list of the top 10, don't despair. The opportunities are nearly boundless, and this is just a sampling to show you what's possible. In researching this book, we found people from all walks of life connecting, expanding, and building their careers through social networking.

I GOT A JOB ON LINKEDIN

Throughout the first part of this book you'll meet many people who have found jobs or additional contract/freelance work thanks to LinkedIn. To get things rolling, we present a few examples here. We could have presented many, many more. LinkedIn is just that powerful.

Consumer Behavior Consultant

Pinny Cohen's consulting business enjoys a new profitability thanks to his efforts on LinkedIn.

In his interesting line of work, Pinny Cohen works with many different types of businesses, from manufacturing companies, to distributors, to retailers, by helping them understand consumers better from a psychology/statistics perspective and to develop plans to increase conversion rates on a site, increase sales in a store, or increase positive feelings toward a company. For example, Pinny has worked with car dealership groups to refine their sites and offline marketing, rug manufacturers to improve their trade-show displays and boost distribution of their products, and restaurants to enhance their patrons' dining experience.

Here in his own words he describes the many ways he uses LinkedIn to drum up business. You'll learn more about these methods in subsequent chapters.

I found clients in the following ways:

By type of company—When I had a service to offer a particular type of person, industry, or geographical location, I used the advanced search to target the decision makers.

By niche—I joined groups in the targeted area and discussed topics that were "buzz worthy" in that group.

By targeted company—If I had a lead for a particular company, or was blocked by a secretary, I could follow the chain of command by looking at all employees from a particular company and get to the right person right away.

Introduction—I built up an army of contacts, all of whom are very kind and will send an introduction to any of the 7.5 million people I end up getting connected to by two degrees away.

Answers—I would answer questions in my niche, and display expertise, and often get a follow-up message which can be converted into business.

Second contact—I would often add a contact to LinkedIn after my initial discussion with them—within 24 hours to keep my name fresh in their head (making use of some of my own expertise on marketing/psych). Then I would follow up with more information a day or week later. In a way, the second stepping stone was LinkedIn.

Profile optimization—I would add keywords into my profile to get ranked well in Google and get the right searchers looking at my profile and getting in touch with me.

Display icons—I place the LinkedIn icon on my blog and other places to make it easy to connect. Someone reading my content is much more likely to already trust me, and LinkedIn is an easy way for them to "officially" get in touch.

Show expertise—I bring my blog into LinkedIn as an application so that any visitor to my LinkedIn profile can instantly see some of my work, and that I'm active on the site. If users don't see that, they won't risk spending time getting in touch with you.

Explain—I explain what I can offer (value wise) to someone reading my profile, so they are thinking about how they can be helped, instead of just "Oh, that's an interesting person" and then leaving.

Financial Representative

Patty Gale and her husband were able to use LinkedIn to locate a job for him between Thanksgiving and New Year's.

Patty Gale and her husband Doug chose to leave Wisconsin and move to Colorado to fulfill a lifelong dream. Then the ground dropped from underneath them.

We live in Wisconsin, and last summer [we] put our house up for sale as our dream was always to live in Colorado. In early September, we went, house had not yet sold. Our plan was to live in an apartment in Colorado, and then when our house sold, we would purchase a home there.

Within two weeks of arriving in Colorado Springs, the stock market crashed, real estate crashed, and our economy came to a head in its downward spin. Showings on our house became nonexistent, while more and more houses were going up for sale in our neighborhood and community.

After giving it much thought, we decided that the best thing to do for our family finances was to put our dream on hold and move back to Wisconsin to live in our house. We just didn't want to take the chance of living in limbo indefinitely not knowing if or when this house would sell.

Once we made that decision, we knew my husband was going to need a job back here. My business is Web-based, so for me, it wasn't an issue. We really had no idea what was going to happen; we just knew that Doug [my husband] needed to be here in order to interview.

I had been using LinkedIn in my own business for some time, so while still in Colorado, I suggested, to him, that he create a LinkedIn profile and start joining groups and networking with business professionals and companies here, which he did. That was in October.

We came back to Wisconsin the week before Thanksgiving. That following week, Doug received an e-mail from a local employer stating that Doug had been referred to this gentleman by a referral on LinkedIn. We still don't know who that third person was, though.

They set up a time for an interview. Doug was asked back for a second interview during the week of New Year's, and the following week, he was formally offered the position, which he accepted. He's been there now since early January. The position is with a local insurance/investment firm, and we are just still amazed considering the economic climate for that industry in particular.

Marketing Associate

In October 2008, Sarah Burris was laid off from her first job—along with roughly 30 other coworkers. Thanks to LinkedIn, she was able to find another job quickly, even in a bruising economy.

To kick start my job search, I knew I had to get aggressive—and fast.

1. I uploaded my revised résumé to almost every job site, including Monster, CareerBuilder, Yahoo!, HotJobs, PRSA job center, and several local Web sites.

2. I updated my LinkedIn profile to showcase all my experience and skills. I asked my recent supervisors for letters of recommendation and received LinkedIn recommendations from a handful of past coworkers.

3. I touched base with all of my contacts in the area and put messages on Facebook, Twitter, and LinkedIn to inform everyone that I was looking for a job.

4. I attended a career fair.

Three months, one declined job offer, and several interviews later, I received an e-mail from someone who found my profile on LinkedIn. She worked for a local PR firm who had a client in search of an in-house marketing associate. She facilitated an introduction, and after exchanging a few direct e-mails with the company, I went in for an interview.

Soon, Sarah started her new job as a marketing associate for Carolina Advanced Digital, Inc. (CAD), a woman-owned, veteran-owned small business specializing in IT infrastructure, security, and management solutions for government, education, and commercial customers. CAD also recruited one of its engineers via LinkedIn.

 Marketing Executive

John Cloonan was happy to share his LinkedIn success story.

Over the last 10 years, I've always kept a small side business going as a marketing consultant, doing everything from brand strategy on down to actually writing and designing collateral. Previously, in its best year, it did about $30,000 in revenue.

John Cloonan has found lucrative consulting work while continuing his job search on LinkedIn.

After getting laid off, I decided to use that consultancy to keep myself afloat until I found another job, but I knew it needed to get bigger, so I started connecting and reconnecting with my network using three primary channels: LinkedIn, Facebook, and Twitter. The pitch was that I was looking for a job, but I also was interested in marketing projects in the meantime to keep myself afloat.

I immediately booked a fairly large project with one of my former colleagues creating a board-level presentation for an initiative he was pitching. Since then, I've booked two other large projects via LinkedIn and a bunch of smaller projects using other social networking constructs.

Public Relations Executive

When Kristen Kouk reconnected with an old college friend, she also found a great new job.

Kristen Kouk was eager to share her LinkedIn success story.

I found my current position [partner of a PR agency] through LinkedIn's Update e-mails. I realized one of my former classmates at the University of Texas had recently started her very own company, and I immediately messaged her through LinkedIn to get more information. I sent her my résumé so she could verify my experience, but she already knew my accomplishments in the PR industry from my LinkedIn profile. She knew I was the perfect fit for her growing agency.

LOOKING AHEAD

Throughout this section of the book you'll learn a great deal about the ins and outs of using LinkedIn. Each chapter will end with a quick look ahead at what the next chapter will bring, but in this first chapter, let's plot your course throughout your LinkedIn exploration and beyond.

The first order of business now is to make your own place on LinkedIn by creating a complete and dynamic profile. Chapter 2 will give you plenty of help. It may take some time to get your profile just right, but every moment you spend on perfecting it will be rewarded. Also, your profile is never exactly finished. As you move throughout your job and career, you'll keep an eye on how you can enhance your profile to reflect your own advancement and goals at the time.

Beyond Chapter 2, you'll learn about building a strong and vibrant network in Chapter 3. Chapter 4 will give you invaluable advice about actually hunting for a job on the site. Chapter 5 will clarify for you the powerful tool that is the Answers section. Having access to a world of experts willing and eager to share what they know will make everything about your work life easier. Chapter 6 will look at the many ways you can use LinkedIn to enhance your job performance. Whether you currently have the job of your dreams or are still in search of the perfect spot for you, once you've got a job you care about, LinkedIn will help you to do it all so much more effectively.

Finally, we'll send you out to explore some other social networks that, although they may be more famous than LinkedIn in many ways, are not well known as great places for job hunting. Facebook, Twitter, MySpace, and Plaxo? Well, let's not dismiss them without a careful look. You may be surprised to find how effective they can be when added to your mix of business tools and social networks.

CHAPTER 2

Create Your Best Profile

How many times have you sat through a presentation for work about a subject you knew so well you could actually have made the presentation yourself? How dreadful is it to have to be polite while someone explains in tedious step-by-step detail something so simple that you could easily have done it yourself? It's a universal human struggle and one you won't be subjected to in this chapter. We know that the mechanics of creating a LinkedIn profile are simple. LinkedIn has worked hard to make them so. If you follow the recommendations on the form you'll use to create a profile, you'll easily be stepped through every aspect of creating a complete and useful profile on the site.

Instead, we're going to focus on the philosophies and theories behind a great profile. We're going to talk about the place your LinkedIn profile will take in your total online presence and existence. When we do give you some nuts-and-bolts advice about making your profile sparkle, we'll ensure that those tidbits have the value-added features you'll need to make your profile work better. For instance, we won't just tell you to include links; instead, we'll tell you how to maximize the links you include. We're simply not going to torture you by repeatedly detailing things that you are clearly able to accomplish on your own. Because you've come to LinkedIn with millions of people already occupying the space, we have a lot of great advice about what makes a terrific profile terrific and also what makes your profile reflect negatively on you. We'll guide you—but only where you need guidance.

THEORIES AND PHILOSOPHIES

You will find almost as many different opinions about what makes a great LinkedIn profile as you will find profiles. Every time someone completes the profile form, another profile comes to life. Some experts will tell you to make sure that you only include the most relevant and detailed professional-looking profile. Others will tell you to be sure to let your own personality sparkle so that people reading your profile will leave feeling like they know a little more about you as a real human. We're here to say that we agree with both those statements.

You don't want to include a lot of trivial personal information on your LinkedIn profile. For example, this isn't the place to declare the minutiae of your life. You can go to other networking sites if you want to update your friends with the latest stomach bug your family is fighting, but don't put that kind of stuff on LinkedIn. As one savvy LinkedIn user told us, "Keep religion out of it, duh!" The things that may be most dear to your heart are not necessarily the things you should include on LinkedIn.

On the other hand, LinkedIn would not be terribly useful if everyone stuck so rigidly to the same information in their profiles. We'd all look too much alike. Your LinkedIn profile isn't just a résumé. It's a snapshot of who you are as a professional, and that means who you are as a person. There's nothing wrong with letting your personality show through. Just do it in a way that supports your professional life. You can easily manage this, for example, by linking your blog or Web site to your LinkedIn profile. It's a way to share more information with people who are already interested in your background enough to want more insight into who you are. They have proven that by their conscious decision to click through to learn more.

Now, the basic information you provide when you first create your LinkedIn account is enough to get a "profile" for you up on the site, but it's far from complete at that point. Once you click on the Profile hyperlink, you can fill in all the details about your work background, education, and much more (see Figure 2-1).

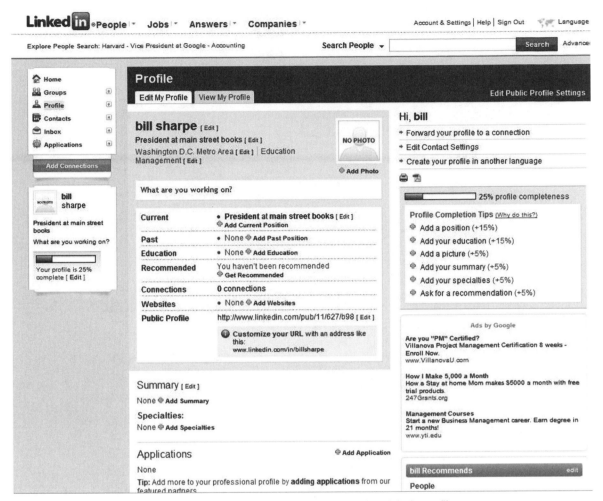

Figure 2-1: Use this screen to fill in all the details needed for a complete LinkedIn profile.

🔲 🔲 A Perfect LinkedIn Profile

There's probably no better way to dive in than to include an example of an extraordinary LinkedIn profile, and for us that means taking a tour of David Becker's (Figure 2-2). David is a maestro of branding. As president and cofounder of PhillipeBecker, his client list includes such recognizable companies as Disney, Microsoft, Wal-Mart, T-Mobile, William Sonoma, Whole Foods, and Safeway's O Organic line of products. He is also a trustee of the San Francisco Chamber of Commerce. Clearly, this man's résumé could open many doors and certainly has during his impressive career. But look a little more closely, and you'll learn so much more about him.

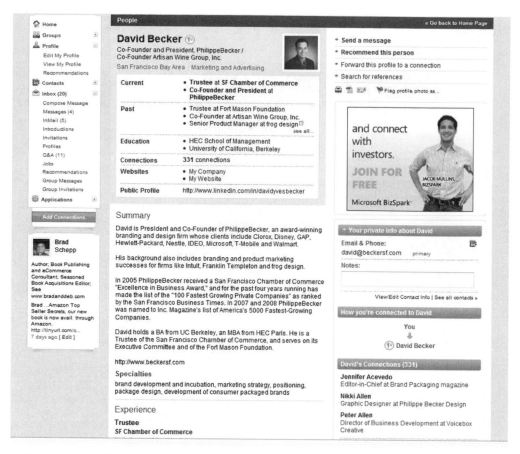

Figure 2-2: David Becker proves his expertise in branding with his own LinkedIn profile.

David's friendly and professional photo presents a warm and lively man. He appears open and accessible. As you scroll down through David's impressive accomplishments, you'll see that he has used his devotion to wine to cofound Artisan Wine Company, Inc. The company launched its first wine, Tableaux, in 2007. David's profile includes links to two Web sites, one for his work at PhillipeBecker and one for his Artisan Wine Company site, shown in Figure 2-3. As an added treat, when you click that hyperlink, you get an immediate and dynamic glimpse of what David could do for you. His wine site is visually beautiful with a happy musical background. Pop-up screens provide you with plenty of information about the wine, but more than that, they combine to make you "feel" the wine. You just can't help but wonder what that wine would taste like.

By the time you scroll through David's complete profile, you've learned that he was a studio musician for a time in Europe and South Korea, playing with

Artisan Wine Group is a unique group of wine veterans from California and France who believe life is about savoring everyday moments and drinking in the scene.

ARTISAN WINE GROUP presents TABLEAUX
The best of the French tradition — a red table wine that is frank, honest, yet structured. It is a Vin de Pays d'Oc: 50% Cabernet, expertly blended by sixth-generation master winemaker François Despagne. This is a wine for the new generation of wine drinkers. Tableaux will surprise and delight both the novice and experienced wine drinker with its structure and elegance.

Figure 2-3: The Artisan Wine Company Web site presents an inviting tableaux for the company's debut wine of the same name.

many well-known bands. You know a lot about David's background and work history. But you will also have learned a lot about what he specifically brings to a project. You can see his taste first hand. You can discern his sense of style from the things he chooses to include about himself in his profile. Although there's naturally quite a lot more to know about anyone than can be learned in a profile format, you certainly can feel as though a decision to consider David for a project is a good one. If you needed branding and marketing advice for your product, you would have every reason to get in touch and schedule a meeting. David makes it easy to for you to think well of him.

Of course, what's right for David may very well be all wrong for you. LinkedIn offers you lots of options for making your profile individual. Although, visually, LinkedIn profiles all resemble each other, what you choose to include in yours and how you present your content will blend to form a profile that's unique to you. Creating the profile that best speaks of you and your work is all that matters. How well you tell your story will be strictly up to you, and that will be shaped largely by your own career goals. The first thing you need to consider is what exactly you want to achieve through your profile on the site. Once you answer some of those basic but core questions, you'll be able to craft the profile that best moves you toward those goals.

For example, if you are a freelancer or consultant, you may want to create a profile that showcases your specialties, such as the one we've just looked at. If you are a writer or artist, the feel of your profile is likely to be quite different from that of an engineer or banker. If you're currently job hunting, you'll choose to highlight certain elements that wouldn't be as important if you were settled in your position and coming to LinkedIn for expertise requests. Those elements might include greater detail about your accomplishments at other companies, complete with lots of figures (e.g., "Boosted global sales 200 percent during my tenure"). But, no matter what you want your final profile to say about you, all profiles have to share common elements.

Go Google Yourself

You should always know what others are learning about you on the Web. We don't know how LinkedIn accomplished this, but your LinkedIn profile is likely to be among the top hits on a search results page when you Google yourself. This is why your profile has to speak well of you, because then you can use it as a dashboard to drive your entire Web presence. Linked to your Web site or blog, the profile becomes a gateway to everything you want professional contacts to know about you on the Web. Once someone is checking out your LinkedIn profile page, he or she merely has to click a quick hyperlink to move over to your Web site.

Conversely, when you put a hyperlink to your LinkedIn profile on your Web site, anyone who happens to find your Web site through a search engine will have your entire professional background available through a single click.

You Need 100 Percent

On LinkedIn, a complete profile means it's 100 percent finished. How do you know you've reached that milestone? LinkedIn notes your progress right on your profile (see Figure 2-4). A brand-new profile is likely to be only about 25 percent complete. "Make sure their profiles are 100 percent complete," advised career consultant Anne Pryor. "Nothing much happens on LinkedIn until your profile is at 100 percent," more than a few successful users told us. Fortunately, LinkedIn will step you through the process as you work your way toward that 100 percent profile. We'll look at the nuts and bolts of maximizing the elements of your profile a little later in this chapter, but for now, know that, among everything else you have to include, you'll need a photo and three recommendations. Let's look at these two elements first.

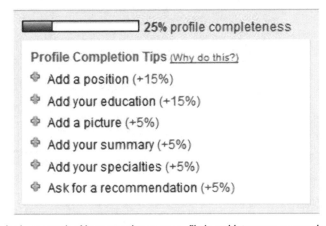

Figure 2-4: LinkedIn keeps track of how complete your profile is and lets you see very clearly the remaining steps you can take as you work your way toward 100 percent completeness.

Your LinkedIn Photo

Throughout this book you'll meet many different LinkedIn users who have chosen their photos for their own specific reasons. Most of us select a photo because we find it flattering. That's good, of course. But remember that the photo you put on you LinkedIn profile will be the only way to get your face before the people you specifically want to attract. It doesn't matter if you're a glamour-puss in this case. It matters that your photo be bright, well lit, and positive. "However you look at work is how you should look in your picture," advised Chuck Hester, a LinkedIn LION. You don't have to wear a suit, for example, although cut-offs on the beach aren't a good idea either. Figure 2-5 makes an interesting first impression. Look a little closer, and you'll see that Theresa Hummel-Krallinger lists "Laughologist" as one of her job titles. This may be just the right impression to attract her particular type of client!

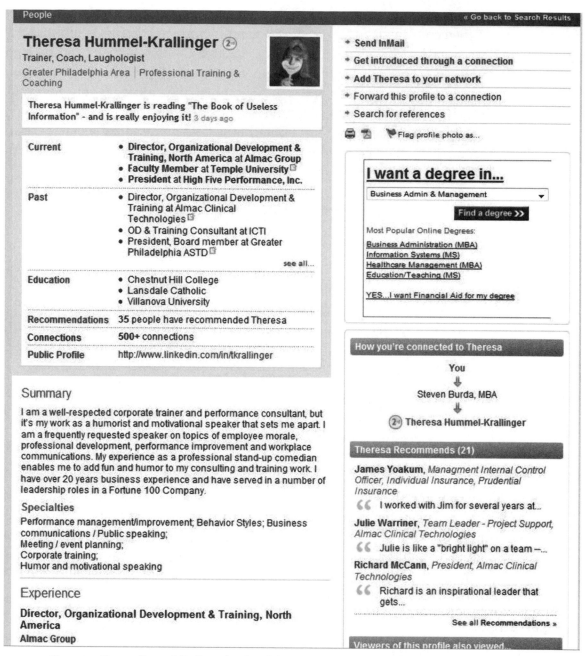

Figure 2-5: Theresa Hummel-Krallinger has found the perfect image for her LinkedIn profile photo. After all, she's a corporate trainer and a "laughologist"!

Recommendations

You can complete all the elements of your profile, but until you've received three recommendations, you're not going to hit the 100 percent mark. Recommendations on LinkedIn don't differ too much from recommendations you'd get anyplace else. It's actually kind of a funny game we humans play. You know you can't make a good professional impression without recommendations, yet you also know you wouldn't solicit recommendations from someone unless you were sure they would be strong and positive. Still, as flawed as the human system of recommending may be, it's vital to your profile. "A lot of people use the recommendation feature," noted David Becker. "I think that's viable if it's done well. It can backfire if you just have one recommendation. It makes people wonder, 'What about all the others?'"

Unlike in real life, on LinkedIn, everyone can view both the recommendations you receive and the ones you leave for others. Bryan Webb, a technical marketing professional, uses recommendations frequently when evaluating someone on LinkedIn. "I look for the recommendations they have given and received," he told us. "But I can tell if you have tit-for-tat recommendations," he said. Keep in mind that not only do your own recommendations speak to your work, but those you leave for others probably reveal even more about your character and values. People are clearly judged by how they present themselves in a public forum, so look at every recommendation your write as an opportunity to show who you are while you shine the spotlight on a colleague or friend.

The immediacy with which others can evaluate you through your recommendations is another thing that separates LinkedIn from older ways of doing business. It used to be that checking references was reserved for the last phase of the hiring process. You wouldn't check references unless you were close to making an offer to a candidate. Now you can use LinkedIn to see what others have said about a prospective employee or business partner before you've even met. "It gives me a better insight into the person," noted Bryan when we asked about recommendations. "With LinkedIn, you don't have to wait to review references from someone." Those recommendations are there and always waiting for the world to see who you are in the eyes of others.

It's best to have at least one recommendation from each of your most recent jobs. If you've had several short stints with companies recently but a much longer tenure with a company before that, then be sure to also include a recommendation from that previous employer.

Ideally, your recommendations are from managers, preferably the people who managed you directly (or, for contractors and consultants, from actual clients who hired you). It's also good to include recommendations from coworkers at your same level, especially if they worked with you in the same group. Finally, recommendations from people who you've managed also can be telling if they attest to your skills as a manager. Just make sure that they're long on specifics and short on saccharin!

Requesting Recommendations

There are several things to keep in mind when you request recommendations from your colleagues, friends, and business partners. "LinkedIn is excellent for demonstrating your expertise," said David Becker. Of course, there are many places on the site for doing so, including the Answers area we'll cover in Chapter 5, but your recommendations also should feature your specific attributes and contributions.

To ask someone to write a recommendation for your LinkedIn profile, use the form shown in Figure 2-6. This appears when you click on the Get Recommended hyperlink shown in Figure 2-1. Note that the form is filled in with a boilerplate note, which you should customize. When you customize that note, include some specific details you'd like to have featured from the part of your career you shared with this person. Give a few specific talking points as suggestions when you send your request. This not only makes it easier for the person who has agreed to recommend you, but it also makes the recommendation more closely tailored to the results you want. Again, what you'd like to spotlight will vary depending on what you're hoping to achieve with your LinkedIn presence. If you're job hunting, you'll want to look across the breadth of your career and request recommendations from people who can spotlight the most important attributes for the type of job you're seeking. Former managers can attest to what you accomplished for them and suggest to your next manager what you are capable of. If you're looking for business partners, on the other hand, you probably want some recommendations that highlight your ability to meet deadlines, manage budgets, and supervise projects, for example.

Finally, when you come across former colleagues who you respected or enjoyed working with, why not write unsolicited recommendations for them? If you send those without expecting to receive any in return, you are living the creed of LinkedIn by doing more for others than you ask for yourself. Your former colleagues will have the chance to review your recommendations before

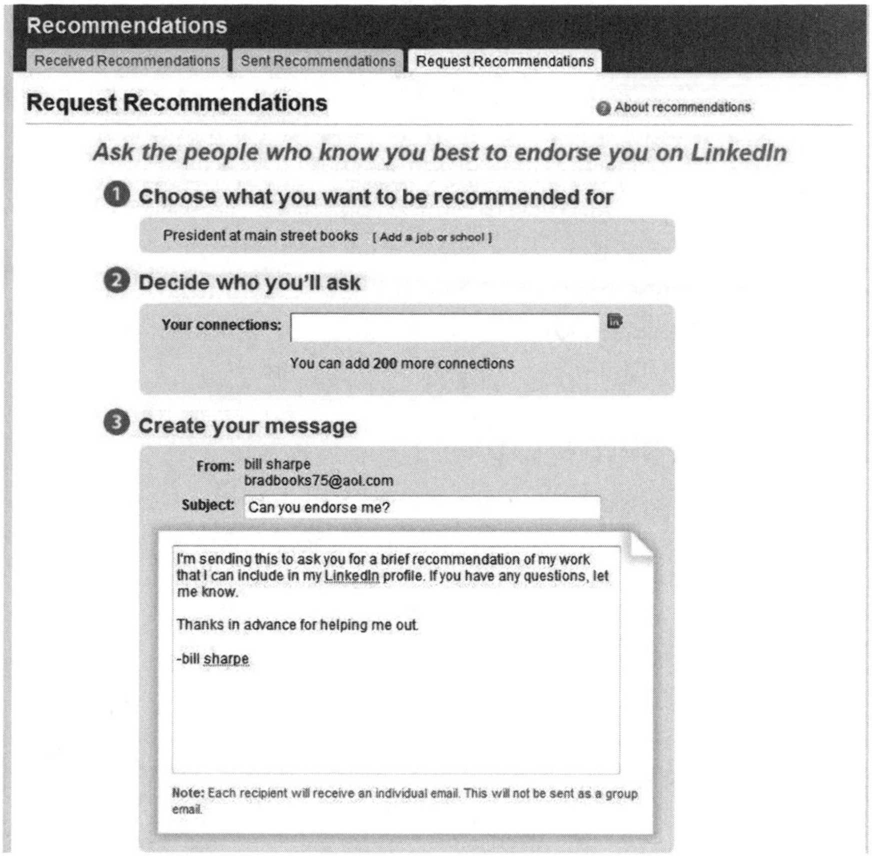

Recommendations

Received Recommendations | Sent Recommendations | Request Recommendations

Request Recommendations   ⓘ About recommendations

Ask the people who know you best to endorse you on LinkedIn

❶ Choose what you want to be recommended for

President at main street books   [Add a job or school]

❷ Decide who you'll ask

Your connections: [_____]   🔲

You can add **200** more connections

❸ Create your message

From: bill sharpe
       bradbooks75@aol.com

Subject: Can you endorse me?

I'm sending this to ask you for a brief recommendation of my work
that I can include in my LinkedIn profile. If you have any questions, let
me know.

Thanks in advance for helping me out.

-bill sharpe

Note: Each recipient will receive an individual email. This will not be sent as a group
email.

Figure 2-6: The Request Recommendation page showing the form note you should always customize.

accepting them into their profiles, so they will know immediately what you've done for them. You'll certainly make someone's day, and it's quite possible that you'll also get a few good recommendations to fill out your profile, too.

NUTS AND BOLTS

Let's turn our attention now to the details of putting together a great profile. You already know you need a photo and some recommendations, but what are the other things to consider as you build your profile? We've gathered some great advice and tips from experts all over LinkedIn to help you create a great profile of your own. "The first thing to realize is that your LinkedIn profile isn't a résumé," said Mike O'Neil, CEO of Integrated Alliances and a LinkedIn trainer. "That's a fast way of getting something up there, but it's not a profile." Your LinkedIn profile lives and breathes in a way that your résumé simply cannot. Since your profile is the home base for everything else you do on LinkedIn, the more active you are on the site, the more activity will show on your profile. Everything you do on LinkedIn from writing and requesting recommendations, to asking and answering questions, to joining groups will show up on your overall profile.

Starting at the Top

Although you're not getting a step-by-step tour of the form you'll use to complete your LinkedIn profile, certain parts of the profile are so important that we should look at them together. Starting at the top of the page, shown in Figure 2-7, you'll see a photo, a headline, and a status update. You've already spent some time planning for the photo, so let's take a look at the other two elements. They actually are more than they seem.

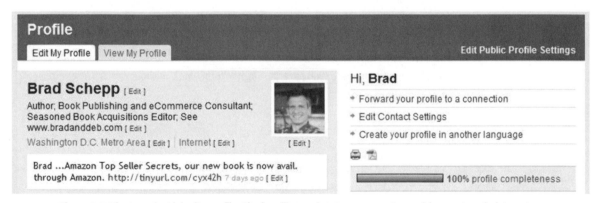

Figure 2-7: The top of a LinkedIn profile. The headline and status area are two quick ways to gain interest and attention from others viewing your profile.

Your headline should consist of the most telling and persuasive things you most want people to know about you. Think of it as the pitch you would use if the hiring manager for your dream job stepped onto the elevator with you in a parking garage. You may only have 15 to 20 seconds to say something that would grab this executive's attention. What would it be? "I'm looking for communication styles," says Chuck Hester. "The writing style should be concise and precise." This advice is especially useful when considering your headline. Get right to the point, leaving no room for speculation about what you offer through your best skills and experience.

Now, if you are currently employed, and especially if you're content where you are and your LinkedIn profile is meant to showcase your employer as well as you, it's perfectly acceptable just to include your full job title within your headline. But we're assuming that you're looking for advice about what to include if you're between positions or at least want to keep all options open.

Here are some actual examples from LinkedIn of status headlines that should achieve results:

- Experienced marketing analyst with GE + Navy leadership experience
- Pricing professional specializing in management, market segmentation, price optimization, and process improvement
- Radio Host, Author, Public Speaker
- Entreprenuer, Executive, Startup Advisor
- Wildly Creative Namer, "Eat My Words"

■ ■ A Complete and Attractive LinkedIn Profile

Monique Cuvelier, CEO/tech consultant at her own Web design firm, Talance.com, has quite an enticing profile on LinkedIn (Figure 2-8). She has honed it to show her best experience and has loaded it with keywords that will attract new clients and potential business partners. You may notice that her status update shows her latest project and includes a link to the case study she's written about the newly designed Web site. From there, it's just another simple click to get to the Web site itself and glimpse first hand what Monique can do in creating a strong and vibrant place on the Web.

Notice also Monique's Specialties. Within this area she details a dozen specific terms relevant to Web design. This list includes everything from the software she's worked with to the details of her job, such as editing, training, and management. She maintains a blog that is linked to her profile through the Wordpress application on LinkedIn, and she adds to it frequently to keep her content fresh and relevant. "My goals with my LinkedIn profile are to try to establish my own expertise and create another entry into my company's Web site and services," she said. "According to my Web site traffic, it does drive people our way, and it's garnered some compliments, so that's another plus!"

Figure 2-8: Monique Cuvelier often receives compliments on her complete and attractive LinkedIn profile.

"I think profile writing is a little like writing a résumé," Monique said. "There are sure-fire mistakes you can make, but a really good one is harder to define. Weird or blurry pictures are a minus," she added. "Poor punctuation is a turn-off, and skimpy information seems useless," she further noted. "Those would be the top picks for what makes a bad profile."

Just below the headline is your status bar. Here's where you can have a little fun and keep your profile lively and dynamic. This status bar isn't un-like those on other networking sites such as Facebook and Twitter. It's meant to be updated frequently and be the most current part of your profile. Just don't update your status with extraneous entries. It's not the place to talk about the weekend hiking trip you just took unless you're looking for work as a hiking tour guide. Instead, use the space to promote your latest business-oriented blog entry, article published, product launched, award won, or anything else that's going on right now in your professional life. The more lively and dynamic you make this, the better it speaks to your productivity and engagement with your career. So update it frequently. It shows you're working and contributing to the LinkedIn community by sharing your news. And be sure to include a hyperlink, if relevant, because it makes your status update that much more useful and provocative.

Some examples of provocative status updates from LinkedIn:

- Monique Cuvelier launched another Web site—we're on a roll! Read the case study http://ping.fm/2JwdP.

- Andy Geldman is catching up with work following Usability Week 2008—a great conference.

- Jay Grandin is trying to blend inflammatory language into a highchair ad.

- Alexandra Watson is naming corporate conference rooms after cereal brands. Meet me in Cap'n Crunch at 3 p.m.

Every Word's a Keyword

As you're contemplating how best to describe yourself, your work, and your goals and aspirations, keep in mind that every word of your profile is a potential keyword. Now that's not to say that a good profile is simply a string of eye-popping keywords because no one wants to read that, and ultimately, it doesn't give anyone a feel for who you are, just what you've done. But keep in mind that keywords help people to find your profile, and you should make sure that you use a lot of them, especially ones that are specific to your own industry. "Southwest Airlines started using 'cheap flights' in their profile, because that's how people searched for flights," said Krista Canfield, LinkedIn's public relations manager. "That upped their search engine optimization (SEO), because that's the search term most commonly used. Fill your profile with keywords that will come up in Google searches."

Okay, fair enough, but how do you know which words to choose? Turn right back to LinkedIn. No matter what your job or level of experience, you're going to find others on LinkedIn who are very much like you. Search for the job title you currently hold or dream of holding. Then search those profiles for keywords that you may not have thought of on your own. "Go to the People search and look for titles you're interested in, like Project Architects," advised Anne Pryor. "See their profiles and the words they use. Then see what groups they're in." Now you have not only the keywords that can add zip to your own profile but also some new destinations to consider as you begin joining groups.

A Citizen of LinkedIn and the World

When you read John Rajeski's profile on LinkedIn (Figure 2-9), you quickly see that he lists himself as a "global citizen." This term appears right in his headline, along with "business developer," "marketing professional," and "photographer." Keep reading, and you'll gain a wealth of well-rounded and dynamic information about this man. He has a long and varied career that's taken him all over the world. His special area of interest is in Asia. When John reviews the profiles of other LinkedIn members, he admits to looking for different features depending on different circumstances. "It could range from who they're connected with, their industry, geographic location, and/or respective expertise," he said.

As you scroll down through his LinkedIn profile, you'll see that he has a long and detailed list of projects completed and areas of expertise achieved. He also has worked to present this information very effectively in a combination of bulleted list and prose. This allows you to quickly pull out the keyword-rich experience he's gained but also to get a feel for how he writes and presents his thoughts and ideas.

When we asked him for advice about creating a great profile, he offered us both objective and subjective wisdom. "Objectively, I would encourage people to be as forthright and professional as possible," he said. "Subjectively, it could be argued that depending upon their respective background/experience, that it is dependent upon what a given individual considers 'informative and appealing.'" We pressed John for even more advice, and he succinctly told us something he actually considered obvious. We think it deserves to be stated quite clearly as you contemplate the words you'll use to represent yourself:

"Remember that whatever you post on LinkedIn becomes a permanent/virtual record. So do be careful regarding using profanity. Refrain from personal attacks or being too critical of a previous employer. Avoid submitting a post that you may come to regret later."

John S. Rajeski ②

APAC Business Development / Marketing Professional |
Photographer | Global Citizen

Singapore | Information Technology and Services

Current	• **Consultant: Mobile, Enterprise & Consumer Strategy** at C Scout
Past	• Vice-President, International Projects at PartnerVision Ventures • Consultant at Hawaii DBEDT & Super Bowl XL • Global Marketing Consultant at CGNET see all...
Education	• Hawaii Pacific University • University of San Francisco
Recommendations	16 people have recommended John S.
Connections	500+ connections
Websites	• rajeski.com • Blogski: Convergence... • ROAD PHOTOS
Public Profile	http://www.linkedin.com/in/johnsrajeski

* Send InMail Free
* Get introduced through a connection
* Add John S. to your network
* Forward this profile to a connection
* Search for references

Flag profile photo ss...

You have exchanged 10 messages with John S., including "RE: McGraw-Hill Book Interview." See all messages.

How you're connected to John S.

You
⇓
David Yaskulka
⇓
② John S. Rajeski

John S.'s Q & A

Expertise in
- Job Search (9 best answers)
- Starting Up (7 best answers)
- Business Plans (6 best answers)
...and 33 others

30 Questions - 30 Answers   See all Q&A »

John S. Recommends (21)

Monty Metzger, *Managing Director, manager tours & CScout Trend Consultancy*

Summary

Career Driver: An opportunity which will allow me to fully apply my passion for developing breakthrough products and services; that solve customer demands and have lasting commercial value in the global marketplace.

Strengths Finder Top 5:

- Strategic

- Input

- Relator

- Focus

- Command

SENIOR BUSINESS DEVELOPMENT & MARKETING PROFESSIONAL

Highly accomplished, experienced, and dynamic Information Technology Executive with more than 13 years in entrepreneurial business development. A superior record of achievement and success developing and closing business in highly competitive markets (with a focus on Asia) complements exceptional tenacity in building new business, securing customer loyalty, and forging strong relationships with external business partners. Highly focused and goal-oriented leader with proven strategic, analytical, organizational, communications, and networking skills.

Figure 2-9: John S. Rajeski is a citizen of LinkedIn and the world.

Your Summary

Your summary is the space for you to elaborate on your professional life. If people reviewing your profile have gotten this far, they've already learned your name and seen your photo, headline, and perhaps status. You don't want to lose them here! You have plenty of room in this space to describe what you do, what you've done, and what spins your propeller. Just be sure to let some of your personality show. The people who read your profile want to come away feeling as though they know something more about you when they're done, so reward them with the tidbits that help to describe you. You're giving them not only facts but also a flavor for what you may be like as a person. Fill it with keywords, sure. Even include some bullet points if that's a good way to detail what you've done. But don't make it simply a dry listing of jobs, tasks, and history.

TIP

Run your spell checker! If you don't have a Web browser that includes a spell-check feature—and Mozilla Firefox does—be sure to cut and paste your text into your word processor and run it through for spelling mistakes. It's a little thing, but that's all the more reason not to let a little mistake turn someone off to your profile.

Your Specialties

Here's the place to really pack in the keywords. Fill this area with every detail you can think of that would entice your next employer to take a closer look. "You should consider where you want to work and tailor your profile accordingly," said Jacqueline Wolven, whose headline proclaims her the "Smartest Girl in the Room" and a marketing specialist for small businesses (see Figure 2-10). The Specialties area of her profile includes nearly 15 separate and searchable keywords describing her services and experience. She noted that attention to her profile significantly increased with the phrase "Smartest Girl in the Room." Just keep in mind that in the wise advice of Chuck Hester, "Everything you put in your profile has to be traceable." Make sure that you can back your claims with hard facts before you make them.

Inside Tips for a Great Profile from LinkedIn

Krista Canfield, public relations manager for LinkedIn, clearly has an advantage over most of the rest of us when it comes to creating a great profile. She was kind enough to share some insider information that will make your profile even better. Here are two of her most important pieces of advice:

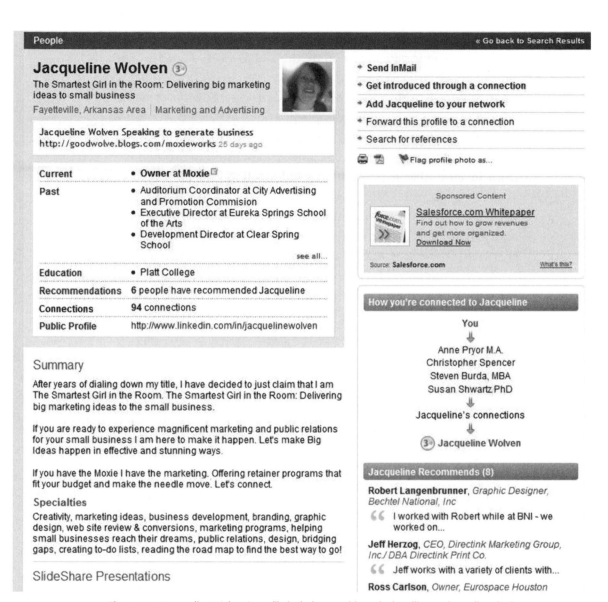

Figure 2-10: Jacqueline Wolven's profile includes a grabber of a headline and a well-crafted Specialties section.

1. When you fill in the box for your Web site, click on "Other." That lets you put your actual Web site's name there instead of the URL. Then use one of the other two links to put your company's Web site so that people can gain more information about the nature of your work. Finally, save your last position in the field for your latest article, award, achievement, or whatever else happens to reside online. That will help you with SEO on your name.

2. Customize your LinkedIn URL. When you first sign on to LinkedIn, you'll receive a generic URL supplied by the site. It's very easy to overlook this simple but practical piece of advice to improve your own branding. Change your LinkedIn URL to be exactly the same as your name is known professionally. For example, if you're a married woman who has taken her husband's name, you might want to put your maiden name in your profile name. That way, people who studied or worked with you prior to your marriage will still be able to find you. However, when it comes to your URL, change it to be the same as the name you are known by professionally. It makes it easier for people to remember you and your profile location if you include that name. No one will search that field for your maiden name. The same will hold true for anyone whose given name is different from their common name; for example, substitute Bill for William or Chuck for Charles if that is how you're known.

Your Experience

As you go about completing your profile, you'll want to detail your experience at your current job and each of your previous employers. This is not the place for dry iterations of the tasks and action items you completed at each stop along your employment journey. You want to make this section sparkle. "You want to make your profile shine," says Bryan Webb. "Add and expand on your experience and what you've done at each position. If I'm reviewing a profile, and don't find it compelling, I will not take it any further. Make your experience compelling and exciting," he advised.

Don't just list what you've done; add details about how you did it. Your well of experience should be broad, but here's the place to also make sure that it's deep. What other departments did you work with to achieve that big project? How did you manage people? What were the proudest moments while you were at any particular job? Give people something to distinguish you from all the others who may share your job titles and your employment history. Make the person reading about your experience want to know more so they'll be enticed to contact you. If this sounds like a lot of work, it is. But it's also your best shot at making yourself desirable in the eyes of that next employer.

LinkedIn Applications

LinkedIn's Applications area was still in beta testing as we wrote. No doubt this is an area of the site that will grow and expand as more people come to want more features and functionality from their lives on LinkedIn. The applications are fabulous tools for making your profile and your life on LinkedIn more vibrant and engaged. Rather than step you through each one, many of which may have changed by the time you read this, we'll look at the purpose of the applications and just what you may be able to do with them.

One favorite application that couldn't be simpler to add to your profile is Reading List by Amazon, shown in Figure 2-11. Here's where you can create your own personal bookshelf that will reside on your profile. Include reviews of books you're currently reading. Spread the word about titles you've found intriguing but haven't yet gotten to read. Creating this list gives you just one more way of connecting to your fellow LinkedIn visitors on a personal and human note. Of course, feature books that support your work life, but don't hesitate to include that latest page-turner, too. Here's a simple, easy, but quite direct way to let your personality and taste shine through your profile.

Bloggers have two options on LinkedIn. You can create your blog through WordPress, a hugely popular member of the blogging universe. Once you create your WordPress blog, you can easily link it to your profile. That way, every time you add a blog entry, your profile will reflect the new addition. Bloglink allows you to connect your existing blog to your LinkedIn profile. Through Bloglink, your network will be notified every time you update a blog entry. Likewise, you'll be notified when members of your network have updated their blogs too. This will go a long way toward building your own personal brand, both on LinkedIn and on the Web in general.

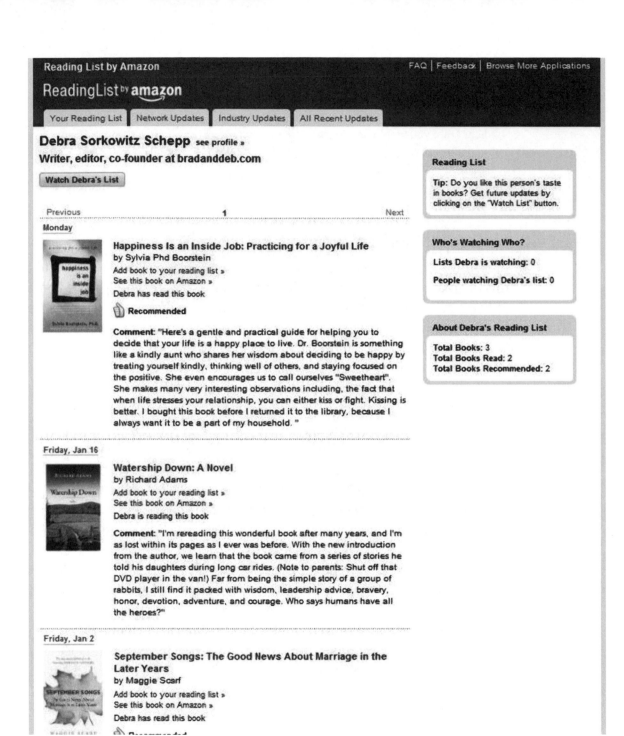

Figure 2-11: The Reading List by Amazon application lets you list and recommend books you think others might enjoy.

Still another useful and dynamic application is Google Presentations. With this feature, you can either upload an existing PowerPoint presentation to your profile or create a dynamic presentation to showcase the work you've done. Anyone visiting your profile can click through the slides to gain more detail about your work life. Figure 2-12 provides an example of a presentation corporate trainer and organizational developer Terrence Seamon included on his profile to spotlight some of his accomplishments.

Figure 2-12: Terrence Seamon used Google Presentations to add a slide show about his career and experience to his profile.

Among the other applications currently offered on LinkedIn are document-sharing functions, a poll-creation feature, a buzz application that lets you tract the word of mouth your company's getting on such sites as Twitter, and even a travel application. Use this last one the next time you're planning a business trip to see if you'll be able to meet some of the members of your LinkedIn network face to face.

Profile Dos and Don'ts

Elizabeth Garazelli is a recruiter who spends hours every day on LinkedIn. She was kind enough to share not only her own insights into what grabs her about a profile but also a detailed list of some basic dos and don'ts to consider as you go about building your profile. "I first look at someone's current job title," she said. "Then I read through their past job titles. Next, I look at the responsibilities that they had at each job, and in some cases, I look at their education degrees and/or their geographic location, if that's applicable." We grant you that this is just a matter of one person's taste and opinion, but it's an opinion built on having reviewed many thousands of LinkedIn profiles.

Do put in as much information as possible. Be sure to include not just your job titles but also your responsibilities at each job. Put down your educational degrees, and include any foreign languages that you speak.

Do put that you are open to "Career Opportunities" under Contact Settings. If you're concerned that this will signal to your boss that you're looking for a job, at least put that you're open to Expertise Requests because then I will feel comfortable asking you who you know who might be right for the position I'm trying to fill. (Then you can raise your own hand if you'd like.)

Do put in keywords that relate to your areas of expertise under Specialties. I have a friend who listed her title as "Multimedia Producer" and discussed CDs and DVDs, but by adding the words *audio* and *video* as keywords, she'll likely have more people contact her.

Do add your picture. It makes people feel more connected to you, and people like to do business with people whom they feel they know.

Do join appropriate professional and alumni groups. It makes you more accessible to recruiters.

Don't put in "cutesy" titles like "Marketing Goddess of the World," "Head Geek," or "Chief Bottle Washer." This will not attract my attention; it will cause me to skip over you.

Don't be vague with your job title. "Experienced Finance and Marketing Executive" is too generic. Much better is "VP Marketing at XYZ Company," and then put *finance* as a keyword under your Specialties.

Don't change your job title to "Consultant" if you're recently unemployed unless you're actively looking for consulting assignments. Just leave your most recent job title there. The dates of your employment will tell me if you're still there or not.

Don't brag about how many connections you have. If you have more than 20, I'm suitably impressed. Boasting "2,700+ connections!" makes me think that you'll link with just anyone.

Office Manager

Cher Lon Malik wasn't even looking for a job when her current job found her on LinkedIn.

Not only did Cher Lon Malik find her current job through LinkedIn, but she's found 75 other people senior-level executive jobs and tripled her personal business from last year. It all began about four years ago when Cher Lon, then in advertising sales for AOL/Time Warner, read in a business magazine that LinkedIn was "The place for lead generation." Furthermore, the article noted that "if you're not on LinkedIn, you're nobody."

So Cher Lon got busy and created a profile. Soon recruiters were calling her daily. Although she had no plans to leave AOL/Time Warner at the time, a persistent recruiter contacted her three times about the same position. "I finally listened," she said, "and I'm glad I did." The job was for an office manager at Informatica, and it called for her to contact some of the same types of people she was already reaching out to at AOL/Time Warner.

Cher Lon attributes her good luck to the quality of her profile. "I believe the recruiter found me because of the keywords in my profile," she said. "At Informatica, I have to reach out to CIOs," she said, and "I've found that LinkedIn gives you a reputation. I've been 90 percent effective in contacting senior-level professionals I've located through LinkedIn." Cher Lon feels that this has a lot to do with the quality of the people using the site. "If you're on LinkedIn, you must be a good guy," she said. "It gives you an automatic reputation." Cher Lon also noted that the LinkedIn community is very protective, working hard to keep the quality of the site high. "They will correct people who misspell a lot of words," she noted.

Cher Lon belongs to 40 to 45 LinkedIn groups and has found scores of job postings on the Groups discussion boards. She's a firm believer in LinkedIn's "pay it forward" philosophy and, as an old hand on LinkedIn, has reposted the jobs she's found in other group discussion groups. As a result, she's helped many people find new jobs all because of her skill at using the site and her willingness to help others.

Consultant

Dhana Pawar is a cofounder of Yojo Mobile and also works as a mobile/wireless strategy and development expert. Yojo Mobile has developed Web and mobile services such as Mizpee (www.mizpee.com) and Yojo Mama (www.yojo-mama.com) that are geared toward women.

> I have benefited immensely from LinkedIn, especially with the consulting side of things. One day, I was contacted by the CEO of a leading women-focused mobile company saying she saw my profile on LinkedIn. She loved the fact that I too had been working on developing mobile services for the female demographic and would love to get me on board full time or as a consultant on one of their key projects. We got talking on LinkedIn, the result of which was a long and extremely satisfying consulting engagement with the company on one of their most important and fun projects.

> The best part is that I now am connected to most of the senior management that work/worked with that company, and we are already helping each other find projects, jobs, partnerships, and the like!

 # Web Designer

Patrick Ortman is a Web designer and producer of original Web entertainment.

> I've been using LinkedIn and other sites since they came out. The best story I have is how a writer found out about our new Web series through LinkedIn. We connected, and our show *Couch Cases* ended up getting featured in *USA Today*.

> One of the great things about LinkedIn is when you make an update to your profile, your network is notified. I've had situations where current or past clients have seen my updated LinkedIn profile and offered me additional work after finding out that we have capabilities they didn't know about.

LOOKING AHEAD

As we began this chapter, we told you that the steps you'll take to complete your profile are carefully detailed and supported on LinkedIn. All the rest is as much an art as it is a science. It would be wonderful to claim that we had all the answers about what you should and shouldn't put into your LinkedIn profile. Honestly, we only had some of those answers. The beauty of LinkedIn is that each profile, created by an individual, is bound to reflect that individual. You most likely know better than most what puts your work history, philosophies, and expertise in the best light. Keep working on it, and you'll have a profile that will make you proud. With that profile complete, you are ready to begin enjoying everything else on LinkedIn. Throughout the next chapters you'll learn about many of the amazing features the site offers and the wonderful things you can learn and accomplish there. Your next step is to take that 100 percent, ever-changing, ever-vibrant profile and start building your network. Chapter 3 will help you with all the necessary details and strategies you'll need to create your own corner of LinkedIn populated with some very interesting people.

Build and Work Your LinkedIn Network

Nothing much can happen on LinkedIn until you've built your profile. But your profile won't take you very far without a robust network to draw on. So now that you've created your own place on LinkedIn and it's at or getting to be 100 percent complete, let's turn to building the network that's going to make everything else take off. Your network on LinkedIn is at once very much like the network you've been working to build ever since you asked your high school teacher for that first recommendation and unlike anything else you've ever experienced.

There are two schools of thought about what makes a great and effective network on LinkedIn:

1. Link with as many people as possible, without regard for whether or not you actually know the person. The larger the network, the better.

2. Link only with people you actually know; be selective when building your network.

We'll look at the differences between these philosophies but leave you to decide which approach is right for you.

In many ways, your network is the hub of everything else that happens on LinkedIn, and it can even serve as the hub of your professional life. You know that networking is important to your professional success. But what happens when you have the power to potentially network with more than 35 million people? The possibilities before you expand quickly and in sometimes unexpected ways.

In the classic 1991 Albert Brooks movie *Defending Your Life,* Yuppie Daniel Miller, played by none other than Brooks, dies and finds himself in Judgment City, where he is asked to defend his actions during his brief lifetime. Now Miller never quite conquered his insecurities to become the assertive, self-confident type of person who gets to move beyond life on earth. But we can forgive him once his defense attorney reveals that Miller uses only about 3 percent of his brain! Please, don't feel too superior yet, because according to Rip Torn, who plays the attorney, no one on earth uses more than 5 percent of their brains. There are simply better parts of the universe for better-wired individuals, such as Torn himself, who happens to use 48 percent of his brain.

Now there's no data to suggest whether we use 3 or 48 percent of our networks, but we *do* know that when it comes to networking, most people are a lot more like Albert Brooks than Rip Torn. Most of us reach only a tiny percentage of the people who potentially could help us find a new job or solve a pressing business problem when we're stumped. It works the other way too. We're just as likely to be overlooked by the people we know who could truly benefit from our knowledge and experience. We're limited by our Rolodexes, our disorganization, our pasts, our personalities, the stack of business cards we all seem to keep, and even time. Computers have helped us to organize some, but the Internet actually can make things even more of a mess. Searching for key business contacts on the Web is hit or miss. Besides, how are you going to go about finding experts when you're not even sure who they may be or where to start looking? Then there's the challenge of vetting them.

LinkedIn improves our networking IQ immeasurably and has the potential to make us all networking geniuses if we use it to its full potential. In fact, this is what LinkedIn is all about—connecting with other people who can help you to accomplish more as a professional. The ability to network is what compelled many of LinkedIn's 35 million members to be a part of the site in the first place. It's why everyone on the site has created profiles and searched for connections and why many have gone on to join groups, answer questions from strangers, and much more.

YOUR VERY OWN LINKEDIN NETWORK

LinkedIn will become whatever it is that you work toward making it. As a tool, you'd be hard pressed to find a more effective way of tracking down colleagues, mentors, apprentices, and friends. "At first I thought, 'Oh no, another site like MySpace or Facebook,'" admitted LION Steven Burda. (LION stands for LinkedIn Open Networker, and as we'll soon describe, a LION is someone who links with as many people as possible.) "But on LinkedIn, I met my professors, business people, those who I have heard at speaking events! I went home and created my own profile." Of course, Steven has pinpointed the essence of LinkedIn. Build a network, and a world of professional experience opens before you. Everyone knows that when you're looking for a new job, it's especially important to network: Speak to colleagues who may know of appropriate openings, neighbors, family, anyone who can help you land that new job. Yet many of us have looked at the prospect of this task and thought, even among all the people I know, I still don't know anyone in a position to help me land this or that particular job.

Dig Your Well before You're Thirsty

Your LinkedIn network can be a valuable asset to your business life whether you're currently working or not. But both Seven Burda and Chuck Hester told us the importance of having an active and vibrant network in place before you need to look for a job. Once you've found yourself in need of a new job, however, you can really crank your LinkedIn networking into overdrive. So don't despair if you happen to be reading this after your thirst has set in. You'll use many of the same techniques to build your job-hunting network as you'd use to cement a network while already employed.

Determine Your Goals before You Dig

It's difficult to create something without an understanding of what it is you wish to have once you're finished. This is not to say that you should be so rigid as to eliminate the delightful serendipity that can come from being on LinkedIn. But just as you thought carefully about what you wanted your profile to say about you before you put the finishing touches on it, you'll need to decide what role your LinkedIn network will play in your life before you can actually create the most effective network for you. Building a solid, well-rounded network not only will help you to find and land that next job, but it also will be there to provide expertise, referrals, and support once you're sitting behind your new desk.

 ## LinkedIn: A Recruiter's New Best Friend

In all her years of matching job candidates with job openings, Virginia Backaitis has seen a little bit of everything. But without question, LinkedIn has helped her to do her job even better. Not only does she use the site to find, vet, and connect with potential candidates and employers, but she also uses the Answers section to research questions and issues to support her journalism work. Virginia writes frequently for the New York Post. She recently described to us what makes LinkedIn such a great place for recruiters, hiring managers, and job seekers.

Virginia Backaitis is a partner at BrilliantLeap! and a recruiter with more than two decades of experience.

If I post a job listing on Monster.com, for example, by the time I get to my office, I may have 500 responses. That's too many to be helpful. But if I get a response from my friend, then at least I'll do a phone interview out of loyalty to that friend. Hiring is risky, so I almost always go with someone who has a recommendation. On LinkedIn, I think, "What companies would hire people to do this job?" Then I go look for people who might know someone who would be right. I generally unearth a candidate, maybe someone who isn't even looking for a job. If you're looking for advancement, but your boss isn't dying, you may need a new place to move up.

I have actually recruited people to fill jobs through LinkedIn, for example, an equity research person at one of our financial companies. I simply put in the names of those companies to see who I might know working in similar positions. Then I ask some questions. Who's good at this? If you were going to leave your company, who would you want to take with you? LinkedIn lets me know these people are already good, because someone I know knows them. My real job is qualifying them through due diligence, but we already know the person can do the job. We're left with a personality, geography, and compensation fit.

Even with all her experience and expertise, Virginia doesn't support the concept of "open networking," or connecting with everyone who asks you to be a part of their network, whether you know them or not. When we spoke, she had about 230 connections in her network, which is significant, but a number that makes her more of a cub than a LION. "Know who you are linked to," she advised. "Some people want to have the biggest network possible. Make sure you're linking to people who really like and support you." Virginia said that although some people seem to be very enthusiastic about building huge networks, seeing large numbers of connections makes her skeptical about how much respect those individuals actually have for their networks.

LINKEDIN OPEN NETWORKERS (LIONs)

A LinkedIn LION will literally link to just about anyone who requests a connection. Some of the LIONs who were so generous with their time and ideas while we researched this book have tens of thousands of connections. Of course, each of those connections has a network, so the more connections LIONs make, the greater number of people they can gain access to. "I have about 16,500 contacts," said LION Todd Herschberg when we spoke. "Of the 30 million people on LinkedIn [at that time], I could reach out to any one of about 18 million people to find a job." Now, for some, that is an absolute windfall of humanity, but for others, the question may remain: What exactly am I suppose to do with 18 million people once I've found them?

The official word from LinkedIn goes against the LION philosophy. You'll find advice all over the site to connect only with the people who you know and trust. What's more, LinkedIn has recently instituted a cap on the number of connections you may have at 30,000. LinkedIn notifies members who are at or will exceed that cap if they attempt to invite or add additional contacts that will push them over the limit.

For the most part, we found that the LIONs were already super networking connectors in their real lives before they discovered LinkedIn. Some of the LIONs we met were actually building their own networks in hopes of someday becoming recruiters themselves. Others used a combination of LinkedIn and in-person networking to connect with as many people as they possibly could. "You don't know what's lurking around the corner," said Gary Unger, LION and LinkedIn trainer. "The downside is that someone may try to sell you something, but I can always delete that person."

A Den Full of LIONs

Let's take a look at some LIONs so that we can better understand what motivates them and see if those same motivations appeal to you. Then we'll consider why becoming a LION may not be such a great idea. By the time we get to the details of actually building your network, you'll have ample information to decide for yourself which side of this coin looks most appealing.

CHUCK HESTER I use LinkedIn as a database. I contact 1,000 people routinely. The others are occasional when we have some common business. When I travel, I reach out through LinkedIn to network within the city I'm visiting, and I do LinkedIn dinners or breakfasts that meet face to face. At a minimum, 10 show up, but I've had as many as 35. When I first came to LinkedIn, I tried to connect with the connectors. There's a top 100 list. I went to the top 50 and invited them into my network. Mostly all of them accepted. For each one I connect with, I find five connections in their network. Once I reached 500 connections, I stopped inviting. Now people invite me.

MIKE O'NEIL Here's the number 41 most-connected member of LinkedIn. When we spoke, he had more than 19,000 connections.

My network is growing at 500 connections per month. I have strategies that can get you there very quickly. I may invite 1,000 in a week, 2,000 in a month. Since LinkedIn is three levels deep, if I have 50 people connected to me, I actually have 50,000. Once you've got your network in place, then you get to go on and tell people what they can do to help you. But you have to start out with a promise to help first.

TODD HERSCHBERG I may be the 46th most linked-in member on LinkedIn. I know I'm in the top 50. I have about 16,500 connections. I've met, in person, about half of those. I'm a very outgoing type of guy. I'm always happy to connect, because you never know where the next opportunity or job offer will come from. I've also founded the largest networking group in Orange County, California. There are now more than 3,000 members.

STEVEN BURDA Is having so many connections a good thing? There are two sides to every story. Some say it's quantity versus quality. I am from the MySpace generation. I was one of the first to use social networking. It's not what you know, but who you know. I keep track of people in three ways. I have a good memory. I remember names, and I put two plus two together. I make a note in my folder. There is no way I know every single person in my network, but I try to add five to ten people each week.

Well, maybe not quite that often. But adding to your network in a more organic and simple way is the other alternative. If you've decided that you're no LION, you'll find that your network can still grow to impressive proportions. Since you gain the connections of all your connections, your network expands at a dizzying rate. For example, if you have 102 connections, LinkedIn is likely to report that your total network gives you access to more than a million people. Although that number sounds a little preposterous, you'll find that depending on your connections' networks, you really do have an enormous pool of potential colleagues and associates.

TIP

"Make sure you're connected to people who are invested in your future."—Krista Canfield, public relations manager at LinkedIn.

Building your network by starting with the people who you know and trust and then moving out in a more gradual way is the path many LinkedIn members recommend. It's also the strategy LinkedIn as a company supports. "LinkedIn was founded to work on the relationships you already have," explained Krista Canfield. "If you connect with people who don't really know you, they can't vouch for you. LinkedIn should be like your Rolodex, and you wouldn't just pass that along to strangers. This site isn't meant to just find people." Instead, LinkedIn was meant to be a gathering place for sharing professional goals and career development. "Look at LinkedIn as if it were a business lunch," said Krista. "You wouldn't just blanket the whole network. You wouldn't announce your needs to a room full of people. Don't forget your manners." If you think of LinkedIn that way, it's a little embarrassing to consider that you'd just blast your requests to everyone at once.

Embarrassment aside, another possible disadvantage of becoming a LION is the amount of time and effort it will take to keep track of that enormous network. Think about it: If you have tens of thousands of connections, every time someone in that network changes his or her status (which, as you remember, is important to do frequently), makes a connection, or answers or asks a question, you'll get an update. Do you really want to know that much about all these people on a weekly or even daily basis? Maybe so, but it does require a good amount of work to tend this network once you've built it. "As you grow professionally," noted Krista, "you know it isn't necessarily how many people you know, but who the people you know are."

These Aren't LIONs, but They're also Not Pussycats

Many people on LinkedIn have large, vibrant, thriving networks without opening them up to anyone and everyone. Through our research, we met people with many dozens of connections, and they call on their networks to support their careers and solve pressing work issues. If by now you've come to think that you're not of the personality or nature to become a LION yourself, don't despair. You actually may be better off.

BRYAN WEBB I came to LinkedIn about three years ago after attending a networking meeting at the University of Waterloo. A facilitator recommended that if you were looking for a way to improve your networking, you should use it. If I am going to connect with someone, I need to have some dialog with them, some e-mails exchanges, for example. Tell me where we met, what common ground we have. It's not just about the numbers; it's the quality. I don't have time to be a LION.

STEVEN WEINSTEIN I have about 400 connections, but I'm not an open networker. I add a connection with a reason in mind. Usually, I've had a real-world connection with them.

JACQUELINE WOLVEN You should have as your connections people you really clicked with at places where you worked, but not everyone. I dislike the LION concept. That distorts your connections. They are not true connections. I don't have a relationship with those people. I don't know their connections. They are so busy connecting! I took out anyone who was a LION in my connections.

WILL THE LIONS AND THE NON-LIONS EVER AGREE?

Will the Democrats and Republicans ever end the partisan gridlock in Washington? Will the Hatfields and McCoys make peace? Will the Trix rabbit ever get his breakfast? All these are questions left to posterity. Your challenge is to decide which type of network you personally feel will serve your professional needs best of all. And you don't have to leave that decision set in stone. Your LinkedIn network is a living and breathing entity. It's bound to change and grow along with your own professional needs and circumstances. Who's to say you won't start out dead set against becoming a LION, only to discover that you've come to believe in the doctrine of "the more the merrier"? On the other hand, you may just find that your own little corner of LinkedIn provides you with ample connections and networking opportunities, and then you'll leave well enough alone. Either way, you've got lots of great ways to build out that network and then use it to advance your business and career goals.

BUILDING YOUR LINKEDIN NETWORK

Soon after you began to complete your profile, you were prompted to add connections to LinkedIn by entering your e-mail addresses and passwords. That's absolutely the fastest way to get your network started. Presumably, some of the people you already have in your address book are people you'd like to include in your network. Figure 3-1 shows you just how simple it is to upload your e-mail address books to LinkedIn to build out your network.

If you're brand new to LinkedIn, you may be intimidated about giving out your e-mail address *and* password, but there's no need to be concerned. This is a secure network, and LinkedIn doesn't store the information you

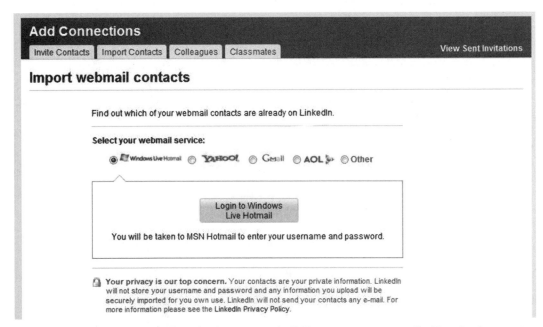

Figure 3-1: LinkedIn provides a simple, secure, and reliable way to use your e-mail address books to start building your network.

provide. Once you supply that information, you'll be able to pick and choose among the people in your address books to invite into your network. For one thing, as you're browsing through an address book, you'll be able to see who among your contacts is already on LinkedIn (there will be a LinkedIn icon next to their names). LinkedIn recommends that you approach those people first. Since they're both on the site and on your radar screen, they're good candidates. Once you've gotten those already familiar with LinkedIn to join you, you'll turn next to inviting your contacts who aren't already on the site to join you there. Whether you decide to invite everyone, as the LIONs advocate, or be more discriminating and invite only those contacts who really know you is your choice.

Using LinkedIn's Outlook Toolbar

For people who use Outlook for their e-mail, LinkedIn provides you with your very own toolbar to make integrating your address book and your LinkedIn network simple. You can download the toolbar from the hyperlink at the bottom of most LinkedIn pages. Once you have it running, not only can you import your contacts into your LinkedIn network, but the toolbar also will track the activity on LinkedIn and notify you when members of your network change their LinkedIn profiles. You also will be able to click through from your e-mail account to LinkedIn with the click of a single button. As an added benefit, your toolbar will notify you when you are frequently e-mailing someone who is not in your LinkedIn network, thereby effortlessly informing you of a potential new connection on the site.

We discussed managing your account through the Account & Settings area in Chapter 1, but it's important to discuss settings here in the context of building a network. To reach that area, click the Account & Settings link on the top right of your homepage, and note the items under the heading Email Notifications. If you were to click on Contact Settings, you would see the page shown in Figure 3-2. From this page you can control the manner in which LinkedIn members can contact you, let other members know the kinds of opportunities you are open to, and provide advice to others interested in contacting you. This is important information because it lets others know how open you are to forming new connections and the kinds of things you would like to be contacted about, such as consulting offers and job opportunities. You may want to update this information as your circumstances change.

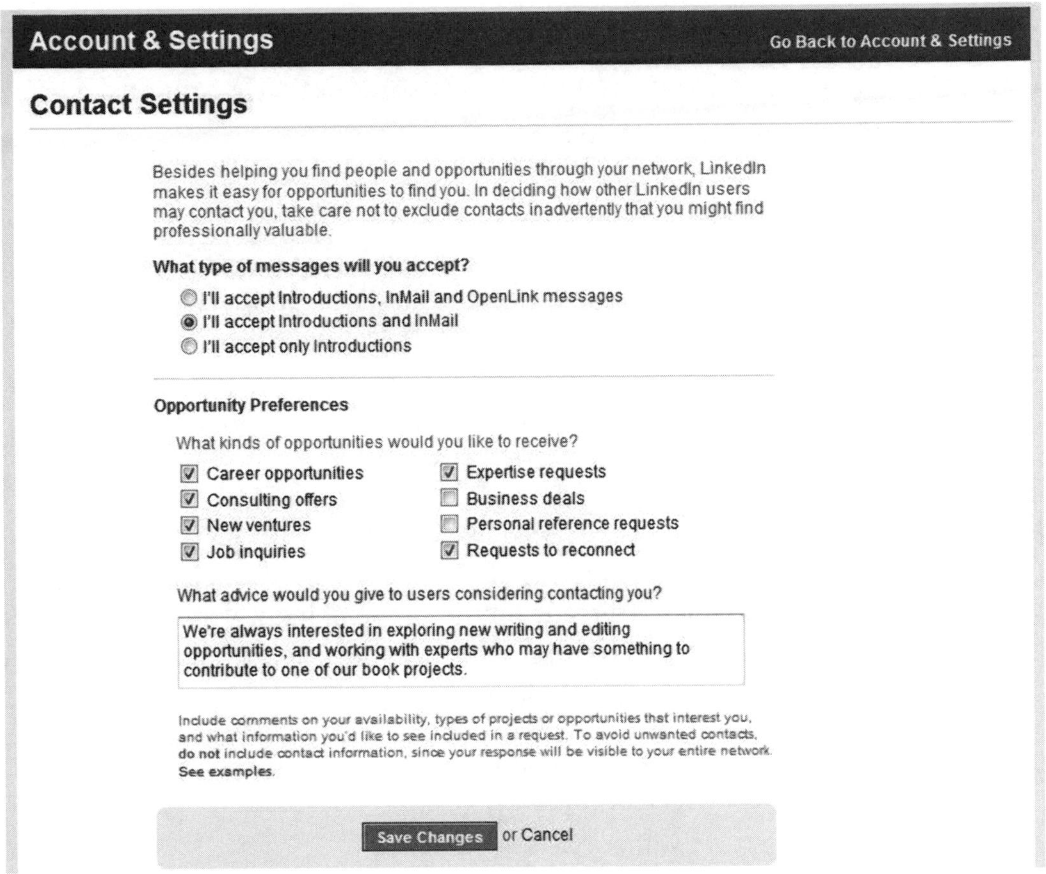

Contact Settings

Besides helping you find people and opportunities through your network, LinkedIn makes it easy for opportunities to find you. In deciding how other LinkedIn users may contact you, take care not to exclude contacts inadvertently that you might find professionally valuable.

What type of messages will you accept?

○ I'll accept Introductions, InMail and OpenLink messages
◉ I'll accept Introductions and InMail
○ I'll accept only Introductions

Opportunity Preferences

What kinds of opportunities would you like to receive?

☑ Career opportunities   ☑ Expertise requests
☑ Consulting offers   ☐ Business deals
☑ New ventures   ☐ Personal reference requests
☑ Job inquiries   ☑ Requests to reconnect

What advice would you give to users considering contacting you?

We're always interested in exploring new writing and editing opportunities, and working with experts who may have something to contribute to one of our book projects.

Include comments on your availability, types of projects or opportunities that interest you, and what information you'd like to see included in a request. To avoid unwanted contacts, do not include contact information, since your response will be visible to your entire network. **See examples.**

[Save Changes] or Cancel

Figure 3-2: The Account & Settings screen allows you to control the way other LinkedIn members can reach you on the site.

Adding Connections

Once you have your network underway by uploading your e-mail address books, LinkedIn will help you to add connections that you may not have already considered. Click on the green Add Connections link on the left side of your homepage. You'll then see four tabs presenting new possibilities for connections on the site. Figure 3-3 clearly shows your choices. You can invite contacts who may not already be in your address book, but you'll have to have their e-mail addresses to do this. You can import your e-mail contacts, which you've already done. You also can browse through the last two tabs, Colleagues and Classmates. Click on the Colleagues tab, and LinkedIn will show you a listing of all the companies you entered when you created your profile. Now you can browse the LinkedIn database to see who else

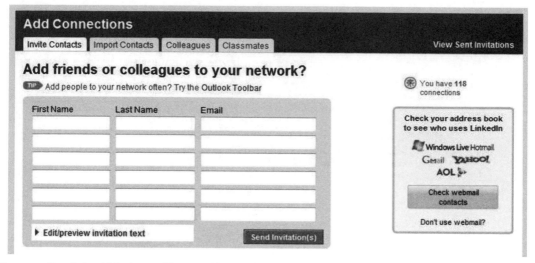

Figure 3-3: The choices LinkedIn provides you with to enhance your network.

from those companies is already on the site, making it very easy for you to find former coworkers to connect with. The next step would be to consider sending direct invitations to those people.

■ ■ Ten Ways to Bother and Annoy the LinkedIn Community

1. Use form e-mails without personalizing them.

2. Post blatant sales pitches disguised as Answers or within e-mail you send to other LinkedIn users.

3. Post nonanswers in the Answers area just to get your name and a hyperlink to your profile posted.

4. Ask questions that have been asked many times before.

5. Invite people to join your network without explaining how you know them.

6. Misrepresent yourself within your profile.

7. Don't proofread your profile and other public comments.

8. Disregard legitimate requests for introductions or connection requests.

9. Treat LinkedIn as though it were Facebook or MySpace by posting trivial status updates, etc.

10. Don't make the most of the site by posting a bare-bones profile, not using the Company and Answers section, or not building your network.

COLLEAGUES Once you've browsed your lists of colleagues on LinkedIn, you can easily keep up-to-date with new arrivals to the site. LinkedIn tracks how recently you've checked for new colleagues and offers you the option of viewing all colleagues or only the new contacts who have joined LinkedIn since you last searched (see Figure 3-4).

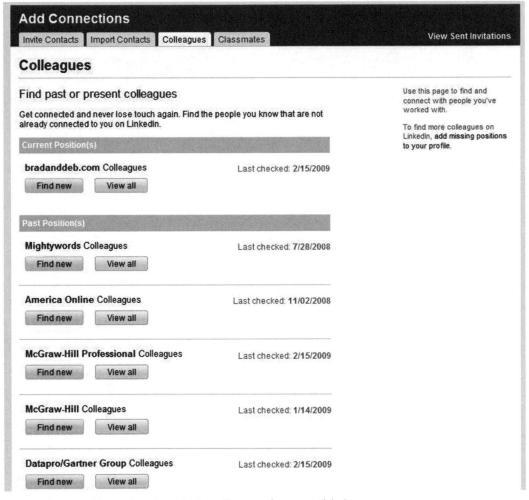

Figure 3-4: Your options for reviewing colleagues who are on LinkedIn.

CLASSMATES If you were to click this tab, you'd see the schools you've included in your profile. Click on a particular school to view profiles for classmates whose attendance overlapped your own. You also can select the option to view only those people who graduated either while you were actually at the school or from up to four years out from your attendance dates (see Figure 3-5).

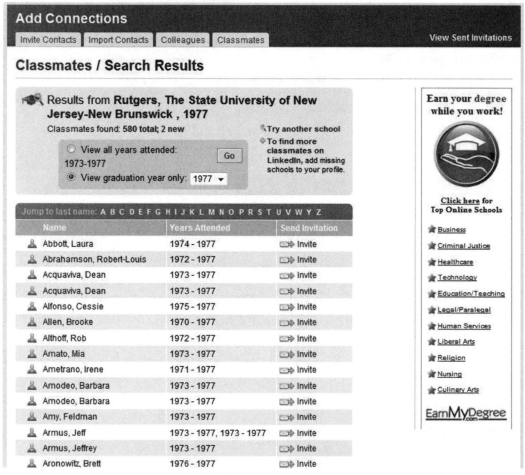

Figure 3-5: When you review classmates on LinkedIn, you can choose to view either classmates whose attendance overlapped your own at some point or who graduated during the year you specify.

⬛ ⬛ Creating Great Invitations

In your eagerness to expand your network, you may be tempted to send off dozens of generic LinkedIn invitations to the people in your address book. This is considered to be universally bad form. Think about it. Do you respond better to junk mail, even well-targeted junk mail or to personalized letters? When we asked LinkedIn's Krista Canfield how receptive people are to invitations to connect, she said, "Very receptive, if you've done your homework. The more tailored and specific you can make your request, the better. Ask yourself, 'If this showed up in my e-mail, would I respond?'"

"If I am going to connect with someone, I need to have some dialog with them. Some e-mail exchanges, for example," said Bryan Webb. "I reject the boilerplate invitations that LinkedIn provides. When I send out an invitation, I personalize it. Tell the person where you met, what common ground you share." At the very least, never approach someone on LinkedIn until you've read their profile. You may find that they are currently not open to more invitations, and knowing that before you approach them can prevent you from accidentally alienating someone who would be a very good contact at some point in the future.

⬛ Using Advanced Search

Before you know it, you'll be ready to search around for new people to include in your network using LinkedIn's advanced search feature. As we write, advanced search is in beta testing, so you may find that the screen you pull up will be slightly different based on feedback from LinkedIn users. Use the advanced search feature to narrow your search for people you share commonalities with. To get to the Advanced People Search screen, just click on the down arrow next to the People hyperlink at the top of most LinkedIn pages. You'll see that you have two choices: People and Reference. We'll look at the Reference Search option in Chapter 6; for now, let's focus on the Advanced People Search.

When you click on that hyperlink, you'll see the form shown in Figure 3-6. Using this form, you can select search parameters to include specific industries, groups, languages, companies, and titles, to name just a few. You also can sort your search results by relevance, relationship, or keyword. You'll want to experiment with this search feature to find the best way to locate

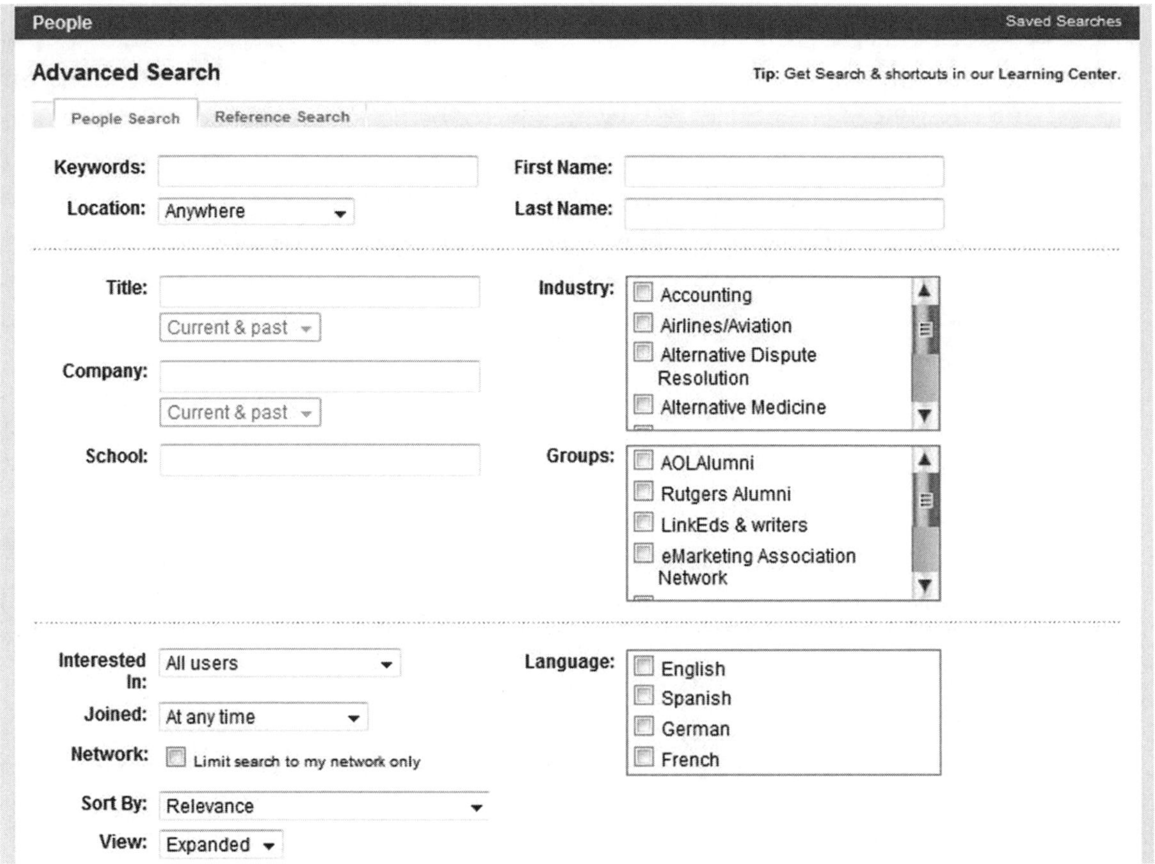

Advanced Search   Tip: Get Search & shortcuts in our Learning Center.

People Search   Reference Search

Keywords: [   ]   First Name: [   ]

Location: [Anywhere ▾]   Last Name: [   ]

Title: [   ]   Industry:
[Current & past ▾]
     ☐ Accounting
     ☐ Airlines/Aviation
     ☐ Alternative Dispute Resolution
     ☐ Alternative Medicine

Company: [   ]
[Current & past ▾]

School: [   ]   Groups:
     ☐ AOLAlumni
     ☐ Rutgers Alumni
     ☐ LinkEds & writers
     ☐ eMarketing Association Network

Interested In: [All users ▾]   Language:
     ☐ English
Joined: [At any time ▾]
     ☐ Spanish
Network: ☐ Limit search to my network only
     ☐ German
     ☐ French

Sort By: [Relevance ▾]

View: [Expanded ▾]

Figure 3-6: An Advanced People Search helps you to locate people relevant to the search parameters you set yourself.

your own good contacts, but we'll step you through an example to help you get started.

Let's say that we're looking for new connections among acquisition editors at book publishers. We'll plug in "acquisition editor" in the Title box and select "Current only" from the drop-down menu below it. We'll also select Publishing as the industry and, lacking foreign language skills, limit our results to profiles in English. We'll also select the basic view for our results and sort by relevance. After we click on the Search box, we're shown 591 different contacts that meet our search criteria (see Figure 3-7). This is a perfectly manageable number, sorted by how they are currently connected to us. We also see generic listings for people who match our search requests but are outside our network. We then can read through our results to see with whom we may want to connect.

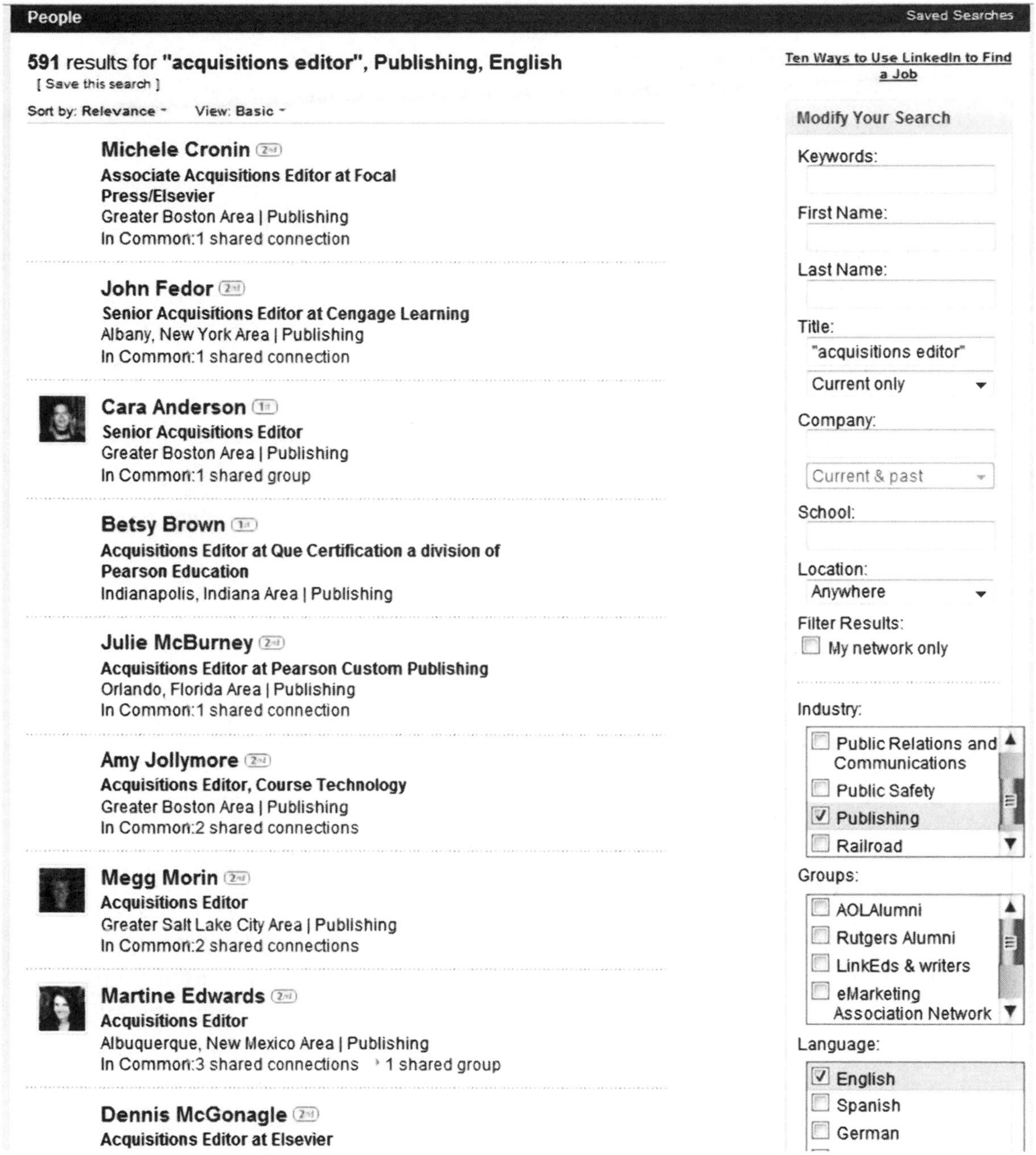

591 results for **"acquisitions editor", Publishing, English**
[Save this search]

Sort by: Relevance ▾   View: Basic ▾

Michele Cronin 2ⁿᵈ
Associate Acquisitions Editor at Focal Press/Elsevier
Greater Boston Area | Publishing
In Common:1 shared connection

John Fedor 2ⁿᵈ
Senior Acquisitions Editor at Cengage Learning
Albany, New York Area | Publishing
In Common:1 shared connection

Cara Anderson 1ˢᵗ
Senior Acquisitions Editor
Greater Boston Area | Publishing
In Common:1 shared group

Betsy Brown 1ˢᵗ
Acquisitions Editor at Que Certification a division of Pearson Education
Indianapolis, Indiana Area | Publishing

Julie McBurney 2ⁿᵈ
Acquisitions Editor at Pearson Custom Publishing
Orlando, Florida Area | Publishing
In Common:1 shared connection

Amy Jollymore 2ⁿᵈ
Acquisitions Editor, Course Technology
Greater Boston Area | Publishing
In Common:2 shared connections

Megg Morin 2ⁿᵈ
Acquisitions Editor
Greater Salt Lake City Area | Publishing
In Common:2 shared connections

Martine Edwards 2ⁿᵈ
Acquisitions Editor
Albuquerque, New Mexico Area | Publishing
In Common:3 shared connections ▸ 1 shared group

Dennis McGonagle 2ⁿᵈ
Acquisitions Editor at Elsevier

Ten Ways to Use LinkedIn to Find a Job

Modify Your Search

Keywords:

First Name:

Last Name:

Title:
"acquisitions editor"
Current only ▾

Company:

Current & past ▾

School:

Location:
Anywhere ▾

Filter Results:
☐ My network only

Industry:
☐ Public Relations and Communications
☐ Public Safety
☑ Publishing
☐ Railroad

Groups:
☐ AOLAlumni
☐ Rutgers Alumni
☐ LinkEds & writers
☐ eMarketing Association Network

Language:
☑ English
☐ Spanish
☐ German

Figure 3-7: We've found 591 potential new contacts through an Advanced People Search.

Join LinkedIn Groups

One of LinkedIn's most powerful tools is its Groups feature, and with more than 220,000 groups on the site, you're sure to find a few that will interest you. Once you join a few groups, you'll likely find many potential new connections among their members.

From your LinkedIn homepage, you can access the Groups directory by clicking the Groups hyperlink on the left. From there, click on the Groups Directory button, and you'll see the screen shown in Figure 3-8. Once you're there, you're ready to start searching for relevant groups. Of course, one of the easiest to find is your college or graduate school alumni group. Also consider joining alumni groups for companies where you've worked, as well as trade groups. If you happen not to find a group that seems right for you, you can always start your own group. "You can create your own group," said Krista Canfield, "as long as it's business-oriented. It has to be business-based. We want to be a site that your boss will want you to be spending time on."

Most groups require that you ask to join, but that shouldn't intimidate you. Simply send a polite and friendly e-mail to the group leader explaining why you'd like to participate in that particular group and how you feel your background qualifies you to become a member. LinkedIn groups are quite well known for being friendly and informative places, so there's no need to hesitate to ask to join. "Joining a group allows you to connect with people without actually connecting directly to them," explained Krista. "You can reach out to anyone in a group, whether you know them directly or not." Once you've joined a group, that group's icon appears on your profile page. Having these icons makes your commitment to your LinkedIn network clear and speaks well of you as an active and engaged member of the LinkedIn community.

Groups

| My Groups | Groups Directory | Create a Group | FAQ |

Featured Groups

UCLA Anderson Alumni Network
We encourage all alumni from the UCLA Anderson School of Management to join this group to maximize the advantage of the UCLA Anderson network.

Business Development Institute (BDI)
The BDI Group on LinkedIn is a global strategic networking platform for marketing, communications and media professionals that greatly extends our member's reach beyond the physical conference.

Caltech Alumni Association
The Caltech Alumni Association is the worldwide network of graduates of the California Institute of Technology, Pasadena, California.

CIO Forum
The CIO Forum, facilitated by CIO.com/CIO magazine, is where members of the CIO community can connect and collaborate to move their business technology initiatives and careers forward. If you are a senior IT professional, we'd love to have you join—apply for membership today.

eMarketing Association Network
The eMarketing Association (eMA) is the largest association for eMarketing professionals in the world. The eMA Network group is open to all professionals with an interest in the eMarketing arena.

Haas/Berkeley Alumni
Haas/Berkeley Alumni Group is administered by the Haas Alumni Network at UC Berkeley's Haas School of Business. All alumni from the Haas School of Business are encouraged to join this group to help us expand our network of people, ideas, action.

HP Alumni Association
The Hewlett-Packard Alumni Association is an independent non-profit association of former HP employees around the world.

Search Groups

All categories ▾
All languages ▾

Search

Create a Group

LinkedIn Groups can help you stay informed and keep in touch with people that share your interests. Create a group today.

Create a Group

Figure 3-8: The Groups Directory makes it simple to find interesting groups to join on LinkedIn.

TIP

Be sure to follow the 80/20 rule after you've joined a group. In other words, contribute four times as much information as you ask for. That's part of being a good LinkedIn citizen. Examples of giving to your group would be posting relevant articles, answering questions on the discussion boards, and generally sharing your knowledge base with others.

Click on a group name, and you'll immediately learn which group members are already in your network. It's a clear sign that you've found a good group for yourself if more than a few members are already in your network. You also will see a brief description of the group and an About the Group box showing when it was created and who owns it (the creator) as well as who manages it. You also will see information about related groups.

Once you've become a member of a group, you'll have access to everything that group has to offer, and we're not just talking about the other members. Most groups include a discussion board, news article archives, and membership lists. If you choose your groups wisely, you'll log on each week to find a wealth of information provided to you by others within your profession. Of course, you'll also be busy providing your own insights and knowledge to help the other group members. "I put my modified résumé up on my groups now that I'm job hunting," said Terrence Seamon, corporate trainer and organizational developer. That's a bonus to other members of Terry's group because they may just be looking for someone with his particular background, making their candidate search just a little bit easier.

Mike O'Neil, LION, LinkedIn Trainer, and Group Advocate

LION Mike O'Neil is a big proponent of joining LinkedIn groups.

"This is one of LinkedIn's best tricks," Mike told us enthusiastically. "When you join a LinkedIn group, and you can join up to 50 of them, it's like a club." Mike went on to explain how you go about finding a group that's right for you. First, he recommends that you search by a keyword relevant to your own background. The groups in the results page are sorted by how large a membership they have.

Then you can approach the leaders of the groups. "The leaders can always be approached," advised Mike. "You're doing exactly what the group founder wants you to do." Ask that leader to please consider you for inclusion in the group.

"You don't solicit help," noted Mike. "You get the connection first; then you go back to thank them and offer your whole network as a resource to the group." The key to the groups is that once you are a member, you are free to search out and approach any other member of the group. You no longer have to work your way through your network connections to find someone willing to make an introduction for you. It completely eliminates the issue of whether you are one degree, two degrees, or three degrees removed from anyone else in the group. You all belong on equal footing.

WORKING YOUR NETWORK

It won't be too long before you'll find your network robust enough to begin making it work for you. There are as many different ways to work a LinkedIn network as there are individuals to make these networks work. No matter what you hope to accomplish on the site, you'll find great ways to bring your network to life and make it a vital part of your professional toolbox. Throughout this book you'll find chapters devoted to some of the most dynamic areas of LinkedIn with plenty of good advice about how to best use those areas. Here, we'll give you a brief but satisfying taste of just a few.

"First, update your status on your profile," said Krista Canfield, when we asked what a job hunter can do to accelerate the job-hunting process. "Answer the question, 'What are you working on?' That lets your network know that you need help."

If you're in the midst of a job search, and you have a lot of connections, it helps to be able to sort them by industry. Click on the Connections link from your profile page and then Advanced Options. From there, you can filter your connections by location or industry.

"I can use LinkedIn for educational purposes," says David Becker of PhillipeBecker. "Let's say one of our clients is a wine company, and they're thinking of doing away with corks, because it's better environmentally to use screw tops. I can go to the group and ask, 'What do you think about this?' I'll get responses that I would have had to pay for before LinkedIn."

Jump-Starting Your Career through LinkedIn

You can use your network to build a career path no matter how freshly minted that diploma may be. Young graduates just starting out can use the job histories of the long-employed to plot their own course. Krista Canfield gave us some great advice to help those just starting out.

"Go to advanced search and search for your dream job title," she said. "Then you can see how the people who have that job got there." What were their educational backgrounds? Which companies gave them the biggest boost? Is there a pattern in terms of where these professionals started and how they progressed? You may not follow along the exact path, but at least, as a newly minted graduate, you'll have a roadmap of sorts to lead you in the right direction.

Using RSS Feeds on LinkedIn

One of the long-heralded pluses of the Internet is that once you identify information you want to receive regularly, you can set up a *feed* so that updates are delivered to you; you don't have go to the Web to retrieve them. This type of technology has had many iterations over the years, from *push* technology to customized daily newspapers that, once set up, are delivered to your computer rather than to your doorstep. The latest version of the technology that delivers regularly updated information to you is called *Really Simple Syndication* (RSS).

There are many different RSS readers (called *aggregators*) that do the behind-the-scenes work for you. If you're unfamiliar with the technology, you should check out an overview such as Wikipedia's http://en.wikipedia.org/wiki/Rss. We suggest choosing a simple Web-based aggregator such as Google Reader if you're not an old hand at using RSS. Most Web browsers, such as Mozilla Firefox, also incorporate readers.

On LinkedIn, you create two types of RSS feeds: public and personal. A public feed brings you information that's available to all LinkedIn members, such as updates on the latest LinkedIn features. You can subscribe to that feed through the Learning Center. Just click on the Learning Center link at the bottom of main LinkedIn pages, and then click the orange icon that appears on the next page.

An example of a personal feed is one that brings you the latest news from your LinkedIn network. Here's how to create an RSS feed for your Network Updates:

1. From your LinkedIn homepage, click on the orange icon next to the heading Network Updates.

2. Click on Enable that appears on the next page (see Figure 3-9).

3. Click on the RSS reader of your choice, or click on the RSS icon.

4. Select Enable.

You also can set up an RSS feed to receive new Answers to question categories you follow. You'll find a complete discussion of Answers in Chapter 5.

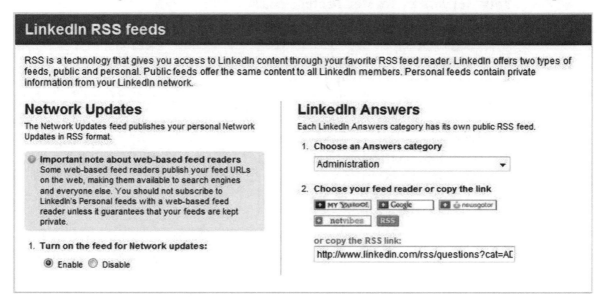

Figure 3-9: The screen that makes it very simple to add an RSS feed to your LinkedIn profile.

LinkedIn suggests that you check to see how your particular reader displays information because some actually will push your feed URLs to the Web. From there, the information can be picked up by search engines. The company advises you not to use an RSS feeder to subscribe to personal information (such as your Network Updates) until you determine that your reader keeps such information private.

Reviewing your Network Statistics

To see who is in your network, as well as the number of people you can contact through your network, go to the navigation area along the left-hand side of your LinkedIn homepage. Under the Contacts hyperlink, you'll see a link for Network Statistics. By clicking that, you'll get the screen shown in Figure 3-10, which will show you how many people are in your direct network, then those who are two degrees from you (friends of friends), and finally, those who are

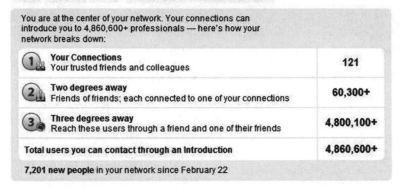

Contacts

Connections | Imported Contacts | Network Statistics   Add Connections | Remove Connections

Network Statistics

Here you see statistics about your network, including how many users you can reach through your connections. Your network grows every time you add a connection — **invite connections now.**

Your Network of Trusted Professionals

You are at the center of your network. Your connections can introduce you to 4,860,600+ professionals — here's how your network breaks down:

①	**Your Connections** Your trusted friends and colleagues	**121**
②	**Two degrees away** Friends of friends; each connected to one of your connections	**60,300+**
③	**Three degrees away** Reach these users through a friend and one of their friends	**4,800,100+**
	Total users you can contact through an Introduction	**4,860,600+**

7,201 new people in your network since February 22

The LinkedIn Network

The total of all LinkedIn users, who can be contacted directly through InMail.

Total users you can contact directly — **try a search now!**	**35,000,000+**

More About Your Network

REGIONAL ACCESS
Top locations in your network:

11%   1. Greater New York City Area
6%   2. Ssn Francisco Bsy Ares
4%   3. Washington D.C. Metro Area
4%   4. Greater Los Angeles Area
3%   5. Greater Boston Area

Your region: Washington D.C. Metro Area

Figure 3-10: The screen that allows you to track your network statistics on LinkedIn.

three degrees from you (people you have to reach through a friend and then a friend of theirs).

Removing Connections

After you have spent all that time and effort cultivating a connection, it seems counterintuitive that you'd want to remove a connection at some point. But it will happen. Relationships sour, a colleague becomes a competitor, and partners decide to go their separate ways. In such cases, you may no longer want that person to have access to your contacts, and the best thing to do in that case is remove that person as a connection.

Since LinkedIn is all about adding connections and not removing them, it's not surprising that how you go about removing someone from your contact list isn't readily apparent. Here's how you do it:

- Click the Connections hyperlink along the left-hand side of your homepage.
- Click the Remove Connections hyperlink on the right side of the blue bar across the top of the page.
- Click on the box next to the name of the contact you'd like to remove.
- Click the Remove Connections button.

Rest assured that LinkedIn wisely does not notify your connection that you have removed him or her, so there's no reason to fear any sort of retaliatory action. You also will be able to reinvite a connection at some other time should circumstances change.

I GOT A JOB ON LINKEDIN

Vice President/General Manager

Dwight Robinson made a solid connection through LinkedIn that brought his company an additional $500,000 in the second half of 2008.

Dwight Robinson is the vice president and general manager of Los Angeles Harbor Grain Terminal, a business his family has operated since 1958. The company provides logistical handling services for grain exporters shipping commodities to Asia.

It is easy for us to think that everyone in our industry knows us since we have been around for such a long time, but I know that is not the case. Last year, the LinkedIn Web site suggested that I might want to link up with "People You May Know," and one of the people the site suggested was from a commodity trading company that I was familiar with but did not have any contacts with. I sent the gentlemen an e-mail, and within 24 hours we spoke via phone, and within 48 hours we came to an agreement on our providing his company some services. We ended up doing about $500,000 worth of business in the second half of 2008, and this could turn out to be a long-term customer. Based on this experience, I have continued to use LinkedIn and have made lots of potential business contacts, and I see very good long-term opportunities because of LinkedIn.

Account Coordinator

Janice Javier was working part time for an event-planning company called Outlined Productions. The owner of the company, Pamela Fishman Cianci, knew that she was looking for a full-time job and was sending her job leads.

> She sent me a job posting that was forwarded to her on LinkedIn. My current employer, Kimberly Charles of Charles Communications, and Pamela had a mutual connection, so they were a "3rd" degree connection to each other. At that point I was already on LinkedIn but had not invested the time into building my profile and getting recommendations. So I did that and applied via LinkedIn to this position.

LOOKING AHEAD

Well, now you have a profile that is complete, or nearly so, and you have the beginnings of a vibrant and growing network of colleagues, classmates, and newly mined connections. You're ready to start pounding the LinkedIn pavement in search of your next great job opportunity. Throughout the next chapters you'll gain lots of insights into how people are using LinkedIn to enhance their careers, move up the ranks, and solve everyday business problems. Chapter 4 will provide you with lots of great ideas for using the site to find your next stop along your career path. Let's get to work!

CHAPTER 4

Use LinkedIn to Job Hunt

With your profile at 100 percent and your network expanding with each passing week, you will be ready to start exploring LinkedIn for new job opportunities any time you want to. Of course, with a keyword-rich profile and a strong network, people with the power to hire may just be looking for you at the same time. "LinkedIn is a tool, not a magic machine that gets people jobs," says Steven Burda. Steven is absolutely right. Like so many other things in life, you won't find a magic solution on the site any more than you can trade a cow for magic beans. But you will find magic in the strong and vibrant network you've built and recruiters, hiring managers, and human relations directors are all over LinkedIn looking for qualified leads. Your challenge will be to identify the ones who have jobs right for you and show them what you have to offer. Freelancers and consultants also will find that LinkedIn is a gold mine. If you already have a job, that's all that much better because the best time to job hunt is while you are still working.

Because you built your network carefully, it's full of people who know you and your work, can vouch for your credentials, and have strong connections of their own to span the breadth of the Internet for opportunities. Your job now is to decide what type of job you truly want, determine which companies hire people for that type of job, and then start prowling your network for people who can introduce you to the decision makers at those companies. Because you are also committed to helping those in your network in the same way, you'll be operating from a position of strength as you go through your search. This chapter will take you step by step through many of the specifics of a job search on LinkedIn, but of course, each individual who comes to the site brings an individual perspective. Your experience is likely to be as individual as and different from those described here as your own tastes and style.

Just a very quick reminder as we begin: Before approaching others on LinkedIn, read their profiles carefully to ensure that they're encouraging In-Mails at the moment. You don't want to approach people in a position to help you and turn them off in the process. If they have specifically stated that they are not open to contacts and you contact them, you'll do just that. It shows that you aren't looking at the network as a whole and instead are just looking out for yourself. That's contrary to the philosophy and scope of the site, and it can be difficult to recover from such a faux pas. So, with a little etiquette reminder and a lot of enthusiasm, let's travel step by step through what happens once you decide to start your LinkedIn job search.

YOUR PROFILE

Yes, we haven't forgotten that you spent hours on your profile after reading Chapter 2, but once you launch a job search, your profile is the first thing up for review. As your identity on LinkedIn, your profile lives and breathes much the same way you do. You are bound to refine your job-search goals as you explore your opportunities. That will surely lead you to discover tweaks that should be made to your profile, so let's take a look. "I think employers don't want to see just credentials," explained David Becker of PhillipeBecker. "They want to see proof of those credentials. Demonstrate your expertise." Now is the time to make your profile as specific and quantifiable as possible. If you increased profits at your last company by 40 percent, say so. If you supervised a staff of 20 people, get specific about what your group actually did and how your leadership led to its success. The more detailed you make your profile, the more a prospective employer will know about you before ever scheduling an interview.

You'll find plenty to think about in terms of the keywords you use in your profile too. As your job search moves along, you'll view profiles of potential competitors, read the profiles of people who work at companies that interest you, and gain insights into what those companies are searching for. Every industry has its own vocabulary, so the more you explore, the more you are sure to discover new and strong keywords that others in the industry are using. Keep a constant eye open for keywords you may have missed that could enhance your chances of showing up in important search results. Then be sure to edit your profile to include them.

Your Status Line

An up-to-date status line can be vital to your job-hunting efforts. "If you are out of work put 'Open to Opportunities,'" recommended Krista Canfield of LinkedIn. "It's better than 'Unemployed.'" Such positive phrasing can mean many things besides "Unemployed," but even if everyone on LinkedIn comes to view the phrases as interchangeable, keeping a positive spin is always important to a job search. Plus, it's the truth.

As tempting as it might be to pad your status with descriptors such as "Freelancer" and "Consultant," use these words only if they represent the truth. "Don't say consulting or freelancing unless it's true," advised Krista. "It will come up in an interview, and that's very awkward." Of course, if you're claiming to be a consultant, a prospective employer will want to know the details about that. Most of us aren't good enough liars to fabricate a whole group of experiences we've never had, and interviewers are pretty savvy at recognizing such fabrications even for those of us who are.

An Updated Status that Landed a Job

Dave Stevens was busy working as a radio advertising representative for two local radio stations near his California home. He'd long been a networker, attending local networking events sponsored by two local Chambers of Commerce. After each event, he'd update his e-mail contacts with the names of people with whom he'd had meaningful conversations. A monthly e-mail about miscellaneous topics helped him to keep in touch with his ever-expanding group of contacts.

At one such event, Dave met Krista Canfield from LinkedIn, who'd been enlisted to give a presentation about using the site. He'd long had a LinkedIn

Dave Stevens quickly found a new job thanks to his LinkedIn network.

account, but this presentation "really opened my eyes to the potential it had," he told us. "Well I imported all of my contacts, and one by one started building my network out there. Before I knew it, I had well over 100 connections. I started getting e-mails from people more and more through LinkedIn, every time I updated my status, answered a question, or posted a question."

Sadly, in October 2008, Dave joined the ranks of the newly laid off. "When the day hit that I was being laid off, I knew I had to alert the network and let my hard work pay off. Going to mixers, being an ambassador, and staying top of mind through my LinkedIn updates couldn't all be in vain. So, instead of sending a massive e-mail out to over 100 people, I simply updated my status." Dave actually changed his status to "I'm up for grabs! Who wants me?" Here's the rest of the story in his own words:

This was on the morning of October 1. Later that morning I received a phone call from the Santa Clara (CA) Chamber of Commerce's chief executive officer (CEO). He informed me that he had spoken with the CEO of the Mountain View Chamber of Commerce, and she was looking for someone. I should call her right away and use his name. So I did. I received a phone call that same day, in the afternoon. We set up a time for an interview, went through the process, negotiated an offer letter, and I was working by the 13th of October. That was it.

USING RECOMMENDATIONS

As you were building your LinkedIn profile, you searched your growing network for good sources of recommendations to include. Simply speaking, it is not possible to reach a 100 percent profile completion without a few recommendations. You're probably quite familiar with the process of asking for recommendations. As a matter of fact, going back into your high school years, you knew you'd have to have a few great recommendations before your college applications were complete. And ever since, you've been told to leave any job on good terms to enhance the likelihood that your former boss would be willing to write you a great recommendation. LinkedIn simply brings this whole process into the Internet age, and that can be, at once, a bonus and a challenge. "I think a lot of people use the Recommendation feature," notes David Becker. "I think that's viable if it's done well."

The bonus part comes with the realization that you can conceivably have dozens, if not hundreds, of different people willing to write a recommendation for you. With each recommendation you request, you can offer a recommendation in return. That way, you never have to feel as though you are imposing on someone. You are merely offering a free exchange of goods. Additionally, whenever you write or receive a recommendation, a notification goes out to the entire network of both parties involved. If you're swapping recommendations with a colleague who has hundreds of connections, your good work is going to be flashed before hundreds of people. Who knows which person in this list may just be looking to hire someone like you?

The challenge in using recommendations is to get good, solid, and specific recommendations from colleagues who actually know you well and to get more than one of them. "It can backfire if you have one recommendation," says David "It makes people wonder, 'What about all the others?'" Fitness expert Karen Jashinsky agrees. "If you're looking for a job, it's always good to have lots of referrals to gain a better perspective of what you're capable of," she said. So your task begins with soliciting at least a few recommendations, but it also goes beyond that. You need to make sure that your recommendations are specific enough so that they actually offer real value to someone who comes to LinkedIn to screen your background. Once your colleague agrees to write a recommendation for you, help that person out. "Scrap the generic request for recommendations, and point out what you need to have included," Krista Canfield told us. "Give them an idea of what you're looking for. The more specific you are, the better. Plus, it makes it simpler for the person filling out the form." As long as your associate has agreed to recommend you, it's time to make sure that the recommendation gives you exactly what you need.

Now, in order to know what you'll need, you can search through your groups and networks to see the types of tidbits your potential competitors include. Your recommendations are prominently displayed on your profile, and so are all the recommendations you yourself have written for people in your network. They are one of the best ways to make your profile a stand out. If you've built your network carefully, you may find that in addition to the recommendations you solicit, every now and again a former or current colleague may just add one spontaneously. Either way, you have the opportunity to review all recommendations before they appear on your profile. You actually post them; your colleagues just deliver them. When you've received a recommendation, you'll get the message shown in Figure 4-1. It's up to you whether or not you wish to add it to your profile.

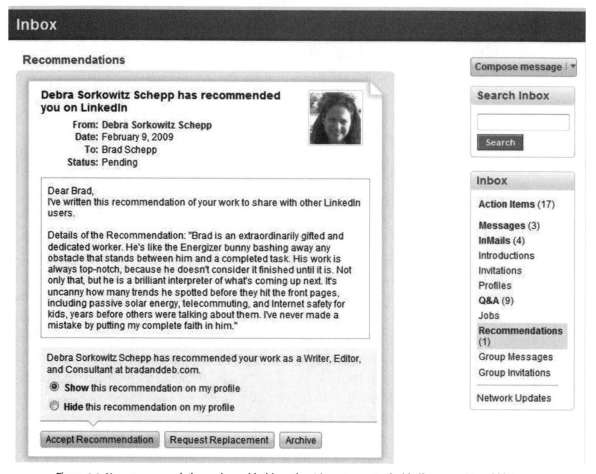

Figure 4-1: Your recommendation arrives with this notice. It's up to you to decide if you want to add it to your profile.

WORKING YOUR NETWORK

With your profile complete, including recommendations, you're ready to start working your network in search of that next job. The most exciting thing about this search is that there's simply no way to know for sure which contact is going to turn the key to your next great opportunity. "It's relationships that get you jobs," said Jacqueline Wolven, owner at Moxie Marketing and Public Relations. "Something I did 15 years ago is helping my client today," she continued. "That's the neat thing about LinkedIn; it allows you to keep connected. I used LinkedIn to connect my client with someone I'd worked with 15 years ago!" Now, all parties are happy and thriving.

As you saw in Chapter 3, the first rule of connecting on LinkedIn is clear. Don't use the standard, canned LinkedIn e-mail forms. Before you approach anyone for help, make sure that you know enough about them to write with a voice that says you know each other. Don't hesitate to remind your contact how you met, where you may have worked together, and what your common affiliation is. "It's not all about connecting with all the people you can," Krista Canfield said. "It's about finding the people who have the 'right' connections." Of course, once you're job hunting, your goal is to find the person who may have an opening to the job you seek. If that person is in your network, you're golden. But, if you have to crawl around your network a bit to find the right connection, don't despair. This is what LinkedIn was meant to do.

When we spoke with Terry Seamon, he was in the midst of a job search himself. With many years specializing in organizational development and corporate training, he was making full use of LinkedIn to locate his next job. Although he was eager to find work himself, he also was happy to help others who were job hunting, which made him a perfect candidate for using LinkedIn. "Since people are joining LinkedIn all the time, I often get e-mails from people who want to link up. That draws me back over to go ahead and approve their requests, if I know them," Terry said. "I may also accept an invitation if I've checked out their profile and found an affinity."

Terry is using his network to reach out to people he may not know. He does this by scouring his connections for connections they may have who are in his field of expertise. Once he finds someone who may be promising, he approaches his 1st degree connection to request an introduction. "You reach out through people who you are connected to," he explained. "I've used it personally, and other people have reached out to me. Usually, I'll help that person, if I can, to meet someone." Terry went on to tell us of a friend who was hoping to get a job in a New York law firm. "I was able to use my network to get in touch with someone there," Terry said. When we spoke, Terry's friend had already had the interview.

Bryan Webb Gets a Job

Bryan Webb, sales manager at AZZ/Blenkhorn and Sawle, Ltd., got his current job through LinkedIn.

Bryan Webb saw a posting on the Canadian Web site www.workopolis.com for a sales manager with a company he knew he'd like to work with. The posting called for him to send his application to the human resources director, but he decided to try a different route. Here's his story in his own words:

I decided to use LinkedIn to see if it could help me reach the hiring manager. I went to the advanced search page, typed in the company name, and found three names of company employees in my expanded network. This list included the chief operating officer (COO), who was a 3rd degree connection. I wanted to get an edge, so I sent a request for an introduction to this person to one of my contacts (a great guy). In my request, I said, "I would like to get an introduction to your contact. Would you mind forwarding this introduction?"

When I contacted the COO, I told him I'd applied to his company and would like more information about the work they do. Within three days, I'd gotten a response through this request. I also got an offer from the human relations department to come for an interview. When I arrived, I found the interview was with the COO, who I'd so recently contacted through LinkedIn.

Normally, first interviews are 45 minutes, but after 90 minutes he asked me when I could start. After two hours, Bryan asked for a formal offer letter to be sent. It turns out that the COO said he'd gotten a request to be introduced to Bryan from a contact of his on LinkedIn, someone he respected very much. The quality of that introduction is what got me the chance to meet the hiring manager. My experience on LinkedIn led directly to my getting my current job.

You're Searching for Others, but Others Are also Searching for You

Soon you'll be learning about how recruiters use LinkedIn to find great candidates for their clients. Remember that just as you are harnessing LinkedIn's power to search for your next great opportunity, you also should assume that from now on, anyone you interview with will have already learned a great deal about you through your LinkedIn activity. This is the reality of social networking, and this reality has caught many a student in its snare. That photo on a social networking site that shows an 18-year-old athlete with a beer can in his hand attending a party in a state where the legal drinking age is 21 certainly can derail the young man's scholarship hopes. Of course, your profile is completely professional after all your efforts based on Chapter 2, but it's still so important for you to comport yourself with total professionalism while on LinkedIn.

"We have not so much hired anyone we've found on LinkedIn," explained David Becker. "But we have used it to screen people. When we're looking at candidates, we'll use it to see how they've presented themselves and to see if what they've said is reality. We see who they are connected with. For the most part, it gives more depth to a candidate. It's an interesting place to see how people interact." David continued to explain that LinkedIn is the perfect place to demonstrate your expertise. "Employers can see that," he said. "If you're an insurance broker, for example, be involved in an insurance group and position yourself as an expert."

Mark Montgomery, a consultant providing college admission and planning advice, agrees. He noted that while he hasn't found a job per se on LinkedIn, he has gotten consulting work from people who first found him through the site. Krista Canfield spoke to us of a wedding photographer who got many jobs from within her network of friends and colleagues simply because she mentioned his work. Steven Burda agrees. "The more descriptive you make your profile, the more people in your field will reach out to you," he said.

RESEARCHING COMPANIES

While you're working on getting noticed and connecting with the decision makers, you also can be researching companies that might be perfect candidates for your next job. You'll use LinkedIn to research companies you're interested in through the Companies tab, shown in Figure 4-2. Behind this tab, you'll find information for more than 160,000 different companies. Please note: At the time of this writing, the Companies area of LinkedIn was still in beta testing. You may find that it looks somewhat different when you begin to explore the site.

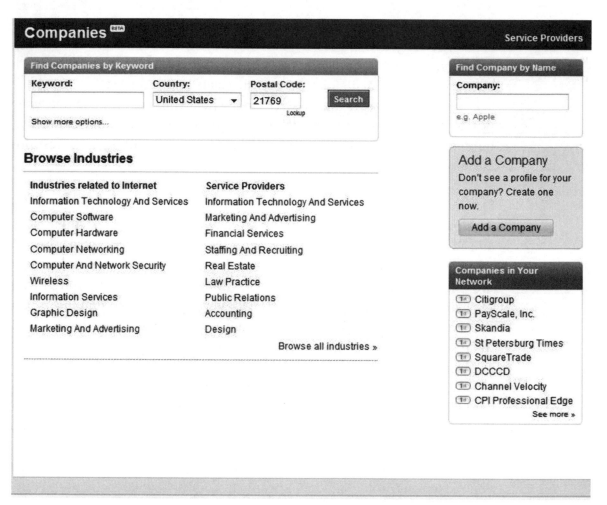

Figure 4-2: The Companies screen will help you to identify the right place to locate your next job.

The best thing about LinkedIn's company data is that they come straight from LinkedIn members and their profiles. Nothing comes directly from the corporate headquarters by way of the public relations department, the latest annual report, or the investor relations department, for example. To create this area of the site, LinkedIn started with companies that have the greatest number of employees. Then LinkedIn staff spoke with representatives at the companies to determine the data that would be most useful to both LinkedIn users and the companies themselves.

You can browse the Companies area by industry. You also can add a company—your own if you're an entrepreneur, for example—if there isn't currently a listing for it. To give you a head start, LinkedIn personalizes this area by showing you companies where people in your network have worked. The assumption is that if you're aligned with these people, you're likely to have an interest in the companies who have hired them. Perhaps best of all, you can see where a company's employees have come from, where they went to school, and who has been hired recently. This is excellent information for all job seekers, but especially for those who may be freshly out of school and wondering just how it is you get to be a product manager at Apple, for example.

Let's use the profile for Google, shown in Figure 4-3, as an example of the valuable information you can find using this tool. Right below the company name, you find much of the same kind of information that's in any directory, although this is written with more of an insider's voice. But that's where the ordinary directory-like information ends. Scan down the page to see the heading, "Google Employees on LinkedIn." There for you to plainly see is the total number of Google employees who have LinkedIn profiles—in this case more than 500 members. You can also spot people who are in your network, presented in order of how closely connected they are to you. Now you can work your way through your own network to find a way of contacting a Google employee first hand. But that's just the beginning. To the right of this information, you'll see a list of companies that Google likes to cherry pick for new hires. Not surprisingly, in this case, new Google-ites come from such computer giants as Microsoft and IBM. You'll also see where these Google folks go most often when they leave the company. If you're plotting a career path as well as conducting a job search, you'll find this information invaluable, and where else are you likely to find it in one single place?

Scroll down the page to see demographic information about the age, educational background, gender, and common job titles of employees at Google. As you glance to the left, though, you find what might be the most important bits of information for job seekers. You'll see the heading "New Hires." With this information, you can scan the LinkedIn members who have most recently joined the company to see where they've come from and perhaps detect a hiring trend at Google. Now is the time to put your research into action.

Google

Find a company

Google is a public and profitable company focused on search services. Named for the mathematical term "googol," Google operates web sites at many international domains, with the most trafficked being www.google.com. Google is widely recognized as the "world's best search engine" because it is fast, accurate and easy to use. The company also serves corporate clients, including... see more

Google

Related Companies

Divisions
- DoubleClick
- YouTube

Career path for Google employees

before:	after:
Microsoft	Microsoft
IBM	Yahoo!

Google employees are most connected to:
- Yahoo!
- Facebook
- Microsoft
- LinkedIn

Specialties

search, software, advertising

Google Employees on LinkedIn

500+ total, 126 in your network

(2nd) **Yael Davidowitz-Neu**, Sales and Marketing Analyst
San Francisco Bay Area

(2nd) **Paul Puree**, Marketing Consultant
Greater New York City Area

(2nd) **Bindu Oommen**, AdWords Specialist

(2nd) **Martin Gajewski Jr.**, Owner, OverSeas Investment Consultant & International Property Broker
Greater Chicago Area

(2nd) **Suchi Kumar**, Account Associate

See more Google employees »

New Hires   What's this?

Koichiro Tsujino, President
was President at Sony - last month

Anil Sabharwal, Product Manager
was Chief Executive Officer at RayV - last month

Kathryn O'Donoghue, Manager, Online Sales & Operations
was Chief Information Officer at GE Money - last month

Ariel Hochstadt, Product Marketing Manager
was CEO at www.madas.co.il - last month

Allen Liu, Regional Compliance Counsel JAPAC
was Chief China Legal Counsel at PPG Industrial - last month

Recent Promotions and Changes   What's this?

David Kruschke, Lead Video Editor - Studio G
was Editor - 3 months ago

Bill Packer, Technical Producer, YouTube
was Account Strategist - 4 months ago

Rob Painter, Business Product Manager, Geo
was Chief Technologist, Federal - 4 months ago

Rosalie Escobar, YouTube Account Manager
was Administrative Assistant to Sales Director - last month

Key Statistics

Top Locations
- **San Francisco Bay Area** (500+)
- **London, United Kingdom** (500+)
- **Greater New York City Area** (500+)
- **Greater Los Angeles Area** (500+)
- Headquarters Address

Headquarters	San Francisco Bay Area
Industry	Internet
Type	Public Company
Status	Operating
Company Size	20,000 employees
2006 Revenue	$10,605 mil (73%)
Founded	1998
Website	http://www.google.com

BW More info »

Common Job Titles	Software Engineer	20%
	Account Manager	3%
	Manager	3%
	Account Strategist	2%
	Engineer	2%
Top Schools	Stanford Univ.	4%
	Univ. of California, Berkeley	3%
Median Age	30 years	
Gender	Male	63%
	Female	37%

Figure 4-3: The information you'll find about Google and its LinkedIn-connected employees will help you to gain a real advantage if you're hoping to secure a spot at the company.

Once you've identified new hires, Anne also recommends that you reach
out to them for information interviews. "Approach new hires, because in the
first month they'll have the time and inclination to be willing to talk," she
advised. What if you find a contact who isn't a recent hire? Well, as long as
you have a connection to that person, you've got an opportunity to touch
base and explore the company for opportunities. Reach out to request an in-
formation-only interview. Anne shared some language you can use to approach an employee who may not be the hiring manager:

> It's great to see you on LinkedIn. I hope you like your position at [this com-
> pany]. I see there's an opening. Can we meet and talk about the culture, the
> work, and who might be the hiring manager? Then, always end with the phrase,
> "Can I do anything for you today?"

If you include an invitation to lunch, you're very likely to get the chance
to talk and get an insider's perspective about life at this particular company.
In addition, now that you've made that person-to-person connection, your
contact is a lot more likely to speak with the hiring manager on your behalf.
Relationships lead to jobs, and you've enhanced this relationship fairly
quickly and easily. Or equally important, you'll find out that the company
you're thinking of isn't right for you.

We spoke with an editor who once enthusiastically went after a job with
a New Jersey publisher. He actually got the offer and was evaluating it in
terms of salary, career-building potential, and the disruption his family
would suffer by moving several hundred miles from their home. In those
pre-LinkedIn days, he scoured the Web for information about the publisher
and fortunately learned that the owners of this publishing company were
known as "the worst bosses in New Jersey." Now that's a bad boss! Luck-
ily, he was savvy enough and dedicated enough to do this research on his
own. Today, it would have taken only a few e-mails to LinkedIn connections
to learn exactly the same thing and also confirm it with others.

You may be fortunate and actually find your next job right on LinkedIn because the site does include job postings from LinkedIn members. When you click on the Jobs link at the top of any LinkedIn page, you'll come to the quick-search form shown in Figure 4-4. This will allow you to quickly search for job prospects. Note: You'll also find the number of times people have viewed your profile and the number of times your profile has popped up in search results. Most of the options on this page are for employers who want to post jobs. But a quick snapshot of how your profile is performing is always good information.

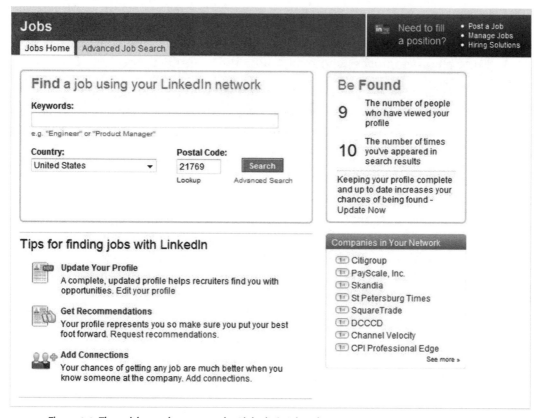

Figure 4-4: The quick-search screen under LinkedIn's Jobs tab.

For job hunters, the Advanced Job Search area, shown in Figure 4-5, is the path to millions of job possibilities, stretching far beyond the relatively few that LinkedIn members actually have posted on the site. Just enter some keywords and then fill in the form to refine your search results in any number of ways (such as how far the opportunities are from where you live). The search-result pages show how you are connected to the company posting the job—that is, if anyone in your network or in groups you belong to works at that company. In this way, LinkedIn makes it easy for you to use your network to help you land a job once you find one that looks promising for you. Let's do a sample search just to show you what information is possible.

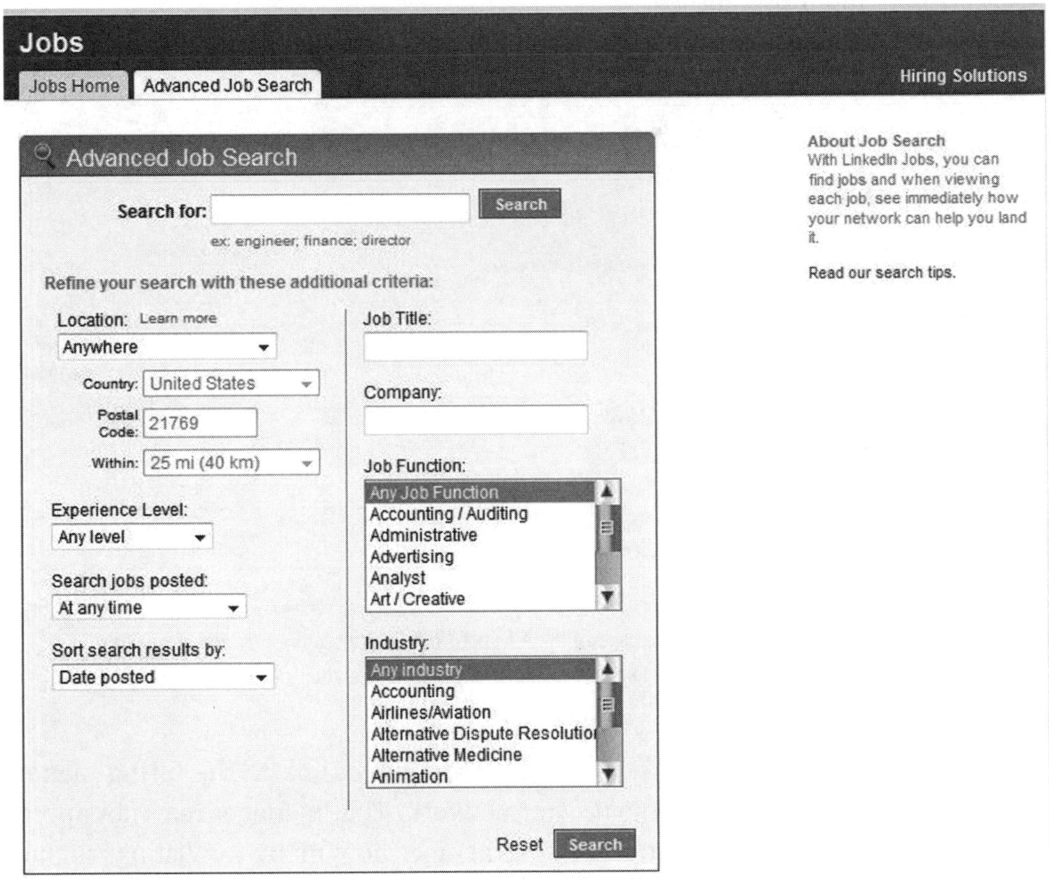

Figure 4-5: The Advanced Job Search screen you can use to identify potential openings in companies near to your home or anywhere at all.

At the Advanced Job Search screen, we searched for all writing positions anywhere within the United States. That search resulted in 42 matches for a variety of positions ranging from medical writer to copywriter. Then we refined our search to include only those opportunities within a 100-mile radius of our 21769 area code. Now we have two job postings. You'll see the results screen in Figure 4-6. One of those jobs, the one with an asterisk, is posted exclusively on LinkedIn and no place else. Next, let's take a look at that job, which is for an information developer. As Figure 4-7 shows, LinkedIn provides information on how we're "linked in" to the company posting the position (Symantec). If we were truly job hunting rather than writing a guide to job hunting, our next step clearly would be to work through our connections to get introductions to people at the company in a position to know more about the job.

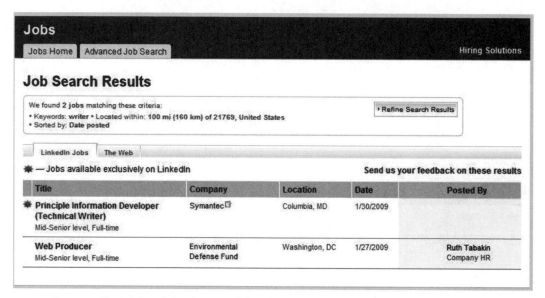

Figure 4-6: The Job Search Results page of the Advanced Job Search feature provides a wealth of information about companies looking to hire people like you.

Don't concern yourself with getting a direct link to the hiring manager when approaching people in your network. That manager may not appreciate being contacted in this way. Remember how many job listings includes words to the effect, "Please, no calls." Random e-mails out of the blue, even from LinkedIn members, may not be welcome either, which is why you should work through a contact to get an introduction to the person if he or she is not a direct contact.

Get Simply Hired

No, this is not hype suggesting that getting hired through LinkedIn will be simple. Simply Hired is a job-search site that's been partnered with LinkedIn

Jobs Home Advanced Job Search   Hiring Solutions

Forward this job to a friend   Back to Search Results | Next »

Principle Information Developer (Technical Writer) at Symantec

Apply Now

Location: Columbia, MD (Washington D.C. Metro Area)
URL: http://www.symantec.com

Type:	Full-time
Experience:	Mid-Senior level
Functions:	Writing / Editing
Industries:	Computer & Network Security, Computer Software
Posted:	January 30, 2009
Job Code:	KT

✱ LinkedIn Exclusive — this job is available only on LinkedIn

Inside connections to the company

You're linked in to **Symantec**

34 in your network work at Symantec and can help you get this job

39 in your groups work at Symantec and can help you get this job

Tip: Land this job with your network's help.

Ask your connections for introductions to contacts at **Symantec**.

Job Description

Be a part of the Endpoint Security Protection product development group, which produces award-winning security products that are deployed on millions of servers, desktop computers, laptop computers, phones, and PDAs around the world. You'll produce user-assistance deliverables for protection software (antivirus, firewall, intrusion prevention, and VPN) and protection management software for the enterprise and SMB markets. As part of a close-knit Information Development community you'll work with some of the brightest minds in the industry.

• Plans and develops large sections or complete information deliverables for large projects.
• Although this is an individual contributor position, incumbents may be responsible for leading a work team on a project section or entire project.
• Collaborates with groups of writers to develop cohesive user assistance for larger projects, working as a content provider or deliverable owner.
• Reviews and provides feedback on User Interface (UI) text to meet

Figure 4-7: The ad for an information developer, showing how we're connected to the company that posted the position.

since 2005. Simply Hired describes itself as the biggest, smartest job-search engine on the Web. The company currently "indexes" more than 5 million jobs internationally, approximately 3 million of which are U.S.-based. These jobs are culled from other job boards, newspaper classified ads, and even company Web sites.

Here's how the two sites work together: When you search for a job through LinkedIn, you'll be shown matches from two sources: the LinkedIn community and Simply Hired. Jobs from LinkedIn appear under the LinkedIn

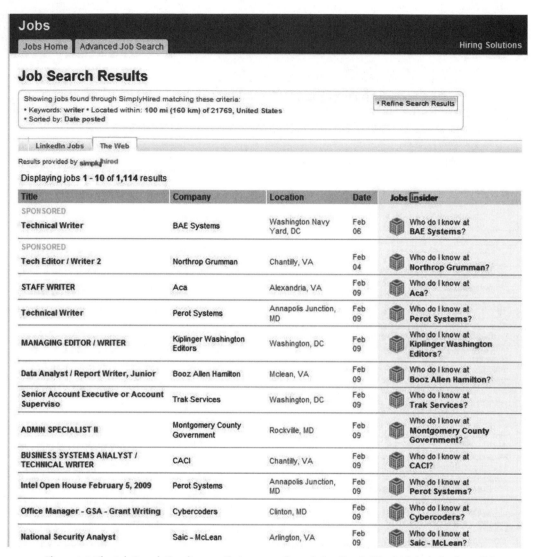

Figure 4-8: The Job Search Results page that appears through the Simply Hired tab includes hyperlinks allowing you to see if there are people in your network who can help.

Jobs tab. The jobs from Simply Hired appear under the tab called The Web. If your search for a new job doesn't result in any matches from LinkedIn, you'll automatically be shown jobs available through Simply Hired. If there are jobs available through both LinkedIn and Simply Hired, be sure to click on the The Web tab so that you can view the Simply Hired positions.

No matter where the job posting is from, you can use your LinkedIn network to help you land the job. In our example, we found seven jobs matching our search term, *writer*. Figure 4-8 on the previous page shows our search results. Note the column to the right. The Who Do I Know at . . . hyperlink appearing for each job lets you instantly scour your network to see if you have a direct or indirect connection within the company to help you learn more about the job and bring you closer to getting hired. Your contacts will appear, starting, of course, with your 1st degree contacts. By now, you know exactly how to proceed for that important introduction.

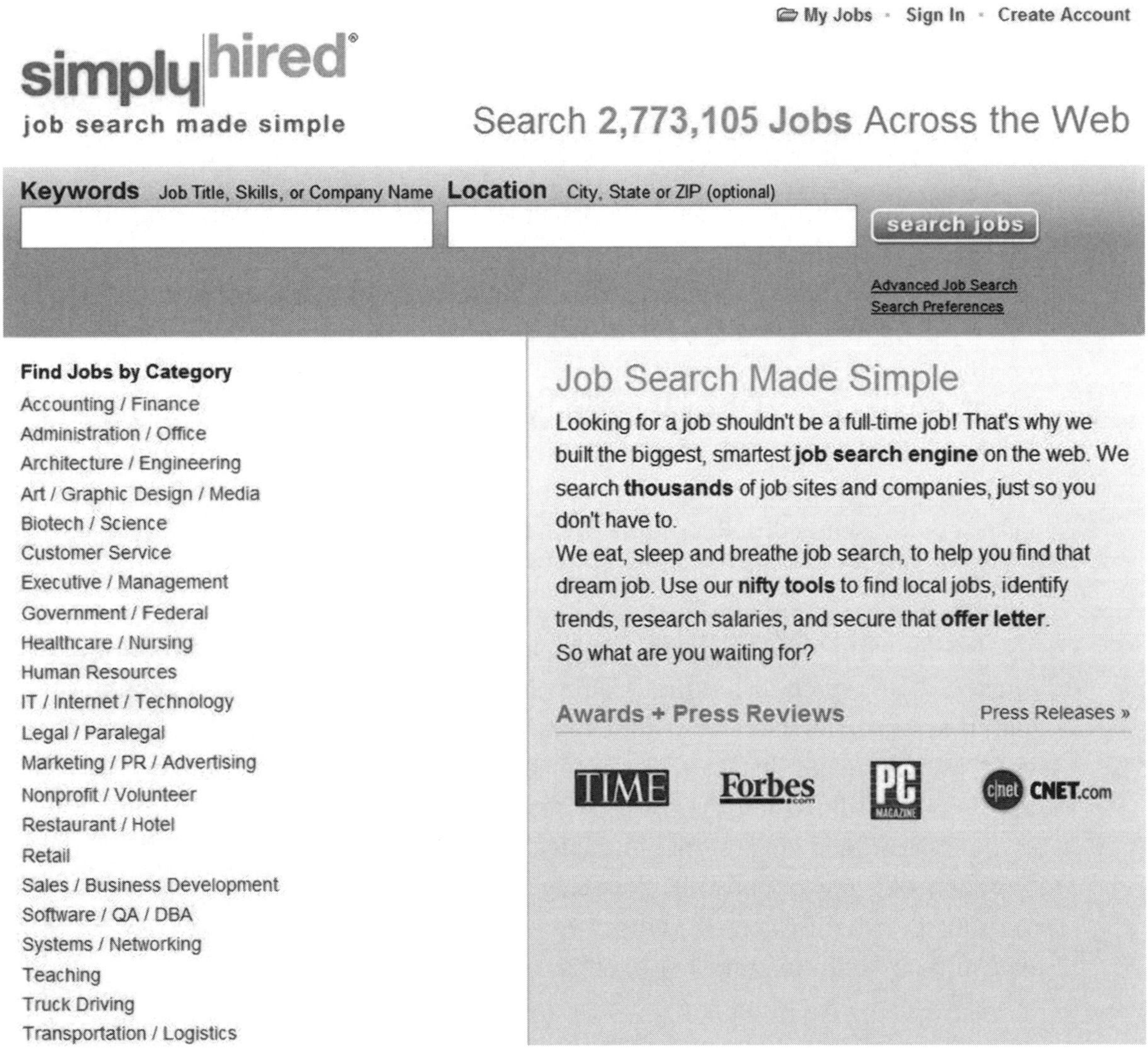

My Jobs · Sign In · Create Account

simply|hired®
job search made simple

Search 2,773,105 Jobs Across the Web

Keywords Job Title, Skills, or Company Name   **Location** City, State or ZIP (optional)

search jobs

Advanced Job Search
Search Preferences

Find Jobs by Category

Accounting / Finance
Administration / Office
Architecture / Engineering
Art / Graphic Design / Media
Biotech / Science
Customer Service
Executive / Management
Government / Federal
Healthcare / Nursing
Human Resources
IT / Internet / Technology
Legal / Paralegal
Marketing / PR / Advertising
Nonprofit / Volunteer
Restaurant / Hotel
Retail
Sales / Business Development
Software / QA / DBA
Systems / Networking
Teaching
Truck Driving
Transportation / Logistics

Job Search Made Simple

Looking for a job shouldn't be a full-time job! That's why we built the biggest, smartest **job search engine** on the web. We search **thousands** of job sites and companies, just so you don't have to.

We eat, sleep and breathe job search, to help you find that dream job. Use our **nifty tools** to find local jobs, identify trends, research salaries, and secure that **offer letter**. So what are you waiting for?

Awards + Press Reviews   Press Releases »

TIME   Forbes   PC MAGAZINE   CNET.com

Figure 4-9: The homepage for Simply Hired, a site you should visit in addition to LinkedIn.

RECRUIT THOSE RECRUITERS FOR HELP!

Recruiters, headhunters, executive placement firms, whatever you want to call them—if you're looking for work, you want to embrace them as part of your job-search strategy. Recruiters love LinkedIn, and many are members actively using the site every day. An article posted on ERE.net, a Web site for recruiters, featured some interesting poll results from a Webinar run by the site. The survey showed that 66 percent of the 500 attendees surveyed used LinkedIn. That's nearly 10 times as many recruiters as the next most popular site, Facebook, which weighed in at roughly 8 percent. It's no wonder that recruiters love LinkedIn. Recruiters, by nature and profession, tend to be active networkers. Having access to a large group of contacts improves their chances of earning money, after all.

Use LinkedIn to find recruiters active in your own industry, and introduce yourself. The search technique is quite simple. Go to the Advanced People Search screen and select your industry. Then plug in "recruiter" as a keyword. When we did this, selecting publishing as the industry, we found 308 recruiters, presented in order of the degrees by which they were separated from us. Just reviewing the list of names gave us ideas for people we could approach and new opportunities we might consider. Second on that list was recruiter Elizabeth Garazelli, who was kind enough to share her methods for using LinkedIn to serve her clients.

Elizabeth Garazelli Shares Her Expertise as a Recruiter

Elizabeth Garazelli is a recruiter based in North Carolina.

Every morning, I look at my 1st degree LinkedIn connections. Often I find interesting new people within the industries that I recruit. When trying to fill a specific position, I go to Advanced People Search and put in endless combinations of job titles, geographic areas, industry specialties, and keywords. For instance, "VP Marketing in the Publishing Industry, located within 35 miles of Boston, with the keywords 'higher education.'" Or, perhaps, "Director, in the E-Learning Industry, located anywhere in the nation, with the keywords 'strategy' and 'product management.'" Then I pull up a list of matches and start clicking on profiles of people who look interesting for some reason (usually because of their title, current company, or geographic location).

Once I identify someone who either looks like a fit or looks like they could refer candidates, I send them an InMail with a brief summary of what I'm looking for and an offer to send them the full position description if they're interested in hearing more about it. If they respond, I send them the position description and then follow up a few days later with a phone call or another e-mail. I have them send me a résumé, phone interview them, and hopefully proceed to a face-to-face interview.

I normally spend about an hour a day looking for candidates on LinkedIn. I have contacted approximately 600 people about nonadvertised, executive-level positions using LinkedIn over the past 10 months. Hundreds have responded, and dozens have turned into qualified candidates. Several have been successfully placed.

Here's one last piece of advice: If a recruiter contacts you about a position that's not right for you, respond anyway. Tell them why it's not a fit. Always refer others if you can. At least you'll be building a relationship, and the recruiter will be very grateful for any help you can offer. That recruiter will be more likely to remember you and contact you again in the future.

Elizabeth can speak with the voice of an insider, but hers is not the only success story we found when LinkedIn and recruiters come together. Her advice emphasizes the need to make sure that your profile is keyword-rich so that your credentials will appear when recruiters go searching. Even if you aren't currently looking for a job, it's a good idea to at least entertain opportunities brought to you through a recruiter. Stephen Weinstein of Cooper Power Systems was quite happy in his previous job when a recruiter approached him. He had been on LinkedIn for about three years when he received an InMail from a recruiter. He told her that he wasn't looking for a new job, but she encouraged him to take the information anyway. She was thinking that perhaps someone else in his network would be a good fit. Once Stephen got the details of the job she was seeking to fill, he decided to apply for it after all. That's where you'll find him happily employed today.

FREE VERSUS PAID LINKEDIN SUBSCRIPTIONS FOR JOB HUNTERS

Once you find yourself looking for a new job, especially if you've been laid off from your former position, the temptation exists to do whatever possibly can be done to find a new professional home. You may be tempted to upgrade your LinkedIn membership by choosing a paid subscription instead of sticking with the version of the site that's free to use. With the free personal account, you'll be able to have five Introduction requests open at a time. You can view 100 results per search, and you'll be eligible for three-day customer service. But you will not have access to LinkedIn's InMail service. If you upgrade to a business account, you'll get 15 Introductions at a time, saved search results with weekly alerts, and have one-business-day customer service. You'll also be able to send three InMails per month with a seven-day response guarantee. This upgrade will cost $24.95 per month, or $249.50 per year if you pay in advance.

You can further upgrade your account to the business plus or pro level. The most expensive choice, the pro level, will cost $499.95 per month, or $4,999.50 per year. Chapter 6 will explain the details of these four options more closely, but we couldn't leave the job-hunting chapter without encouraging you to carefully assess which of these account types is most suitable for your current situation. Many of the dozens of people with whom we spoke as we researched this book never went beyond the free account type.

Professional recruiters may well make use of the most expensive account options, but what should a job hunter do? It's clear that when you're looking for work, you may be watching your expenses more closely than ever.

But it's also true that you may have to spend money to make money. Work with the free personal account for a while to see if it is truly meeting your job hunting needs, but do consider upgrading to the business account if you find yourself constrained by the limits of the free account. The more robust site offerings may justify the cost of the upgraded account.

WHEN LINKEDIN CAN'T HELP

As much as we enjoy and admire LinkedIn, the site is a tool that can greatly enhance your job-hunting experience, but it won't necessarily answer all your career-building needs. Offline strategies for communicating with employers and job hunting in general may seem antiquated in view of your newfound power, but they still should take a vital place in your job search. Liz Ryan, *BusinessWeek*'s "workplace communist," goes so far as to suggest that candidates send paper, rather than electronic, résumés to companies. "The response rate is higher than using an e-mail," she wrote in a recent column. Of course, many companies have explicit instructions for applying for positions, and they may include only accepting online applications. But once the interview is over, an old-fashioned "snail mail" follow-up letter may be just the right key to open that employer's door.

I GOT A JOB ON LINKEDIN

 ## Programmer

Tim Kassouf is one of the many recruiters who turn to LinkedIn every day to do his job. That's nothing unusual. What is unusual is the person he was able to find through the site to meet a client's very specific requirements.

> I work for G.1440, an IT [information technology] staffing firm in Baltimore, MD. We recently had a unique job requirement come in. They were looking for a developer versed in a rare and outdated programming language—it was so rare that no one in our candidate database of tens of thousands met the requirements. [Note: The client was hired to do project work for the federal government and needed a specialist with a Plone/Python programming background.] In search of this rare skillset, I performed a quick search of my network on LinkedIn. I found three people with the necessary expertise, two of whom were willing to apply for the job we had available. The client interviewed both and hired one. They've been a client of ours ever since.

LOOKING AHEAD

As you've seen in this chapter, providing proven evidence of your accomplishments and professional experience is an important part of getting noticed by your next employer. Chapter 5 will give you a look at LinkedIn's Answers area. You'll be hard pressed to find a better, more efficient route toward building a fine reputation on the site and within your industry than by being an active contributor to this part of LinkedIn. Every time you post a question or answer, you bring recognition and exposure to your profile and your background. By the time you get to Chapter 6, you'll be so busy building your reputation and enjoying the results that you may just forget that you once thought of this process as work.

CHAPTER 5

Questions? LinkedIn Has Answers. Answers? LinkedIn Has Questions.

O n a winter afternoon otherwise darkened by cold, clouds, and a "wintry mix," as we call the dreary intermittent snow and freezing rain that plagues the Northeast, warm sunshine eventually broke through the day. No, the weather had not taken a sudden turn for the better. It happened within two hours of posting a question to LinkedIn for this book. In just that brief time, we received 12 excellent answers and were off and running despite the weather! Here was the question:

WHAT ARE THE BEST WAYS TO USE LINKEDIN ON THE JOB? I'm working on a book for McGraw-Hill and was wondering about LinkedIn's value for those happily employed. There's no disputing that LinkedIn can be a big help if you're looking for work, but what if you have a good job and aren't really prospecting for something else? How can LinkedIn be of value to you? If you have anything to share on that score, especially personal accounts, I'd love to hear your thoughts and possibly include them in the book.

The answers? You'll find that wisdom spread throughout this book, particularly in Chapter 6. But this experience proved once again that for anyone who needs relevant, high-quality answers quickly, LinkedIn is the best tool since e-mail. If you're a reporter, market researcher, writer, product or brand manager, or just about anyone who has business-related questions, LinkedIn is a gold mine. Where else could you so quickly get input from such high-caliber worldwide experts? Not only that, the information they provide is free.

This chapter covers not only asking questions on LinkedIn, but answering them too. As you'll see, answering questions has its own rewards. But, whether you're on the asking or the answering end of a question, LinkedIn's Answers tab is one of the most valuable parts of the site. As a matter of fact, it alone justifies the time and effort you'll put into using LinkedIn.

THAT 80/20 RULE

When you discover the ability to get timely, expert information from LinkedIn members, it's only natural to be like a kid with a great new toy and fire away whenever you have a question. But this is a community where karma counts, and for the community to really work, you must give as well as receive. This means that you should plan to answer questions and not just ask them. More than one LinkedIn expert advised that members abide by the 80/20 rule and answer four questions for every one asked. You may not have to be quite so exacting about it, actually keeping a score of each question asked and answered, but answering more questions than you ask is definitely the way to be a valued LinkedIn neighbor.

Looking for Work?

The Answers section is not the place to announce to the world that you're looking for a new job. If you do post such a question (for example, "I'm looking for a job in pharmaceutical sales. Can anyone help?"), you may well get flamed by more experienced LinkedIn members who resent that you posted your personal query so publicly. Or they can flag your question as inappropriate, and LinkedIn may well remove your question. Ooops!

As you saw in Chapter 4, you'll have much greater success job hunting by clicking on the Jobs tab and searching from there. Now once you have a job, take full advantage of the Answers section to show your boss how smart she was for hiring you. "LinkedIn is a site that your boss doesn't mind your being on," said Krista Canfield. With the first-rate information and advice available through the Answers link, you'll quickly agree.

THE ANSWERS LINK

Okay, it's time to open the lid to that treasure chest. Simply click on the Answers tab at the top of any LinkedIn page. You'll see the screen shown in Figure 5-1. As you can see, the options under the drop-down menu are:

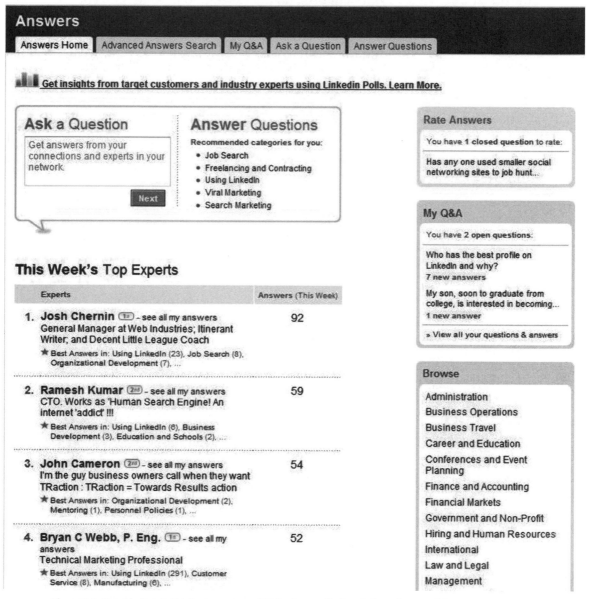

Figure 5-1: Your choices in the Answers area of LinkedIn are displayed along the top of the Answers Home tab.

Answers Home. Here, you'll find some current questions up for consideration. You'll also be able to see the degree of separation between you and the questioner.

Advanced Answers Search. From here, you can search the huge database of questions and answers already posed on LinkedIn to see what may be of use to you. You'll find a wealth of information here with no need to reinvent the wheel.

My Q + A. This is your personal repository of the questions that you've asked and answered. Having complete and concise access to this information here is valuable because it allows you to easily keep this information well organized for retrieval when you need it.

Ask a Question. This takes you to the form you use to craft a question and designate who will receive it.

Answer Questions. Click this tab to go to the pages that list open questions you can answer. The questions are presented in order of how many degrees the poster is away from you.

You may be wondering why people would go to the trouble of answering questions from complete strangers. Some LinkedIn members answer hundreds of questions a week! Part of the motivation to do this rests in the philosophy behind LinkedIn, the idea that you have to give more than you receive. "The more you give, the more that comes back to you in different ways," said Gary Unger, author, public speaker, and advertising consultant. "Normally, consultants would hesitate to give too much information away, but I always give advice," he added.

Another, perhaps less altruistic reason to answer questions is, in a word, *exposure.* Each time you answer a question on LinkedIn, you get the chance to display what you know in an area that may be aligned with your livelihood. Right next to your answers will appear your name, title, and hyperlinks to other answers you've provided. Your name actually is a hyperlink to your LinkedIn profile. So don't be reluctant to post questions; people are glad to answer them. It's good for you, and it's also good for them.

 ## Susan Shwartz, Ph.D., Is Available to Answer Your Questions

Susan Shwartz is very generous with her time and energy in the Question and Answer section of LinkedIn. She was equally generous with our request to help us understand the best ways to approach asking and answering questions and in explaining her motivation for doing so. She has a doctorate degree in English from Harvard and a long list of books and stories published. In addition, she's currently working as a financial writer on Wall Street. Despite all these tasks that lay before her, she was kind enough to help us explain how newcomers can get started on LinkedIn. We'll share with you our questions and her answers:

Why do you choose to answer so many questions on LinkedIn? For you, what's the payoff, considering the time you put into it?

I have been on the Internet for 20 years, starting with the bulletin boards and Usenet. I enjoy the ongoing conversations of online communities. On LinkedIn, the questions are fascinating because they come from people who are well advanced in careers in so many different areas and geographies. I've got a lot of curiosity, and I love participating.

How do you recommend those who are new to answering questions proceed? Any advice to share?

First, I think they should complete their profiles to whatever extent is possible. Many of us check profiles before answering a question or after reading an answer to understand how a person's background and experience have informed what they've written. Newcomers really do want to create a context that gives them credibility. Then I think they ought to read some questions and answers, perhaps check out the profiles of people who have a lot of expertise points, and then answer their first questions in fields of which they're very sure. I wouldn't start by being flippant. You can get away with more once you're online "friends" with people.

In actual fact, I organized my profile first, saw the questions, realized that they were really interesting, and jumped right in. The "scream and leap" approach has its drawbacks, but it's a lot of fun.

Have you been able to leverage your LinkedIn status as someone with so much earned expertise? Do people tend to contact you more as a result?

More people do tend to contact me as a result. I find this very satisfying. What, frankly, I find the best of all is the custom on LinkedIn that you reply, at least to say thank you, to everyone who answers a question that you've put up. I've made some of my best coxnnections through those dialogues because I go back, check their bios, and realize that there are synergies between the two of us. Then, usually, one or the other of us will ask to connect.

GOT A QUESTION? GLAD YOU ASKED!

First off, LinkedIn recommends that you ask questions that call for one of three things: knowledge, experience, or opinion. That said, click on Answers, and then choose Ask a Question from the pull-down menu. You then can use the form shown in Figure 5-2 to craft your question. The first box you fill in will become your question's headline and is the most important one you'll complete. But the box below it, where you have the option of adding details, is also quite important. In fact, those details and the way you phrase them have a lot to do with the quantity and quality of the answers you will receive. Provide the information and details needed for people to really understand your question and be enticed to answer it. Next, categorize your question by clicking on the category that best describes it.

There are more than 20 categories of questions, including several quite relevant to job hunters (shown in Table 5-1). Once you select a category, you may be shown a number of subcategories to further refine your question's topic. For example, if you were to select Career and Education, the following subcategories appear in the next box: Certification and Licenses, Education and Schools, Freelancing and Contracting, Job Search, Mentoring, Occupational Training, and Résumé Writing.

Table 5-1

Question Categories

- Administration
- Business Operations
- Business Travel
- Career and Education
- Conferences and Event Planning
- Finance and Accounting
- Financial Markets
- Government and Non-Profit
- Hiring and Human Resources
- International
- Law and Legal
- Management
- Marketing and Sales
- Non-Profit
- Personal Finance
- Product Management
- Professional Development
- Startups and Small Businesses
- Sustainability
- Technology
- Using LinkedIn

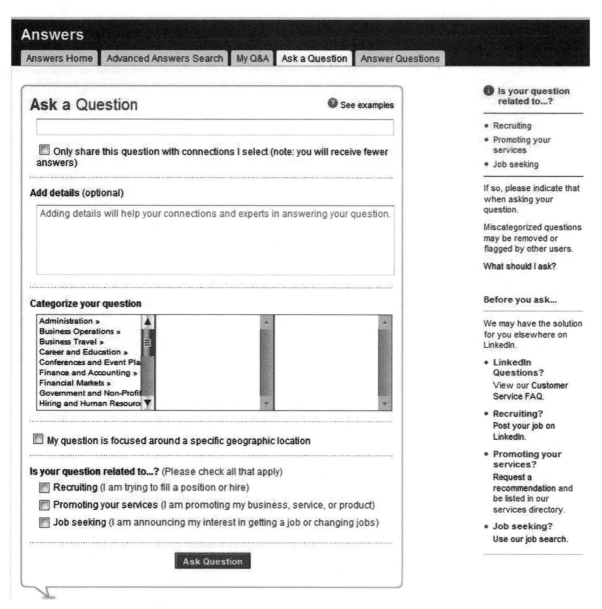

Figure 5-2: The form you'll use to pose your questions on LinkedIn.

Once you post a question, it remains open for seven days; then it closes, meaning that you will no longer receive responses. You can close it yourself sooner than that if you find your question is answered sufficiently or it's apparent that LinkedIn's members aren't going to help you with your dilemma of the moment. After that seven-day period, you can reopen a question if you'd like. Just click on the Answers hyperlink at the top of the page, and then click the My Q&A tab. You'll find a hyperlink on the question that you want to reopen. Simply click "Re-open this question to answers."

Use Advanced Search First

Before asking your question, it makes sense to search the Answers section to see if similar questions have been asked before, how they were answered, and when. The information you need may already be there. However, if the question hasn't been asked for a while, or if you are seeking other information, go ahead and ask the question again. No one will mind.

Further, you can use the advanced search feature to keep up-to-date with your own particular industry. "Use advanced question search to see what's going on in your area of interest," said Krista Canfield. "It helps you to keep current. Questions pop up with relevance sorting. The numbers can tell you what's hot in that particular field," she added.

Examples of Good Questions

All kinds of questions are posted on LinkedIn, and you'll see that some can get 50 or more responses, whereas some only get one or two. Why the variation? There are many reasons. One may be just how provocative and timely the question happens to be. Another may reflect the effort the questioner took in crafting the question.

Let's start with the obvious. If it's apparent you just fired off a question without giving it much forethought, rambling on perhaps, you've made the task more difficult for the experts who may consider answering your question. Frame your question concisely. Make sure that you've actually asked a question and not just stated something that you want people to respond to. Remember, you have the ear now of a brain trust that's 32 million strong, so don't waste your opportunity. Besides, people who ask good questions are viewed in a positive light among the LinkedIn community. Of course, be sure that your question is free of grammatical or typographic mistakes. This shows that you took the time to think and proofread your question. If you don't show this level of interest in your question, why would others be interested in spending their time creating an answer? Finally, if you're at all unsure of how best to proceed, review questions that have been asked before to see which of those received a lot of on-target responses? Once again, this will take you back to the advanced answers search function.

Here are some examples from LinkedIn of actual questions that produced a lot of good answers. You'll see that they're all in the form of a question, they invite discussion, and they're challenging to people with the expertise to answer them. No one had to try to figure out just what these people were asking. With so many questions posted, you can't afford to make the expert's job too difficult.

- What is the best city and country to locate a European headquarters?
- What is the future of the newspaper industry?
- What influences the choice of commercial database versus open-source database?

Just for fun, here are some examples of questions that produced a lot of responses, even though they may not seem as buttoned down as the preceding examples.

- Mind teaching me something new today? (202 answers)
- The Reality: What you know? Who you know? Who (do) they know? Or who knows *you*?! (98 answers)
- When is it really okay for a man *not* to pay? (55 answers)

There Really Is Such a Thing as a Bad Question

It's only fair that we also provide examples of bad questions. These are also courtesy of LinkedIn.

- Data about consumers contacting magazines and big company customer service departments.
- What is a home equity line of credit (HELOC), where can I get it, and what are the advantages and disadvantages?
- What are the three best companies?

Why I Answer Questions on LinkedIn

Joshua C. Chernin, a general manager for Boston's Web Industries, Inc., has answered dozens of LinkedIn questions, having achieved expertise in more than 20 areas! (You achieve an expertise point when the person who asked the question selects your answer as the "best" answer.) We asked Joshua why he spends so much of his valuable time helping people on LinkedIn. In answering our question, he once again proved how generous he is in sharing his time and expertise:

I am first and foremost just fascinated with the possibilities that the Internet and sites such as LinkedIn present to all of us. How else could one ask a question and get informed, diverse answers from 30 million+ people all over the world—in hours? How cool is that? I just love to be a tiny part of this process.

Second, I learn a tremendous amount from the Q&A on LinkedIn. As a general manager (I like to say that I "generally manage"), I have wide interests, and there are some great Q&As on a kaleidoscope of issues on LinkedIn. Often, with a question that I'm interested in but don't have the expertise to answer, I just read.

Third, I like to contribute. I really believe in the "pay-it-forward" concept. I have seen it in action too many times to mention. I especially like to answer questions from people who are truly trying to figure something out and are genuinely asking for help ("I need help rewriting my résumé" or "I need help figuring out how to manage a project") rather than the opinion-type questions ("What do you think of the budget deficit?"). Although I also answer the interesting ones of this genre too. I skip the weird ones and the ones that are just advertising fronts, although on the latter, I'm not beyond flagging them either. I believe that the users have to take responsibility for maintaining the integrity and the purpose of the site.

I try to contribute something new. I don't repeat what others have said, and if someone has already offered the answer that I would have added, I skip it. Sometimes I'll amplify an answer already given or reference it in my answer to give credit, and once in a while, just to be provocative and stir the pot, I'll play devil's advocate. It's fun!

I try to keep my answers short, punchy, and concise—a couple paragraphs. I think that is more useful, and brevity of writing breeds focus of mind.

Determining Who Sees Your Question

You can either share your question with the entire LinkedIn network, or specify that only members of your network will see it (up to 200 members), or both. After you've created your question, you'll see that below the text box you can check a box that says "Only share this question with connections I select." Questions open to everyone are deemed *public;* those only intended for your network are termed *private.*

We've tried posting questions both ways—allowing them to be visible to everyone and specifying that they go only to our direct connections. We've found that if your network of direct connections is large enough and chosen carefully enough, there are advantages to sending a question just to your network. You may receive answers sooner because the question is directly e-mailed to your connections. Also, because your network members know you, they may do a more complete job of answering and even tailor the answer to you. They have a connection to you beyond the overall LinkedIn community and are motivated even more to help you out.

Most often you will want to open your questions up to everyone. After all, you don't know who among LinkedIn's 32 million members may have just the information you need. Despite your best efforts to create an A+ network, it's likely that there are many people who are outside your direct connections with something of value to share. Give them the chance to do so.

Hiding Embarrassing Questions

Okay, confession time—it's good for the soul. The first question that one of your authors (no names, but this one takes out the trash and shovels the snow) ever posed on LinkedIn was a request for job leads. It was definitely a LinkedIn faux pas. Happily, if you also make a mistake, your mistake does not have to glow in cyberspace forever. We learned from that early experience that LinkedIn allows you to "hide" a question. To do that, you must first close it. Then, from the My Q+A tab, choose the question you want to hide. Once you are actually on the screen that shows you the question, you'll find a hyperlink box on the left, shown in Figure 5-3, that includes the option to Completely Hide Question. Of course, then you may want to resist the urge to write a book with your wife, who will happily reveal your little social slip to everyone!

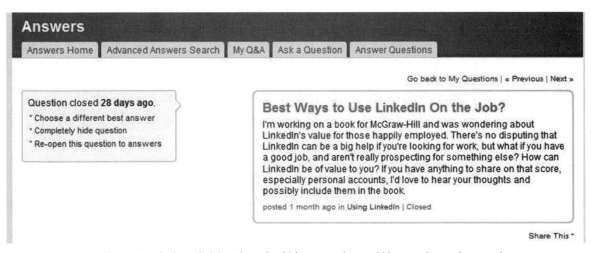

Figure 5-3: The hyperlink box through which you can forever hide an embarrassing question.

How Job Seekers Can Use the Answers Section

While it's against LinkedIn protocol to ask for job leads outright, there's no reason why you can't use the Answers section to get advice about conducting your search. As we mentioned earlier, the Career and Education category includes many subcategories of questions that would interest job seekers. Here are some examples of excellent actual questions posted in the Career and Education category that would provide food for thought for many job seekers:

- What are you doing to make yourself "findable" these days? (21 answers)

- What do hiring managers and human resources (HR) professionals want to see in a résumé? (11 answers)

- What are your Career or Freelance Consulting resolutions for 2009? (7 answers)

- When choosing a career, do you focus more on the salary or more on the level of happiness that you believe you'll achieve? (17 answers)

Choosing Good/Best Answers

As a good member of the LinkedIn community, you'll want to rate the quality of the answers you receive. You should do this after you've received enough answers to give you the information you need or sufficient time has passed (say, a week). Figure 5-4 shows the screen you'll use to do just that. We like to reward any answer with a good rating as long as the person who answered it actually added something of value. And we always choose a "best" answer.

Does Posing a Question Result in Actionable Information?

We think the Question & Answer feature of LinkedIn is brilliant, but don't just take our word for it. Robin Wolaner, author and founder of the social networking company TeeBeeDee, checked the history of all the questions she had asked on LinkedIn for us. "Every one of them got helpful business answers for me in starting my company," she said. Here are some of the results she achieved from the questions she posted:

Can you write a better tagline? 49 answers, June 25, 2007, in Writing and Editing

Figure 5-4: After sufficient time has passed, you should take the time to rate the answers you have received. You can do this through the screen that shows your question and its associated answers.

Does anyone have a great employee handbook? 11 answers, May 30, 2007, in Personnel Policies

Do ComScore ratings generally overstate, understate, or roughly reflect companies' own logs of their Web traffic? 10 answers, April 25, 2007, in Web Development, Starting Up

Do you know someone who can paint our logo on the interior wall of our new office? Cheap? 6 answers, March 1, 2007, in Starting Up

What is an ergonomic chair that is also affordable? 12 answers, January 29, 2007, in Facilities Management

ANSWERING QUESTIONS

The payoff you receive when you ask questions is apparent. Hopefully, the information you get in response will be useful to you whether you're looking for a new job or just trying to solve a task or research challenge for your current job. But answering questions also has its rewards, as we've said. The two main ones are

Every time you answer a question, your name and contact information appears next to it. Free advertising! The answers also become part of your profile.

It feels good to help other people out. And answering questions on LinkedIn is a great way to share the knowledge you've accumulated.

Finding Questions to Answer

Click the Answers link and then the Answers Home tab. First off, you're shown the latest questions posed by people in your own network, as shown in Figure 5-5. It's more than likely that you'll be able to answer one or more of these questions because people in your network share your interests. Plus, since you know them, you're likely to understand more clearly the information that would be most useful to them. It's a great place to start.

Next, click the Answer Questions tab. From there, you can browse open questions. By default, the questions are presented according to how many degrees away from you the person who asked the question is. You also can choose to sort the questions by the date they were posted.

Now, while you're at it, please don't answer questions just for the sake of getting your name on the site. If you don't have anything of value to contribute, move on to another question. We've actually seen people respond, "That's a good question, but I don't know the answer." Hmmm, then why did they bother responding? Quite likely, just for the exposure, but the exposure in that case is not the kind of exposure you want. If you prowl the

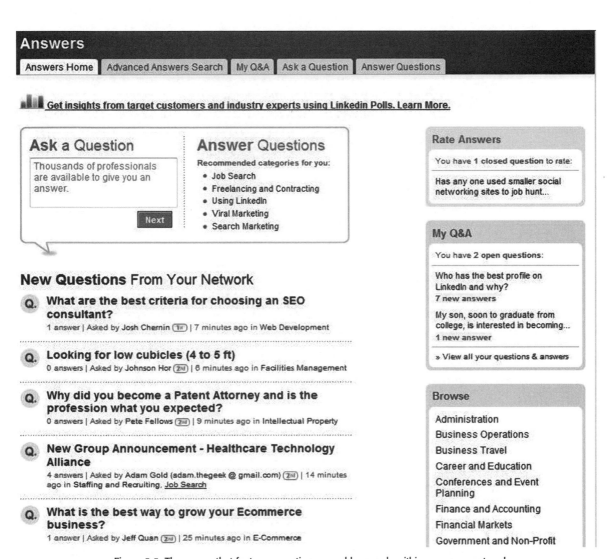

Figure 5-5: The screen that features questions posed by people within your own network.

boards enough, these kinds of opportunists become known to you. You don't want to be one of them.

Gaining Expertise

If someone chooses your answer as a "best" answer, you have cause to celebrate. You will have earned "expertise" in the area of that question, and that fact will be displayed on your profile and on the form you use every time you answer a question in the future. You can see what this looks like in Figure 5-6. The ability to earn expertise and then have that displayed for

Josh's Q & A

Josh Asks

 Q. What are the best criteria for choosing an SEO consultant?

posted 17 minutes ago | answer

Expertise in

 - Using LinkedIn (23 best answers)
- Job Search (8 best answers)
- Organizational Development (7 best answers)
- Staffing and Recruiting (5 best answers)
- Business Development (5 best answers)
- Economics (4 best answers)
- Starting Up (4 best answers)
- Government Policy (3 best answers)
- Personnel Policies (3 best answers)
- Planning (3 best answers)
- Equity Markets (3 best answers)
- Project Management (3 best answers)
- Quality Management and Standards (3 best answers)
- Career Management (3 best answers)

Figure 5-6: The LinkedIn proof of your expertise that will follow you on the site.

the entire world to see is one of the things that makes LinkedIn so valuable to business professionals. The expertise serves as proof that someone else has found you knowledgeable in a given area, and that can't help but give your future answers and your profile as a whole more weight. If your profile notes that you have expertise in solar architecture, for example, your answers are going to carry more weight among people interested in green energy or even in other alternative-energy categories. From then on, when you reach out to a potential client on LinkedIn, you have more than your résumé to attest to your expertise. You have put yourself ahead of the pack should someone be looking to hire an expert. Your answers demonstrate the knowledge your profile describes. So by all means answer questions with an eye toward putting your best work out on the site.

Business development and marketing professional John S. Rajeski is a LinkedIn Question & Answer guru. He has earned expertise in 31 areas, including Job Search, Business Plans, Antitrust Law, and Green Products! Here are three simple rules he's shared to help you make a great impression on this part of the site:

Be brief in your reply.

Be as specific as possible regarding whatever information you're posting.

Be sincere and have a genuine interest in assisting others. Towards that end, I subscribe to the "pay it forward" model regarding networking.

RSS Feeds Your Brain

If there are categories of answers that you find yourself checking regularly, set up an RSS feed (RSS most commonly refers to Really Simple Syndication; if you're unfamiliar with this valuable tool, see the Wikipedia entry for it at http://en.wikipedia.org/wiki/Rss) so that you are automatically notified when new questions in that category are posted. You can set this up easily from the Account & Settings page. You'll see the option for this along the bottom left-hand side of the page. Choose a category and your RSS reader of choice. You'll receive an automatic stream of data.

From LinkedIn to the National Theatre of London

Stephen Weinstein has become an expert at answering LinkedIn questions and more, too.

Marketing communications guru Stephen Weinstein not only landed his latest job through LinkedIn, but he also was able to arrange an internship for his daughter at the National Theatre of London. Stephen uses LinkedIn's Answers section a lot, posting and answering dozens of questions. His questions range from business-related queries to more philosophical ones. He posts these questions not just for himself but also for other people. On behalf of a podiatrist friend, for example, he asked whether a referring physician was due a commission for referring a patient to another doctor. He got 36 replies!

When Stephen receives a helpful response, he reaches out to the person who answered, inviting him or her to be a part of his network. On one occasion, he connected with someone who had a connection at the National Theatre of London. He asked his new connection if she would send an Introduction for him, and the rest is LinkedIn magic. Once Stephen was connected to that person, he mentioned his daughter, a student at Carnegie Mellon, and her need for an internship. His newfound contact encouraged him to have his daughter get in touch. From there, she landed her internship at the National Theatre of London!

I GOT A JOB ON LINKEDIN

 ## Career/Business Coach

Sharon DeLay is a small-business owner who, like many people in her position, must balance generating revenue (actually doing work for a client) with marketing her business.

> I find LinkedIn to be a critical tool to marketing my business, Boldy Go Coaching, and reaching new customers. As a matter of fact, it has been so successful for me that I actually teach other small-business owners how to use the tool to do just that (I started just teaching my career clients how to use it to find a job). I spent 20 minutes on LinkedIn one day answering questions and ended up getting two clients from that that could be calculated at an approximate 500 percent return on investment. Granted, my price points are lower than something like a GE giant, but for just me, it's a great motivator and example.

 ## Social Media Entrepreneur

Brennan White's company, PandemicLabs, is a viral and social media marketing firm that found its very first customers through LinkedIn.

> We've never sought or needed funding and didn't have a network to tap into when we started this business, so using LinkedIn to let our expertise shine through was important. We used the LinkedIn Questions & Answers section to answer questions to spread the message of marketing based on a social platform. From our answers, we made a small batch of really tight contacts and landed our first con-

sulting and business deals. This was early on, before viral marketing and social media marketing became buzzwords, so there was little competition (now the platform is much more swamped with people looking for business). Once we had our first case studies and references (from the clients we met via LinkedIn), we were able to win much larger brands and grow the business. Leveraging our initial success from our LinkedIn clients, we're now a very successful business with international brands like Dunkin' Donuts and Puma for clients.

LOOKING AHEAD

Now you know how valuable LinkedIn's Answers section can be, whether you're looking for a new job or just trying to get insider, expert information relevant to the job you have. But there are many other ways LinkedIn can help you to shine at work or win that next promotion. Turn the page to Chapter 6, and you'll see the many different ways your life on LinkedIn can help you increase your efficiency and performance, no matter what your job status.

CHAPTER 6

Using LinkedIn on the Job

"Linked In seems to have a reputation of being somewhat of a job-hunting board," said digital marketing consultant Susan Emmens, "I can't recall a time I've ever used it that way. And yet, I'm on it at least an hour a day." Undoubtedly, LinkedIn is a fantastic resource for job hunters, but you may be surprised at how frequently you'll use it as an invaluable tool once you have a job. Even with relatively high unemployment rates of 7 to 9 percent, which is where they hover as we write this, more than 90 percent of workers remain employed. This is especially true for LinkedIn's target market of college-educated white-collar professionals, who may not be immune from unemployment but historically enjoy lower rates than those in other demographic groups.

In this chapter you'll learn some very creative answers to the question: How can LinkedIn help me with my job? We're happy to say that the site can be invaluable in making you more effective and productive with nearly any aspect of your job, and this holds true for nearly any kind of job you may have.

Here are some suggested ways for using LinkedIn at work, which we'll explore in detail in this chapter:

- Using LinkedIn to locate vendors
- Doing market research, including online focus groups
- Locating industry experts
- Tracking sales leads
- Supporting purchasing decisions
- Staying current with your industry
- Scouting for possible new hires
- Conducting reference checks
- Finding other recent hires once you've joined a company

Of course, exactly how useful LinkedIn is to you initially may vary with the industry you're in. Unquestionably, people in media, marketing, e-commerce, human resources and recruiting, high-technology, consulting, and related fields are especially well represented on the site. But this doesn't mean that you won't find people from other industries there as well. All told, representatives from more than 150 industries are on LinkedIn.

BEHIND THE COMPANIES TAB

A good place to get a feel for how LinkedIn can help you at work is the Companies area that you've already learned so much about in support of a job search. As you know, this unique resource, the opening screen for which is shown again in Figure 6-1, provides information on more than 160,000 companies. This is information that you simply will not find elsewhere. To create it, LinkedIn started with the companies that have the greatest number of employees. It spoke with representatives there to determine the data that would be useful for both LinkedIn users and the companies themselves.

We did a search for our publisher, McGraw-Hill, and found the page of information shown in Figure 6-2. Now, visit LinkedIn and view the New Hires area. Now you can see areas in which the company is hiring and what the company seems to value in new hires. This is great information for job applicants, of course, but it's also valuable to competitors seeking clues about where the company is putting its resources right now. Note that the people who show up there are present LinkedIn members only, and as a result, the information isn't complete. Not every recent hire, for example, appears there. The ones who are there appear because they noted on their

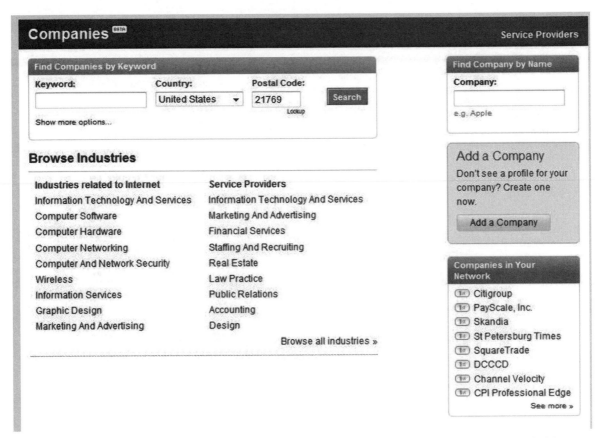

Figure 6-1: The Companies area of LinkedIn will prove to be an invaluable tool for success on the job.

LinkedIn profiles that they recently started working at McGraw-Hill. Other categories of employees are those recently promoted and those who have changed jobs within the company.

You'll also find what LinkedIn calls "popular employees"—the ones who show up in LinkedIn searches the most or appear most often in the news and blogs and participate the most in industry groups. These are the movers and shakers in their own corner of the world, and you'll do well to search your network for ways of connecting with some of them. Even if you never seek a job with this group, you'll find that they provide a wealth of information and guidance within their own areas of expertise. Plus, you already know they are willing to share what they know, which is one reason why they are so popular on LinkedIn.

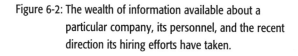

Companies **BETA**　　　　　Add Company | Company Directory | What's this? | Feedback

McGraw-Hill

Find a company

The McGraw-Hill Companies, Inc. provides information services and products to the education, financial services, and business information markets worldwide. Its McGraw-Hill Education segment operates as a global educational publisher. This segment comprises School Education Group, which provides educational and professional development materials to pre-kindergarten to 12th... see more

Capital IQ | **BW** More research »

Related Companies

Divisions
* JD Power and Associates
* e-Builder
* McGraw-Hill Higher Education
* McGraw-Hill Construction

Career path for McGraw-Hill employees
before:　　　　　after:
* The McGraw...　　* The McGraw...
* Standard &...　　* Pearson...

McGraw-Hill employees are most connected to:
* The McGraw Hill Companies
* CTB McGraw Hill
* BusinessWeek
* The Grow Network/McGraw-Hill

Key Statistics

Top Locations
* San Francisco Bay Area (91)
* Columbus, Ohio Area (347)
* Greater Chicago Area (253)
* Greater Denver Area (110)
* Greater New York City Area (500+)
* Greater Los Angeles Area (95)

Headquarters Address

Headquarters	Greater New York City Area
Industry	Publishing
Type	Public Company
Status	Operating
Company Size	10,001 or more employees
2007 Revenue	$6.772 mil (8%)

Figure 6-2: The wealth of information available about a particular company, its personnel, and the recent direction its hiring efforts have taken.

If you were to search for your own new employer, you could use the company's LinkedIn profile to see who else has been hired recently. This is especially helpful when you join a large company where new hires may be spread among a large population and lots of different departments. The information along the right-hand side of the profile is again a blend of what's likely to be in similar directories (for example, related companies and details on the industry of which McGraw-Hill is a part) and insightful data that's unique to LinkedIn. This includes demographics on the McGraw-Hill work-

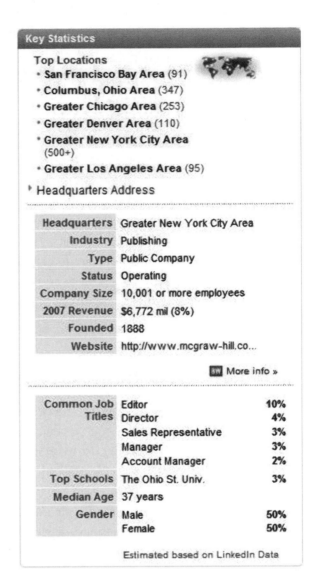

Key Statistics

Top Locations
- **San Francisco Bay Area** (91)
- **Columbus, Ohio Area** (347)
- **Greater Chicago Area** (253)
- **Greater Denver Area** (110)
- **Greater New York City Area** (500+)
- **Greater Los Angeles Area** (95)

▸ **Headquarters Address**

Headquarters	Greater New York City Area
Industry	Publishing
Type	Public Company
Status	Operating
Company Size	10,001 or more employees
2007 Revenue	$6,772 mil (8%)
Founded	1888
Website	http://www.mcgraw-hill.co...

BW More info »

Common Job Titles	Editor	10%
	Director	4%
	Sales Representative	3%
	Manager	3%
	Account Manager	2%
Top Schools	The Ohio St. Univ.	3%
Median Age	37 years	
Gender	Male	50%
	Female	50%

Estimated based on LinkedIn Data

Figure 6-3: The Key Statistics box gives you a quick fix on the company's relative size and where it stands among its competitors.

force, such as age and sex, common job titles, the colleges employees were most likely to have attended, and the companies to which employees are most often connected on LinkedIn.

Notice the BW icon (the BW stands for *BusinessWeek*) at the bottom of the company description shown in Figure 6-2. Clicking on the icon brings up a wealth of financial and news-related data. The Key Statistics box, shown in Figure 6-3, gives you basic information on where the company has offices, the number of total employees, the company's Web site address, and so on.

Serving Up Service Providers

Looking back at Figure 6-1, you'll find a list on the right headed Service Providers. This is another valuable section of the Companies area, especially once you're working in a new job or starting your own business. Check here to locate fellow LinkedIn members who may be able to help you with a specific task. You will find profiles of people from accountants to writers, even dentists and doctors, and personal trainers! These are all people who have at least one recommendation on LinkedIn, with the number of recommendations the service provider has received clearly marked (see Figure 6-4). You can sort service providers in one of two ways: those with the newest recommendations appearing first or by the total number of recommendations they have received. You can get listed in the directly yourself if you're a service provider with recommendations, which you'll have, of course, because you followed our advice in Chapter 2.

USE LINKEDIN TO LOCATE VENDORS AND EMPLOYEES

Now let's put the shoe on the other foot for a moment. In Chapter 4 and throughout this book you've seen how LinkedIn can help you get your next job or work assignment. But you may be in a position yourself to hire someone using the site to prospect for talent. Recruiters know this all too well, but so do managers. "I've also seen people use it when they are trying to fill a position," said Jan Brandt, vice chair emeritus at America Online. "A recommendation from a friend or close business associate has always yielded great candidates for me," she said.

The same goes for vendors you're thinking of doing business with. While there are many directories of professionals that can be tremendously helpful, they also can be costly. And if they're not online, you can imagine how quickly they're outdated. For Scott Rogers, however, an executive with Mc-Graw-Hill, "LinkedIn is, increasingly, a great way to find professional colleagues and/or look up the background of a potential business partner." Scott went on to note that the information on LinkedIn is often more detailed than what you're likely to find through other resources. "Typically [they] provide only partial information, and you must be a paid subscriber to access information—making LinkedIn the better choice."

Figure 6-4: The first page from the Service Providers page for attorneys. This list is sorted by number of recommendations.

Prospect for Sales Leads

Michael Jansma, owner of online jewelry retailer, Egems, Inc., uses LinkedIn to make introductions or get introductions. "Say, for instance, I want to meet a buyer at Home Shopping Network," he explained to us. "I can visit their

Figure 6-5: David Becker of PhillipeBecker uses LinkedIn to track down sales and marketing leads, saving great amounts of time and money in the process.

site, get his or her name, then put that name in LinkedIn, and most times, I know someone who knows that person. Then I can send my friend an e-mail saying, 'Hey, can you introduce me to so and so?' You can dig deeply into people's backgrounds to locate very specific resources—get in front of the decision makers who can aid you."

Jennifer Murphy, a salesperson for an employment screening service, also finds LinkedIn useful for digging up contacts and leads. "LinkedIn is a great tool for networking and for introductions to potential clients," she explained to us. "I do a lot of cold calling in my line of work, and often times I can at least get a name from LinkedIn as a starting point."

David Becker (see Figure 6-5 on previous page) of the branding and packaging firm PhillipeBecker is a LinkedIn maestro when it comes to using the site for tracking down sales leads and conducting market research.

"I'd go into advanced search functionality and type in 'Gardenburger,' and see who has that on their résumé," David said. "We want to get in front of the marketers. We also want to be in front of brand managers and creative people. I could search for all brand managers of Stanley Tools, for example. That's very valuable information. There are services that provide this, but they're very expensive. You might have to spend $50 per name." This strategy may work even with very large companies. "Proctor & Gamble is a huge company with hundreds of brands," David said. "I could hire someone to find all the brand managers, but I can go to LinkedIn and do it for free. It's a huge time and money saver."

Check Those References!

One of the greatest benefits of LinkedIn is that you can easily locate people who worked at a particular company at the same time your job candidate or potential business partner worked there. What an improvement this is from the old-school route you used to have to take to check someone's references. You no longer need to be satisfied calling a company's human resources department and getting just the most basic of facts. To locate potential references, go to the People tab's pull-down menu, and then click Reference Search. You'll see the screen that appears in Figure 6-6. Enter the company name and then the years during which your candidate or potential business partner worked there. The next screen that appears will list the names of people in your network who also worked at that company sometime during the time span you specified. Viola! You now have the names of people you can contact for impressions of that person's work. But remember, while you're checking out vendors and potential new hires on LinkedIn, they may be doing the same for you! So, once again, keep that profile up-to-date and complete so that it's as positive a reflection of you as possible.

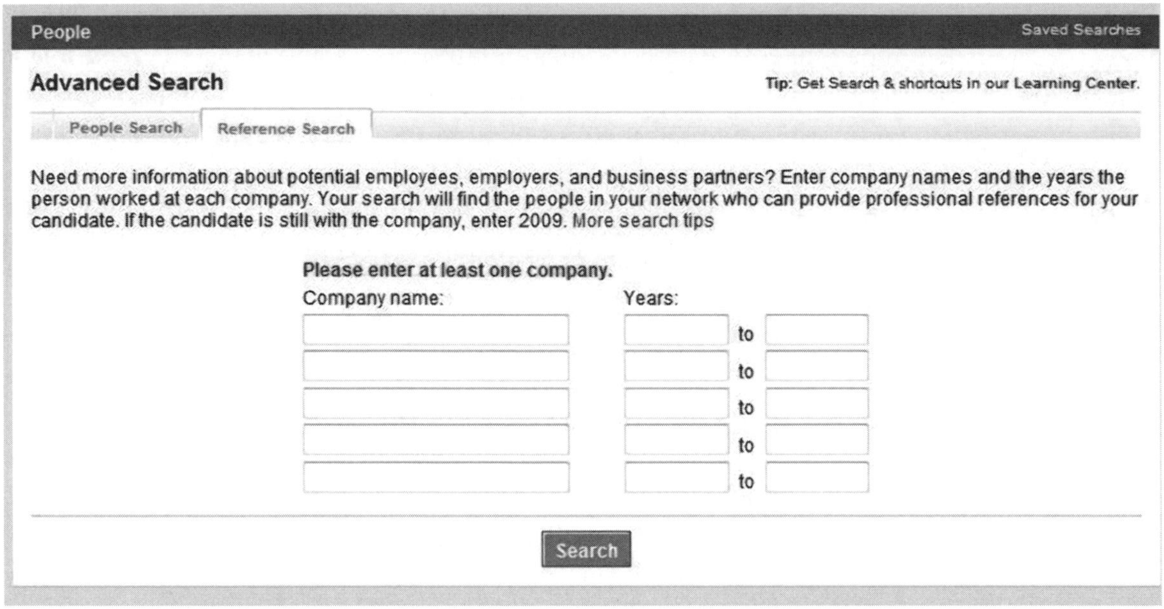

Advanced Search

Tip: Get Search & shortcuts in our Learning Center.

People Search | Reference Search

Need more information about potential employees, employers, and business partners? Enter company names and the years the person worked at each company. Your search will find the people in your network who can provide professional references for your candidate. If the candidate is still with the company, enter 2009. More search tips

Please enter at least one company.

Company name:	Years:
to
to
to
to
to

Search

Figure 6-6: You can use this Reference Search screen to find people who may have known your prospective new hire or business partner from a previous company.

Your Future LinkedIn Contacts

Just a reminder: Never forget that LinkedIn is at least a two-way street. Once you join a new company, you should view your new coworkers as possible future references. Cultivate them. Get to know them. They may be your future LinkedIn contacts, and you may need them sooner than you think. The next time a prospective employer goes looking for the people who worked with you, you'll want them to find fellow employees who will speak well of you when they pop up in your reference search. Everything about your LinkedIn profile should be a real-time résumé that reflects your up-to-the-minute status.

ENTREPRENEURS EAT WELL ON LINKEDIN

 Teen-Oriented Personal Fitness Business

In 2005, MBA candidate Karen Jashinsky knew she wanted to start a business in the fitness industry but wasn't sure how to go about contacting advisors who

Karen Jashinsky used LinkedIn to help her launch her personal fitness business.

could assist her. Her task was especially challenging because she wanted to break new ground and work with teenagers. Despite the rise in childhood obesity levels, the fitness industry was pretty much ignoring this population.

When Karen began her business plan, she turned to LinkedIn, which her classmates were just starting to use and talk about. "I started just doing keyword searches for 'youth fitness,'" Karen said. "I got a list of names to go through to see if we had any connections in common. That helped me meet people who could help me. Anytime I try to make a contact at a certain company," she explained, "I look for links that might help me get in contact with someone at the company. If I'm determined to find someone, I'll just be persistent and spend the time I need until I find them. Today, thanks in part to the help of the contacts she met on LinkedIn, Karen is the owner of O2 MAX, a Santa Monica, California–based fitness center for teens.

Promote Yourself as a Freelancer or Consultant

It's the rare consultant or full-time freelancer who doesn't have his or her own Web site these days. The only challenge with a Web site is making sure that people can find it. Of course, you can give current contacts your Web address, but what about people who are just prospecting for someone with your background and skills? Unless you become a search engine optimization (SEO) pro, prospective customers may or may not come across your site when using a search engine such as Google. However, if you have a LinkedIn profile, LinkedIn does the advertising for you and leads people, if not to your front door, then certainly to the neighborhood that includes you. Because you made your profile keyword-rich, that profile will attract clients and employers. Once they find you, there's no better way to showcase your work and therefore get more business than through LinkedIn. For now, it remains an exclusive club with a feel of respectability about it. Including LinkedIn applications such as Portfolio make demonstrating your skills and prior achievements even easier.

As freelancers ourselves, we use LinkedIn all the time, and not just because we're working on a book about it! Through our LinkedIn profiles, we can describe what we've done before and what we can offer new clients. But we also use LinkedIn to research prospective clients, to pose questions and answer them, and to stay on top of the publishing industry.

Boost Your Marketability

It's easy to get mired in your own little world when you work in an office by yourself most of the time, as many freelancers and consultants do. Try as you might to stay on top of trends, it's challenging, even with the Internet. In fact, the Internet can make your task seem more daunting because there's just so much information available through Web sites and blogs alone that the noise can drown out the music that's truly worth "listening" to. Once again, LinkedIn comes to the rescue. "I think it has given me tremendous insight into what clients need from consultants such as me," consultant Susan Emmens told us. "People like us are good at what we do, but how can we be great? What kinds of issues do people commonly run into when they try to find people who offer my services? It gives me great insight into habits or things I might take for granted that leave clients confused or uncomfortable in any realm."

For example, as a digital marketing consultant, Susan Emmens has learned that a lot of clients have questions about SEO. "SEO is a very technical and complicated field when you really get into it," she said, "and customers know they need it for rankings, but they didn't really get what they were paying for. SEO can get very pricey, but there seemed to be a lot of mystery around why and what exactly was being done to their Web site for that kind of cost." Plus, Susan has learned that it's not just clients who are misinformed about SEO. "On the flip side, I think a lot of consultants in this particular field take for granted that consumers 'get it.' When anyone would approach me about their SEO, I never did package prices, because ultimately it was important that we had a conversation. They needed to understand what kind of time goes into things like keyword research, Web site page name changes, etc. I get the sense most clients ask an SEO firm for help, get a complicated document about their recommended changes and a price, but they might as well be speaking Latin."

The Answers area, discussed in Chapter 5, is a great way to get a feel for what the hot buttons are in your field and what the current thinking is toward

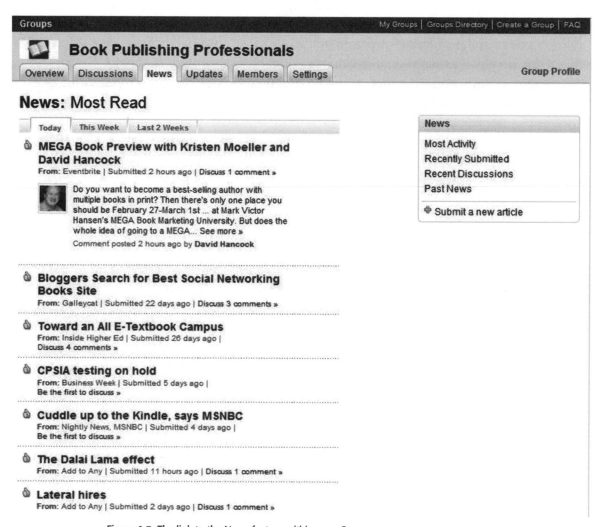

Figure 6-7: The link to the News feature within your Groups pages.

them. But you also should stay abreast of what's going on through LinkedIn's Groups, introduced in Chapter 3, and the articles members post there. The articles are likely to be very on target and helpful. "The articles keep us in the loop regarding other publishing companies, and professionals can share information such as recommending agents," said Cara Anderson, an editor with a major science and technology publisher. To find these articles, try clicking on the News tab for the groups you've joined. You'll see an example in Figure 6-7. You are bound to find at least a few on-target articles from newspapers, magazines, blogs, and other sources. Search results are sorted in several ways so that you can zero in on the latest news, as well as the articles members are commenting on the most.

Here's another way to get market intelligence through LinkedIn. Go to your Groups area (the link is along the left-hand side near the top of your profile page), and click on the Discussions hyperlink that appears under each of your groups. What are people in your groups discussing? While there will be the usual Internet noise ("Wishing you a Happy New Year"), you also may find discussions about other companies in the industry, helpful software tools, and industry-rattling events.

TIP

When searching for discussion topics within your groups, be sure to check the box to the right, which allows you to sort the discussions by several criteria. Use "Most Activity" to zero in on the more lively and potentially valuable discussions.

USING LINKEDIN'S APPLICATIONS ON THE JOB

We discussed LinkedIn's applications in Chapter 2. Many of these applications are especially useful to people on the job. For example, if you'd like to monitor what Twitter users are saying about your company in real time, you should check out Company Buzz (see Figure 6-8). Install the application and then customize it for the topics, trends, and companies you want to track. You also can retrieve historical data through Company Buzz. Other applications you might want to use include LinkedIn Polls, where you can survey members of your network (no charge) and even selected targeted groups, such as software engineers, within the LinkedIn membership at large. (There's a minimum fee of $50 per response to distribute your poll outside your network.) Huddle Workspaces and SlideShare are also good tools to use as a way to collaborate on projects and share information. Be sure to read LinkedIn's terms of use before adding these applications because the information collaborators provide can be displayed publicly.

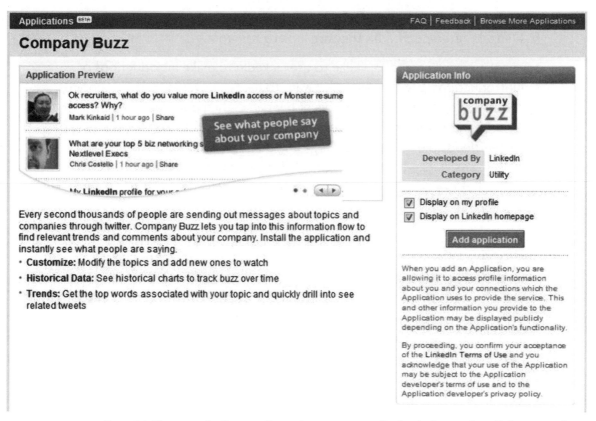

Figure 6-8: The screen for Company Buzz, where you can see first hand what people on Twitter are saying about your company, your competitors, or your potential business partners.

⬛ ⬛ But Don't Just Take Our Word for It!

We used LinkedIn's Answers to see exactly how real people were using the site on the job. As we've come to expect, the answers were quick and abundant. We've pulled some together to share with you so that you can clearly see what's possible for the happily employed on LinkedIn.

Jan, vice chair emeritus at America Online: "I've also seen people use it when they are trying to fill a position. A recommendation from a friend or close business associate has always yielded great candidates for me."

Cara, senior acquisitions editor: "It is definitely useful to those happily employed. The articles keep us in the loop regarding other publishing companies, and professionals can share information, such as recommending agents. It is also helpful when publishers are actually looking for freelancers because freelancers often post when they are looking for work."

Michael, owner, Egems, Inc.: "I like to use LinkedIn to make introductions or get introductions. Say, for instance, I want to meet a buyer at Home Shopping Network. I can visit their site, get his or her name, then put that name in LinkedIn, and most times, I know someone who knows that person. Then I can send my friend an e-mail saying, 'Hey, can you introduce me to so and so?' I also like to use LinkedIn for questions on how to handle business problems, simpler ones like 'Should we send Christmas cards to vendors or customers?'"

Susan, digital marketing executive and social media enthusiast: "I've found that a lot of value comes from the Answers section here. Frequently, people that are in the position of finding vendors and need recommendations, input, or what they should look for regarding certain services comes up. For example, am I overpaying on my SEO? My design firm is using an open-source checkout process; are there any pitfalls? Things like that. On the flip side, I think it has given tremendous insight into what clients need from consultants such as myself. People like us are good at what we do, but how can we be great? What kinds of issues do people commonly run into when they try to find people that offer my services? It gives me great insight into habits or things I might take for granted that leave clients confused or uncomfortable in any realm."

Dennis, founder at KareerKit: "Sites like LinkedIn definitely help happily employed people, and if you aren't using these networking sites you should be. Here are some benefits:

1. Maintaining relationships with existing contacts in your field.

2. Making new contacts in your line of work.

3. Creating an online identity that brands your professional expertise.

4. Keeping up-to-date on the latest developments in your field.

5. Having a dedicated forum from which to seek advice on challenging issues."

Jennifer, sales at background investigation bureau: "LinkedIn is a great tool for networking and for introductions to potential clients. I do a lot of cold calling in my line of work, and often times I can at least get a name from LinkedIn as a starting point!"

Christopher, Kosmic Network content strategist, network building: "I belong to a number of LinkedIn groups and find them useful on many levels. I get a feel for what others are doing in my field. I sometimes read about opportunities or alliances that can be created. I also post replies to group discussions to contribute something to the industry I'm in, but also to get the name of my company out there a bit. I've had more than a few connections and business relationships come from my participation in the groups."

Julie, marketing consultant: "I've been inspired by other people's questions and answers and have actually gotten ideas on how to do my job more proficiently. I've been exposed to ideas that I would have never thought of. It is also good to connect to people in your area and invite them to events such as workshops that we hold at my place of work."

Zachary, information technology (IT) technician at RunPC Computer Repair: "Personally, I am using LinkedIn to learn about the IT field. I'm still in college and plan to start a career in computer networking once I get my degree. I use LinkedIn to meet other people who are already working in the IT field. By talking with these people, I can learn what my future job environment may be like, hiring and salary trends, what skills are most in demand, generally just what I can expect as an entry-level network technician. I've learned a lot about my future career from LinkedIn. For the time being, I'm a self-employed computer technician, so I'm not using LinkedIn to try to find work, but to learn about my future career and better prepare for it."

FREE VERSUS PAID ACCOUNTS

We've mentioned that LinkedIn offers a standard account for free access and then options for those willing to pay for more in-depth research and communication capabilities. It's time now to explore just what you get when you pay for an upgraded account and whether doing so may be worth it for you.

LinkedIn refers to its standard free account as a Personal account, and that entitles you to do all the things we've described in this book, including build and maintain a profile, ask for recommendations, use the Questions & Answers area, perform company research, and take full advantage of the Groups area. You also can build a network, although you will require

	Personal	Premium Business	Premium Business *Plus*	Premium Pro	Enterprise Corporate *Solutions*
Cost per Month/Year	FREE	$24.95/month or $249.50/year (Get 2 months FREE) Upgrade	$49.95/month or $499.50/year (Get 2 months FREE) Upgrade	$499.95/month or $4,999.50/year (Get 2 months FREE) Upgrade	Recruiting • HR Research • Sales Learn More
Receive Requests for Introductions (?)	✓ Unlimited	✓ Unlimited	✓ Unlimited	✓ Unlimited	Many find LinkedIn to be mission critical to their personal success.

The only thing more powerful than your network is a well coordinated team connecting multiple networks.

Corporate Solutions' Accounts enable you to:

• **Expand** your reach

• **Work** your network with exclusive tools

• **Take control** of your searches

• **Share** information

• **Build brand awareness** for your company

• **Manage and optimize** user access and cost

Learn more... |
Send Requests for Introductions	✓ 5 at a time [1]	✓ 15 at a time [1]	✓ 25 at a time [1]	✓ 40 at a time [1]	
Receive InMails™ (?)	✓ Unlimited	✓ Unlimited	✓ Unlimited	✓ Unlimited	
Send InMails™	-	✓ 3 per month	✓ 10 per month	✓ 50 per month	
Receive OpenLink Messages (?)	-	✓ Unlimited	✓ Unlimited	✓ Unlimited	
Reach over 30 million users	-	✓	✓	✓	
Reference Searches	-	✓ Unlimited	✓ Unlimited	✓ Unlimited	
LinkedIn Network search results	✓ 100 per search	✓ 300 per search	✓ 500 per search	✓ 700 per search	
Saved Searches	✓ 3 maximum, weekly alerts	✓ 5 maximum, weekly alerts	✓ 7 maximum, weekly alerts	✓ 10 maximum, daily alerts	
Expanded LinkedIn Network profile views	-	✓	✓	✓	
OpenLink Network membership (?)	-	✓	✓	✓	

Figure 6-9: The various types of LinkedIn accounts that are available and what each one offers.

introductions through your 1st degree contacts to reach out to those who are within their networks but outside your own.

If you're willing to pay for a premium account, then you will have the ability not only to receive but also to send InMails (the quantity will vary with the account), retrieve additional results for each network search that you do, and save more searches than you otherwise could so that you can repeat them easily. You also will receive upgraded customer service.

These premium features are especially important to recruiters and human resources personnel, as well as those with a desire to use the LinkedIn member base for extensive research. For recruiter Elizabeth Garazelli, for example, a paid account is worth the expense. "I have a paid membership because it allows me to contact people immediately and directly with InMails," Elizabeth told us. "Asking for and then waiting for an Introduction takes too much time in my line of work." She said that paid subscribers should be part of OpenLink, which allows them to receive an unlimited number of direct contacts from LinkedIn members. (You opt in for OpenLink by clicking the Account & Settings hyperlink at the top of LinkedIn pages and proceeding from there.)

We agree with Elizabeth, who feels that "for your average user, a free membership is quite sufficient." In fact, even those who use LinkedIn often to prospect for valuable sales leads and conduct market research may find that a free account is all they need. "I've found thousands of leads," said PhilippeBecker's David Becker. As you've seen, David uses his free account to track down prospects to approach, to keep up with his industry, and to conduct extensive market research. He even conducts "online focus groups." A breakdown of what you get with each type of LinkedIn account is shown in Figure 6-9. Please note that space limitations prevented us from showing the entire screen, so for those last couple of rows and updated information, click on the Account & Settings hyperlink at the top of a LinkedIn page and then click on Compare Account Types.

LOOKING AHEAD

LinkedIn is *the* spot for business networking. It's nearly unbelievable how in just a few years it's become the first place that comes to mind when people think of social networking online for business purposes. But you may be surprised that there are also many other Web 2.0 sites that may be valuable to you both as a job seeker and as a business person looking to network with others. Now that you've been firmly rooted in the LinkedIn soil, you're ready to branch out and see what some of the other destinations have to offer. Part 2 of this book is dedicated to some of those other destinations. Some are even more famous than LinkedIn, and some are sites that you may never have heard of. As you develop your social networking career strategy, though, you need to consider all your choices to see which ones will be most useful.

PART 2

Facebook, Twitter, MySpace, Plaxo and Beyond

CHAPTER 7

Facebook: For College Kids and Their Parents, Too

Do you have a Facebook page? Chances are you do, your kids do, or you know people who do. By now, just about everyone has heard of Facebook. And with 150 million members, there's no need to wonder why. When people think of social networking, Facebook most often comes to mind.

But maybe you associate Facebook more with college kids and pictures of frat-house fun, silly messages on "walls," virtual gifting, poking, and a lot of other things that have nothing to do with serious business networking, let alone job hunting. Bryan Webb, one of LinkedIn's most connected LinkedIn Open Networkers (LIONs), when asked about his use of Facebook, had a response typical of many of the "LinkedIn people" we spoke with. "I'm on Facebook," he said, "but not that much because I'm too busy to be a social butterfly." Another LION, Steven Burda, was even more specific in describing the line between LinkedIn and Facebook. "I keep Facebook just for my friends, pictures of my wedding, and my baby," he said. It has "nothing to do with my professional life."

While we agree that many people use Facebook, shown in Figure 7-1, mostly for personal or social networking, there is also a lot of business being done through the site. And while the college crowd may get a lot of the at-

Figure 7-1: The homepage of Facebook, where you'll soon find lots of connections.

tention, the face of the Facebook community is changing quickly, with older demographics among the fastest-growing groups. So pigeonholing Facebook as just a place for casually keeping up with friends would be a mistake.

As of January 2009, Facebook claimed more than 150 million active members, making it roughly five times the size of LinkedIn. While Facebook started out as the province of college-aged kids, the company now says that more than half its users are "outside of college." Not only that, the fastest-growing portion of the Facebook population is made up of those who are 30 years of age or older.

When you consider the look of some parts of the Facebook site, it's apparent that lots of Facebook users aren't thinking much about business when they post things. They're uploading personal pictures; writing about the snow, their vacations, or whatever else on their friends' "walls"; and showcasing personal videos and Web links. Yet, as you'll see, people of all ages are realizing that Facebook is a great way to connect with employers and others who can be helpful in a job search. Plus, to enhance the site's value to job hunters and recruiters, Facebook is adding applications and features just for them. At the same time, LinkedIn is becoming less stuffy and more social as it adds applications such as Amazon reading lists. As in all Internet things, the lines are blurring, and you're in position to take advantage of that blur.

People *are* finding real jobs through Facebook, jobs that support families and lives. In this chapter you'll learn about how others are using Facebook to find new work and how you can do the same. We'll close with a summary of people who discuss, in their own words, the new jobs they found thanks to Facebook.

FACEBOOK IS FOR JOB HUNTERS

In April 2008, staffing and recruiting giant Robert Half International surveyed 150 executives from the nation's largest companies about whether they thought "professional networking sites" (like LinkedIn) and "social networking sites" (like Facebook and MySpace) would be useful when searching for candidates over the next three years. The results were interesting for two reasons. First, nearly 66 percent felt that the professional sites would prove useful, but only 35 percent thought that the social sites would. Those are impressive numbers. As the economy worsened in the last half of 2008, the role that sites such as LinkedIn and Facebook can play for job hunters and employers alike drew even more attention. Second, Robert Half's distinction between social and professional sites is important and represents something you should keep in mind as you devise your strategy for using these sites. No, Facebook isn't LinkedIn, but it still has value for job hunting.

Building Your Facebook Network

By now you know how easy it is for social networking sites to connect you with people you already know. It's the same for Facebook. After you sign up, one of the first things Facebook prompts you for are your e-mail addresses and passwords so that it can search your address books for people you might want to connect with.

You also can search through Facebook's 150 million member base yourself to find people you may know. You start this process from the Friends pull-down menu at the top of the page and conduct one of the following searches:

- Classmates Search (enter a high school or college)

- Coworkers Search (enter a company)

- Name Search (enter a name or e-mail address in the Search for People box)

Further details about how to build your network are right on the site itself.

Getting Help on Facebook

If you ever need help, Facebook's Help hyperlink is at the bottom right of any page. Just click on that link, and you'll wind up on Facebook's Help Center (www.facebook.com/help.php), shown in Figure 7-2. From there, you'll find quick links to and about every part of the site.

Figure 7-2: Facebook's Help Center shows just how easily you can find help while working on Facebook.

CREATING A FACEBOOK PROFILE FOR BUSINESS

Facebook is a place for being you, connecting with friends, sharing thoughts and events, and otherwise being social. But you're planning to go to Facebook now in search of a job. Your profile needs to reflect this. Yet, at the same time, you still want to make people glad that they stopped by. Facebook is a great place to let your own personality sparkle a bit. After all, visitors to your page have almost endless choices of where to go on the site. They may have 500 Facebook friends. They may belong to 50 groups. If you're boring them or depressing them, they can just move on. Wouldn't you?

What Your Page Says about You

It's true that Facebook is more relaxed than LinkedIn, and your page should reflect that. People go to different places with different expectations, and on Facebook, no one wants to hear or even think about how much you need that new job, whatever it may be. They may not need to know all the details of your past jobs either, although your accomplishments there may have been impressive. You need to really think in terms of elevator pitches or perhaps a block-party pitch. These would be more apt for Facebook. Write down your answer to the question "What do you do?" until you have a cogent, interesting statement to make that would get the attention of a friendly stranger. Beyond that, think of your Facebook page as a billboard that shows you as a person, yes, but specifically what makes you a great catch for a company. Some things to include, then, might be:

Links to articles you've written, such as a thought-provoking blog entry (For example, on his Facebook page, consultant Terry Seamon had a link to an article called "Refreshing Advice for the Job Hunt." Now that got our attention.)

Presentations

News about new projects you're working on

Interesting music

Photos of "your life" that get people thinking (For example, University of Maryland student Laurel Hughes studied abroad in Spain during the spring semester of her junior year. The pictures she posted from that trip and the blog she wrote might well intrigue those considering her for various internships.)

At the very least, don't forget a photo of yourself. It doesn't have to be as business-like as your LinkedIn photo, so pull off that necktie or kick off those heels, and be sure to smile. You want to come across as someone an employer would want to add to an already existing team.

Finally, use the Update Status area (at the top of your page) to let people know that you're in the job market, but do it in a "look what Company X is missing" sort of way. For example, Chris Schlieter, a former marketing executive looking to reenter the field wrote: ". . . is happy to work for a privately held company that still wants to grow." That shouldn't make anyone feel uncomfortable and may just make the right person take a second look at his page.

Content That's Pertinent

Let's narrow the focus just a bit. If you're on Facebook, your page should feature content that's *relevant to how you earn your living*. Artistic people will have more to explore about this in the upcoming multimedia section, but for here, let's use the example of a person with a background in marketing. You would want to include items that validate your knowledge and interests as someone who knows how to put products into people's hands. Good things to feature on your page thus would be links to advertising campaigns you've created, relevant articles, and especially articles you have written yourself.

Dr. Scott Testa, professor of marketing at St. Joseph's University in Philadelphia feels that recent grads should display an interest in something as well as their knowledge. In other words, when he reviews someone's Facebook page, he wants to see evidence of genuine interest in the profession affiliated with that person's field. He believes that having these things on your page gives you an advantage over people who don't include that context.

Multimedia Content

Facebook gives you the ability to add to your page lots of multimedia content, including brief messages, "graffiti," videos, and pictures. If you're looking for a job and you have samples that would help sell you (for example, you're a writer, a graphic designer, an illustrator, or even a musician), it's a real boon to be able to include such content right there on Facebook. Just be sure to share things that would appeal to employers you target, such as a portfolio, writing samples, music, scripts, and so on. And put that best foot forward by choosing your samples carefully! If you're in business for yourself, one thing you can do is post videos showcasing your latest products to push people to a Web site where they can make an actual purchase.

Use the Information Tab!

Once you have a Facebook profile, if you click on your name, which is hyperlinked at the top of the page, you'll be taken to your main page. Notice the three tabs at the top, shown in Figure 7-3. Click on the Info tab, and you'll find the spot to put all the résumé-type information that normally might comprise a good part of your LinkedIn profile. Your education and complete work history can go here, as well as business-related Web sites, if applicable. It's "safe" to place this information here because if someone goes to the trouble of clicking that tab, they're already interested in learning this type of detail about you. As a job hunter, it's essential that these basic facts about you and your career background be there.

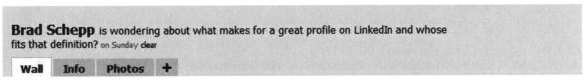

Figure 7-3: The Info tab on your Facebook page, where you'll be able to list your professional history and details relevant to your job search.

Finessing Facebook's News Feed

Every time you log on to Facebook and check out your page, you can view your own customized News Feed, showing what the people in your network are up to. This may include new photos they have posted, networks they have joined, "wall" postings, relationship news, status updates, videos they have posted, and more.

Of course, it works both ways. People in your network get to see what you've been up to also. It's not often you get to address such a diverse group of people, who may well know you and be interested in what you're doing. Use the items that people will see about you to your best advantage. This is your chance to show how clever and smart you are, not how mundane and ordinary life can be. We all have to feed our pets, eat, and deal with nasty weather, so, instead, tell your network about the incisive commentary you've just read, the mind-expanding video you saw, or even that you're looking forward to your next job interview with an ad agency in New York. This way, your Facebook page boosts your own personal stock.

Be sure to use your Privacy settings, shown in Figure 7-4, to control which items about you your Facebook contacts receive. As someone who is seeking a new job, you may want to adjust those settings for a while so that every time you write on a friend's "wall," for example, that action isn't visible to everyone in your network. And if someone writes a comment on your "wall" that reflects poorly from a business point of view, use the Block People option to remove it. You'll find more specific suggestions along these lines in a moment.

🔒 Privacy

Profile ▶
Control who can see your profile and personal information.

Search ▶
Control who can search for you, and how you can be contacted.

News Feed and Wall ▶
Control what stories about you get published to your profile and to your friends' News Feeds.

Applications ▶
Control what information is available to applications you use on Facebook.

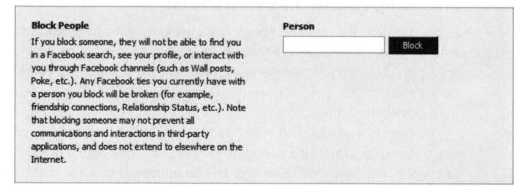

Block People

If you block someone, they will not be able to find you in a Facebook search, see your profile, or interact with you through Facebook channels (such as Wall posts, Poke, etc.). Any Facebook ties you currently have with a person you block will be broken (for example, friendship connections, Relationship Status, etc.). Note that blocking someone may not prevent all communications and interactions in third-party applications, and does not extend to elsewhere on the Internet.

Person

[   ] [Block]

Figure 7-4: The Privacy settings you can control to make sure that your Facebook page is making the right impression. You'll find this page on the Settings drop-down menu at the top of any Facebook page.

Here's this chapter's top tip. One of the best ways to use Facebook is to search for people who can help you get a job once you have an interview or have pinpointed a company that interests you. But first use LinkedIn to pinpoint such people. Keep reading to see exactly how this can happen.

Let's say that you learn there's a job available as a product manager for America Online (AOL). You have the job description, perhaps you e-mailed a résumé, and now you want to stand out from the pack of applicants. You know from previous chapters that you can use LinkedIn to search for people in the department at AOL you're interested in or for others who seem in a position to shed light on the job or put in a good word for you. (Remember our discussion of Advanced People Searches in Chapter 3 and Company searches in Chapter 4.) It's true that through LinkedIn you could then contact these people. But to do that, you'd have to use InMails if those people aren't part of your network. These cost money.

Try to contact those people on Facebook, instead of LinkedIn, suggested Lorne Epstein, CEO of the InSide Job Web site (myinsidejobs.com). On Facebook, there's no cost to reach out to people. Plus, you can approach them on a site they probably check even more often than LinkedIn and at a time when they may be more receptive to what you have to say.

Here's an example of the note Lorne suggests you might send to a business contact on Facebook:

Hi Khalid,

I am scheduled to come in for an interview with your organization very soon and would like to learn more about your company to see if I am a good fit. What can you tell me? I appreciate your help in advance.

Sincerely yours,

Lorne

It's a Two-Way Street

You're reaching out to companies and their employees on Facebook, but others are checking you out, too. It's a fact of life now that companies use sites such as LinkedIn and Facebook to get a feel for candidates that a one-dimensional résumé won't give them. If you're under 30 especially, your employer may even be *likely* to search for you on Facebook to see what they can learn about you, according to Professor Testa, the social marketing expert. If it's down to two or three candidates, he explained, a savvy human resources (HR) manager may visit candidate Facebook pages to help make a decision.

Professor Testa had the following advice about Facebook for job hunters:

- Be careful of what you put on your Facebook page.

- Be careful of what others put on your "wall."

- Don't post anything that you wouldn't want your mother to see.

JOB POSTINGS ON FACEBOOK

Yes, there are actual job postings right on Facebook! This is just another piece of evidence in support of the blurring that is occurring between social and business networking on the Internet. On Facebook, two sources for possible job postings exist. These are third-party applications and Facebook Groups.

Applications

There are thousands of third-party programs and Web sites that work in tandem with and on Facebook. Many of these are games such as Scrabble, but others will be of great use to you as a job hunter. The advantage of using them on Facebook is that they are right there on the site; you don't have to go elsewhere on the Web. Another advantage is that since they are integrated with Facebook, certain searches may bring up Facebook members you can approach for help. Checking out these pages should become part of your Facebook routine. Here's a look at just one of them.

CAREERBUILDER CareerBuilder is an authorized Facebook reseller, and it has a page on the site with many good features for job hunters. Now, we're not the biggest fans of sites like Monster.com and CareerBuilder because they can be real wheel spinners. With so many résumés posted on them, the competition is fierce. But CareerBuilder is definitely worth your time to check out if you're on Facebook anyway.

Here are some of the features you'll find there:

Job listings. You can search for jobs or browse by job categories such as engineering or health care.

Quick links to resources. You can use these in your job search, such as salary calculators. It's handy to have tools that you may need all in one place.

Career fairs. CareerBuilder sponsors career fairs all across the country, and news of upcoming fairs is available right there on Facebook. You can even see if other Facebook members have confirmed that they are attending a local fair. That way, you can go with a Facebook friend who also may be checking out new opportunities.

Discussion boards. These cover all sorts of career issues.

CareerBuilder's blog. Called The Work Buzz, there is a link to subscribe to it in your Really Simple Syndication (RSS) feeder.

Finally, you can become a CareerBuilder fan by clicking the link to receive special promotions from the company. Just remember that doing so will place a CareerBuilder icon on your profile, so decide first of all if that's something you'd like.

SIMPLY HIRED Simply Hired has a variety of applications on Facebook that allow users to connect and network to find jobs. For example, Workin' It helps Facebook members who may be looking for jobs to connect and discuss the process. Simply Hired also has I Am [insert profession here] applications that allow members of certain occupations to connect with each other and talk about issues specific to their jobs. I Am Nurse is one of the most popular applications with 28,214 monthly active users.

OTHER JOB APPLICATIONS ON FACEBOOK Other companies are joining Career-Builder and Simply Hired by providing Facebook applications to help job hunters. One is InSide Job, a page that "connects you to helpful people at places you want to work by giving you access to where people have interviewed, worked, or are currently employed."An authorized Facebook developer, InSide Job was on the site but only in beta testing as we wrote this. It's only reasonable to expect that as demand for job-hunting support grows, similar applications also will come to Facebook.

Facebook's Groups

Facebook isn't just about connecting individuals. It's also about connecting people who share common interests. One way Facebook does that is through the Groups area. Facebook hosts thousands of groups. These are broken down by Type, such as Entertainment, Internet, Organizations, and Student groups. Figure 7-5 shows a Browse Groups page and will give you an idea of the broad range of subject areas included there. Group types then are further broken into subtypes. For instance, the Group type Common Interest has further groups under it dealing with everything from activities to wine.

As a job hunter, the two types of groups you'll want to focus on most are Business and Organizations. Let's use the Business category for our exam-

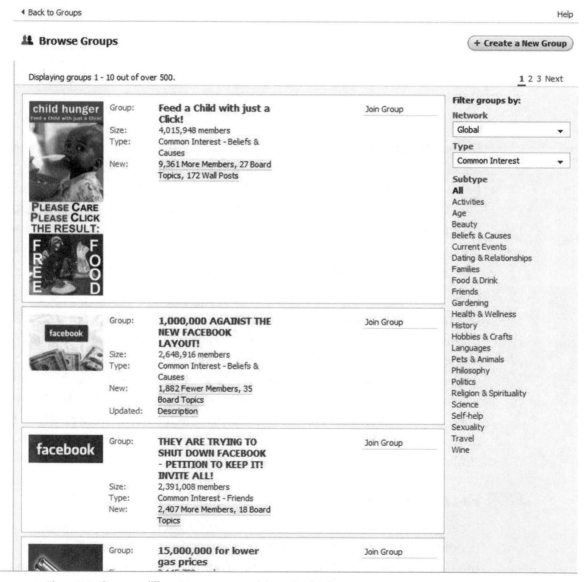

Figure 7-5: The many different groups you can join on Facebook.

ple. If you select the Business link from the drop-down menu on the Groups homepage, you'll see that it includes the following subtypes:

- Companies
- Consumer Groups
- Employment & Work
- General
- Home Business
- Investing
- Marketing & Advertising
- Public Relations
- Real Estate

Not only does Facebook present you with these options, but the site automatically tailors these results to things it already knows about you from your profile. When we checked, for example, lots of our results were based in South Jersey because we had already identified ourselves as having an interest in that area.

To join a group, go to the Groups area and search for groups of interest using precise keywords. We say *precise* because there are a lot of groups on Facebook with only a few members, and they may be of limited value to you. Then there are the gems. So you may have to try some different searches to zero in on groups that are worth your time. When we entered "book," for example, we were served up a buffet of more than 500 groups to choose from; that seemed too daunting. Also, many of the groups struck us as a waste of time because their main purpose seemed to be to sell products. So we entered "book publishing professionals." That resulted in 18 hits, which wasn't enough. We then tried "book business." That gave us the mix of results we wanted, and we were off and running, joining groups that seemed truly valuable!

To find those jobs and contacts, keep digging. Under Public Relations, for example, you'll find The Official Facebook Public Relations Group, shown in Figure 7-6, which has more than 10,000 Facebook members. It's defined as "a space for Facebookers in PR to post job listings, search for jobs, ask advice, vent, et cetera." It's considered an "open group," meaning that anyone can join it. This is definitely Facebook's home for public relations (PR) professionals.

If you're looking for a job, group discussion boards are probably where you will want to spend much of your time. Topics sure to interest you are up for discussion, and actual jobs may be posted, too. The Public Relations

👥 The Official Facebook Public Relations Group
Global

Basic Info

Type: Business - Public Relations

Description: A space for Facebookers in PR to post job listings, search for jobs, ask advice, vent, et cetera...

Contact Info

Email: mlewicki@mjl-media.com

Recent News

Recently there has been a great number of requests from group members for me to msg all the members with events etc...
I do not have the ability to msg all the members, but you are more than welcome to post it on the wall or in the discussion board. That way, it becomes the members choice to check it out....

Members

Displaying 8 of 11,048 members   See All

Jonnice Slaughter   Jim McClure   Shalimar Blakely   Tim Hurley   Hallema Sharif   Diego Barceló   Aqeel Khan   Chris Gent

Discussion Board

Displaying 3 of 376 discussion topics   See All

Senior PR Officer Wanted Chesterfield UK
1 post by 1 person. Updated 42 minutes ago

How to be heard in Ottawa
1 post by 1 person. Updated 19 hours ago

Ethical PR Study
1 post by 1 person. Updated 23 hours ago

The Wall

Displaying 5 of 840 wall posts.   See All

 Randa Arafa wrote
at 3:40am

View Discussion Board
Join this Group

Share +

Group Type

This is an open group. Anyone can join and invite others to join.

Admins

- Michael Lewicki (Ottawa, ON)

Related Groups

The PR and Communications Network
Business - Public Relations

Public Relations Society of America (PRSA)
Business - Public Relations

Six Degrees Of Separation - The Face book Experiment
Just for Fun - Facebook Classics

PR Job Watch
Business - Public Relations

Karma Experiment - Pay it forward
Just for Fun - Facebook Classics

Figure 7-6: The Official Public Relations Group on Facebook. It is just one of many business groups you'll be able to join to promote your job search.

group also includes photos, a "wall," and posted items (including announcements of upcoming meetings and video clips from past meetings). Other groups in the Public Relations category include PR Job Watch and Marketing Job Watch.

One group you should be sure to join is Facebook for Business. Once you read the description, you'll see why: "Do you think Facebook is a viable solution for business? Do businesses need social networking? What would make a great social networking application for business? Business is social, and that's what this group is about." The group has 28,000 members, an active discussion board, and lots of posts about upcoming Webinars. There are definitely people who use the group to push their own products and schemes for making money quickly, but once you push that stuff aside, you're bound to find that this is a worthwhile stop to make on Facebook.

FACEBOOK ADS

Want to advertise that you're available for a new job to the Facebook community? Facebook has a full array of ad types for people who want to target certain Facebook members. Say that you're into designing energy-efficient green buildings. You can create an ad that includes a link to your Facebook page, your LinkedIn profile, or your Web site. To begin, simply click on the Advertising link at the bottom of Facebook's homepage.

Facebook makes it simple for you to reach your audience by targeting your ad by

- Location
- Sex
- Age
- Keywords

- Education
- Workplace
- Relationship status
- Relationship interest

The ability to use keywords to target people is especially powerful. It helps to ensure that people in your industry or who otherwise share your professional interests see your advertisement. If the keywords you specify when you create your ad appear on someone's profile, in a group they belong to, or on pages they're fans of, for example, they will receive your ad. Keywords are based on interests, activities, favorite books, TV shows, movies, or most important, job titles that users list in their Facebook profiles. They also may come from the names of groups users belong to or are fans of.

Pricing for Facebook ads starts very reasonably; you can set a daily budget of as low as $25. Facebook then runs your ad in the Ad Space part of members' pages, within News Feeds, or both. You also can choose when your ad will run, such as continuously or only on specified dates. For more information, see Figure 7-7.

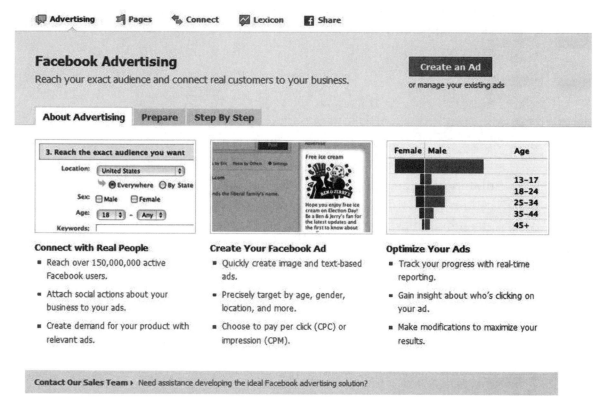

Figure 7-7: The opening screen of Facebook's Advertising area.

WE FOUND OUR JOBS THROUGH FACEBOOK!

Nothing is quite as encouraging as reading about the success others have found through following the path you are taking yourself. Here are some short but very inspiring tales of people who once came to Facebook without job prospects but soon found a spot for themselves in the world of the happily employed.

Information Architect/Business Analyst

Jocelyn Wang found her current position on Facebook almost without realizing it. (Photo by Arden Ash.)

Jocelyn Wang was celebrating her one-year anniversary at her job with speakTECH (a design and technology company) when we spoke, and she has a Facebook connection to thank for making it all possible. Her story is interesting because it reflects both the unique social environment of Facebook and its potential for bringing together people who may have never met otherwise.

I have been in my current job for one year now, and it was through a Facebook connection. At the time, I had joined Facebook for general networking opportunities; I was not specifically looking for a new job. I was contacted by a person I mistakenly thought was someone I knew from high school. In reality, he was simply someone connected to a friend of mine. He added me because he saw me on our mutual friend's list and thought I "looked interesting." We spoke over the course of several months, but what I didn't realize at the time was that he had been sizing me up for a specific position at his company. I thought he was simply being friendly when he asked me about work and also what I was doing in business school (I was in the process of getting my MBA at the time). About three months after we first began talking, he made a formal job interview request, and we continued the process until I was eventually hired.

Consultant

Eric Kiker has plenty of new work thanks to Facebook.

Eric Kiker used Facebook to land a six-figure consulting job. As someone who has kicked around in the advertising business for more than 20 years at the time, he may not be the type of person you associate with Facebook, but after reading his story, you probably won't look at Facebook in the same way ever again.

I'm an advertising writer/creative director/strategist—been in the business for around 20 years. Ten years ago, I was working at a Denver ad agency, where I was serving as an associate creative director. I interviewed a young writer named Alex who was relocating from South Africa—she was awesome. We hired her; she did great; the agency went out of business.

I went out on my own as a freelancer and didn't see Alex for six years. No reason really, just different circles. Apparently, she did great, had a bunch of kids; I grew the heck out of my business. All was well.

A couple months ago, I received an offer to become a partner in a firm with which I had worked increasingly closely with over the past six years. Interestingly, it was a firm I first met two decades ago, right out of college—only now, it's second generation—the son bought the business from his dad. I've become friends with the son and his partner. And together, we're doing great.

My partner, Kelly, came in one day and said, "Set up a Facebook page and link your address book to find all the people you know." I did it and got lots of "friends." But certainly no immediate business leads. The following day, apparently through the "People you may know" tool, Alex found me—asked if I was still writing, said she had a possible gig for me as a freelance art director. I suggested she meet with me and my new partner since, as a group, we could offer much more service than any freelance team. She agreed, liked us, introduced us and a number of other hopefuls to the client. The client picked us. We're four months into the relationship and still together—good client.

 ## Freelance Web Consultant and Writer

Ruth-Ann Cooper now uses Facebook as her primary source of new assignments!

I am a freelance Web consultant/writer/editor, and over the past year, I have had multiple leads that resulted in freelance jobs from connections on Facebook. In fact, it has been my primary direct or indirect source of new work. The leads did not come from posting a status update that I was looking for work; they came from networking.

For example, I reconnected with an old college friend and looked up the company she worked for. Out of curiosity, I looked at their job openings. I ended up applying for a freelance position with them and, using my friend as a reference, was hired for the position.

Freelancer Ruth-Ann Cooper keeps busy with work she's found on Facebook.

In another example, a Facebook friend from my college years saw that I was freelancing and heard of someone looking for a writer, so she connected us. She did that another time as well, and I have done repeat work with both the people she connected me with.

An example of indirect networking is that I became friends on Facebook with someone I knew from college, and when I was looking into joining the alumni board for my college, I saw that he was the head of it. After talking with him, I was able to join the board. Attending a board meeting, I met the new dean of the college and am now working on a couple of projects for him.

Another small project came in creating a Web site for a friend on Facebook. In that case, I knew she had her own business, and I soft pitched her on the idea of me helping her out.

I was contacted the other day by my former college roommate, and a friend on Facebook, about possibly helping her company with some writing for their Web site. I had sent her a soft-pitch message through Facebook as well.

Graphic Designer

When we first spoke, Tim McMahan had just finished speaking with a client about designing a personal budgeting and financial advice Web site for him, a client he met through Facebook.

I just had a meeting with someone last night about designing a Web site. We were friends-of-friends already, but he made the initial contact to inquire about working together through Facebook. Our first couple of interactions about the project were all made through Facebook. It's likely we would have hooked up without Facebook, but it certainly made it easier. It surprised me that he used Facebook to contact me. I was not at all expecting that. Until that point, it had just been a way to connect with old friends and laugh at old pictures.

The next day, Tim shared the good news with us that he had just received a signed contract.

Public Relations Consultant

Tracy Bagatelle Black is a PR consultant who actually has gotten two assignments through Facebook.

> One was someone who I didn't know but was a friend of a friend, and the other was someone that I knew in high school. We reconnected on Facebook. Since that success, I am continuing to pitch for new work using it. I'm "friends" with several people from PR agencies and hope to pick up work from them. When I see them online, I use the opportunity to chat via instant messaging and find out when they may need some help.

LOOKING AHEAD

As you can see, it's quite possible to find work through Facebook, as the preceding accounts point out. Now it's your turn to get that profile in shape, start connecting, and get ready for what happens next. But that's not all. To help with your job search, Chapter 8 will show you how you can get a job lead through 140 simple characters, that is, when you put those characters together on Twitter to answer the ever-important question, "What are you doing?"

CHAPTER 8

Twitter Your Way to that New Job

It's easy to dismiss Twitter (Twitter.com), the most popular microblogging site, as nothing more than a way to fritter away your time to no good end. If you do this, though, you're making a mistake that could delay the successful end to your job search or cut off a steady stream of new business.

Twitter, shown in Figure 8-1, is the site that asks you to answer one simple question for the rest of the world to consider: *What are you doing?* You must answer in 140 characters or less. Twitter came into its own in 2008. Actually, it was never designed to be time waste but rather a fast way to reach customers and communicate with possible clients and employers. It's fulfilled that purpose for sure, but it also has become a fun and simple tool beloved by millions.

Consider that no less than Guy Kawasaki, the former Apple evangelist with an unassailable reputation among techies, told the respected publishing industry blog MediaBistro that while "many people view e-mail and Twitter as kind of an adjunct to their main function, for me, it is my main function, and everything else is adjunct." He continued, "Twitter for me is not something I do when work is done for fun; Twitter is what I do."

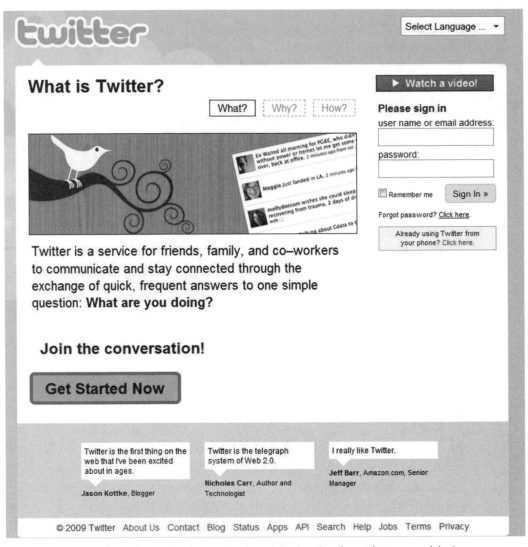

Figure 8-1: Twitter asks one simple question through its clean interface: What are you doing?

So how do we get from a place where Twitter seems like a silly thing to do to a place where it's more important that virtually all the more robust choices we have for social networking today? It's a good question that formed only as we delved more deeply into researching this book. The story is actually quite fascinating. The microblogging site asks no more of you than to tell the world, in a very short phrase, what you're doing right now, in this moment. What about that makes a fellow like Guy Kawasaki use it all day long? Beyond that philosophical question, and more important for you as someone exploring new job options, how can you use Twitter to get that next job or freelance gig?

THE LOWDOWN ON TWITTER

Twitter launched in 2006 as a way for people to track what their friends were doing between e-mails, blog posts, and other slower types of communications. No one expected at the time that businesses would grow to use it to communicate in real time with customers and that individuals would use it to find new jobs. Yet that's just what has happened.

Twitter has taken off like a wildfire. In October 2008, *Website Magazine* reported that unique visitors to Twitter grew by more than 570 percent year to year (from an average of 500,000 per month to 3.5 million per month). By January 2009, the *Wall Street Journal* estimated that about 4 to 5 million people use the service, "with about 30 percent or more being very new or limited users."

While in the real world people tend to be either leaders or followers, on Twitter, most are both. That is, you can sign up to follow people whose "tweets" (messages) you want to receive, and then others can choose to follow your tweets of wisdom. Log on, and you'll see the latest tweets from your own network, as shown in Figure 8-2. You can choose to observe whenever you like. You can participate when the mood strikes or ignore the "tweetering" entirely when the mood passes. The choice is yours, and as in so many things, the more you put into Twitter, the more you get out of it.

Your Twitter Profile

Twitter, which is free, doesn't ask you to input your life story or even anything nearly as detailed as what you entered for your LinkedIn profile. You just need to input the basics about who you are and why someone might want to take time out of a busy life to follow you on Twitter, that is, listen to your tweets.

In fact, aside from your username, you have just the following ways to explain yourself to the world:

1. A one-line bio that can be no more than 160 characters

2. A More Info URL (for example, your Web site's address)

3. A picture

As you can see, Twitter doesn't give you much opportunity to distinguish yourself. So tweak your profile before you do much tweeting.

And then make those tweets count! To get started, go to https://twitter.com/signup, shown in Figure 8-1. Once you've filled out the form, Twit-

Figure 8-2: The screen where all your tweets will appear on Twitter.

ter asks you to check to see if your friends are on Twitter. As with LinkedIn, you'll need to enter your e-mail addresses and passwords for sites that Twitter supports. Twitter then loads your address books and shows you which of your contacts are already using the site.

The next screen, shown in Figure 8-3, displays your contacts from that source and shows you which of those are already using Twitter. If you'd like to start following anyone, leave the box next to their picture or icon checked. If not, uncheck it. Next, Twitter gives you the option of inviting the people who are in your address book but not yet on Twitter to join the social networking site. Twitter will send "invites" to them for you. Tweet! Finally, Twitter shows you some famous folks who are on Twitter in case you'd like to start following them. That's it. From then on, you'll start receiving tweets from the people you are following each time you log on. And soon people will start following your tweets, too, so get ready to tweet yourself!

Figure 8-3: You can easily designate who you interact with on Twitter simply by checking or unchecking the box next to each user's name.

Those 140 Characters

As you know, you have just 140 characters to work with when you answer the question "What are you doing?" and send off those Twitter updates. You'll see people send tweets at all times of the day. It's no wonder you will learn that people are putting their kids to bed, feeding their dogs, and so on. Certainly, tweets range from the mundane to the useful. You may be thinking, "Okay, but why do I care?" Fair enough. But stay with us. Soon you'll see how all this twittering can result in queries from employers and possible job opportunities.

We've deleted any identifying information, but other than that, here are some examples of actual tweets (messages sent). The true purpose of Twitter will be far more clear when you get to the end of the list:

"Drinking my 2nd cup of Java, catching up on e-mail & ready to work on my eBay listings. Finally over this bronchitis!"

"My day has taken the wrong turn today."

"Sears tries new take on online shopping http://jijr.com/u19."

"Affiliate Summit Recap: http://is.gd/g4V7. And the parties: http://is.gd/g7Ao #asw09. TONS of pictures."

"Any SEO experts out there? Looking for guest suggestions to join my podcast show next week."

If your interests lie in e-commerce, you've got several tidbits to consider. What does our coffee-drinking eBayer sell, and how successful is that business in today's tough economy? Do I know (or even am I) an SEO expert? What is retail giant Sears doing in their online efforts right now? Although you're certainly relieved that your Twitter partner is feeling better, the other tweets are likely to be more relevant to your e-commerce interests. You most likely will click through to at least a few of these hyperlinks to see what more you can learn. That's a pretty powerful use of 140 characters.

WHAT ARE *YOU* GOING TO TWEET ABOUT?

As someone who is looking for new job opportunities, you may focus on tweets that showcase articles you have written, very brief first-hand accounts of meetings and conventions you're attending, news you've come across related to your industry, and anything else that would demonstrate to a potential employer that you're bright, connected, ambitious, and hard working.

Of course, who you tweet to is even more important than what you tweet about. As you move through this chapter, you'll see, in the section on people who have gotten jobs through Twitter, that they not only happened to say the right thing, but they also said it to the right person. But first, let's take a close look at the structure and vocabulary of Twitter. Let's start by looking at Twitter vocabulary and creating great tweets. Then you'll move on to building your connections with people you follow and those who follow you.

The Ways of Twitter

Just to get started:

> Here are 140 characters including the spaces. You can easily have your say within these limits. So have fun and make progress by twittering!

Twitter (like all communities) has its own vocabulary. Here are a few words to get you started:

Tweet   A message, also called an *update.*

Twitter Badge   A bit of software code that enables you to add your latest Twitter updates to your blog, MySpace page, and so on. The type of program that makes this possible is called a *widget.*

Follow   When you decide to follow someone else's tweets.

Public Timeline   The steady stream of messages from Twitter members who have chosen to keep their tweets public.

Follower   When someone is following your tweets.

Direct Messages   Messages you send directly to another Twitter user.

Tweet-up   A face-to-face meeting of Twitter users.

Tweeple   People who use Twitter.

As you go about creating your tweets, you can choose to have them be public or private. The setting is absolute, so if you do select to keep your tweets private, only the people within your Twitter network will be able to view and respond to them. For the purpose of job hunting, it seems most beneficial to keep your tweets public. How can a vast network of potential opportunities come your way if you've limited yourself to only those within your Twitter network? Plus, since you are exploring Twitter for job-hunting purposes, you are most likely making professional or at least responsible tweets. This is not the time or place to share your wild weekend plans with all the world, so there's no harm in letting others see what you're up to. As a matter of fact, there's a lot of good to it.

You may find a tweet to which you would like to respond. That's easy. Simply mouse over the lower right-hand corner of the tweet, and you'll see two icons pop up. One is a star that will allow you to highlight that particular tweet as a favorite. The other is a curved backward facing arrow that is called a *swoosh* on Twitter. Clicking that swoosh automatically adds the username of the tweet to your dialogue box. Now it will say, for example, @bob432 before your tweet. You also can just put an @ sign before any username to respond to a tweet directly. The detailed mechanics of using the site are beyond the scope of this book. All the details you'll need are right there on the Twitter help pages, and you'll learn a lot by moving your way through the simple instructions posted on the site. We're going to focus on using Twitter for job hunting and trust that you will very quickly be up to speed on using this simple tool for all your other reasons. And besides, you can read all about it on the Web for free.

Tiny URLs for Twitter

After so many years of living online, you've probably noticed that some Web addresses are incredibly long. Cutting and pasting makes it easy to put those long URLs into e-mails or reports or even books. That's okay if you have plenty of space in your document, and everyone knows to expect this serving of alphabet soup, but what if your space is limited to a tweet of 140 characters? For example, one retailer's URL for our McGraw-Hill book, *How to Make Money with YouTube,* is 121 characters long. Obviously, we couldn't use this in a tweet and still have anything useful left to say about the book. But, thanks to an amazing and free Web site, TinyURL.com, at http://tinyurl.com/create.php, you can enter the longest of URLs and come back quickly with something quite manageable. We shortened our URL to one that was only 25 characters: http://tinyurl.com/7vlkjm. You'll be using this site or one like it a lot once you're busy tweeting on Twitter.

Good Tweets for Job Seekers

It's one thing to tweet about what you're eating, the latest funny thing the dog did, or how your toddler embarrassed you in public yesterday if you're not in the market for a new job. Twitter is a fun place for just "being social." But if you've come to Twitter to have a business communications tool, you'll want each of your tweets to shine as an example of who you are and what you can do. Here are examples of tweets with a purpose. They're good because they provide useful, actionable information and/or cast a positive light on the tweeter.

"See my latest blog post on network security and social networking sites at tinyurlxxx.xxx."

"Have a Fully Integrated Marketing Plan http://short.to/lsy."

"Obama Girl duets with Obama. http://tinyurl.com/7y6vtu."

Don't Let Your Tweets Turn Out Like This

At some point, you may want to use Twitter for fun, and lots of people do. But that point will come only after you've secured your next job and are happily enjoying your new life. By now, you've seen how important it is to behave well on all social networks. They really are your new public persona as much as the clothes you choose to wear or the company you keep. Here are some examples of tweets that really could derail you. So please don't forget for a minute that you are on a public forum that could easily be explored by that hiring manager comparing your credentials with those of your competitor for that single job opening.

"Trying to convince this 2-year-old to sleep!"

"Just ate dinner and am now ready for a nap."

"The Ravens gave it their best but the Steelers are just a better team!"

"Any jobs out there in sales or marketing? I'll take anything."

FINDING PEOPLE TO FOLLOW

Start by clicking the Find People hyperlink at the top of most Twitter pages. From there, you'll see the screen that appears in Figure 8-4. You'll see a search box to let you get right down to finding friends on the site, but you also can let the site help you search by using the tabs that run along the top of the page. Those tabs let you search Twitter, search another social networking site, send e-mail invitations to friends who may not yet be using Twitter, and lastly, take a look at some suggestions from Twitter itself about groups you might want to join. (When we checked, the suggested groups ranged from NPR Radio to Britney Spears).

Figure 8-4: The many options for searching for new connections on Twitter.

Of course, you will want to follow people from your e-mail address books and other sources that may be in a position to hire you or help you with a job-related question. Perhaps some of the people you follow are just intellectually stimulating or competitors you want to track. Often, if you read articles mentioning Twitter or, increasingly, social media sites in general, the authors will give their Twitter address, such as "Follow me on Twitter—www.twitter.com/bschepp."

You can also send e-mails through the Find People screen to people who you would like invite to become Twitter members. Last of all, but perhaps the easiest option, you simply can enter a person's name to see if they're currently on Twitter.

If you are looking for a job in a given field, it definitely pays to follow people in that field who happen to be on Twitter. The fact that they are even on Twitter says something about them because relatively few people use Twitter as a way to communicate right now. If you are using Twitter as well, that says something about you, too. You and your "tweeple" are kindred spirits who recognize the value of seeing updates from someone's "lifestream," as the people in social networking often call it. It's getting more and more difficult to be a trendsetter for very long these days, but for now, people on Twitter fit that bill.

GETTING PEOPLE TO FOLLOW YOU

Your goal should be not just to follow people of interest but also to get people to follow you, especially if you are a person with something to sell, such as a great work history. Once you have followers, you've become a publisher, and any publisher will tell you that they want as many people (subscribers) to see their messages as possible. Your group of followers will be sure to receive your tweets and thus will be the first to know if you've published a savvy new blog entry. Other people can come across you by doing a Find People search, or they may come across your tweets if they're posted on the Public Timeline.

If you're building a following, however, as someone seeking new opportunities should be, invite people to follow you on Twitter by promoting your Twitter address. You can do this in many ways. For example, include it as part of your e-mail signature, within blog articles you write, or on your Web page. Include the line, "Follow me on Twitter: http://twitter.com/yourname."

Note that you can opt to "protect your updates" and have just the people who you approve be able to follow your tweets (also known as *updates*). You do this by checking the Protect My Updates box on your Settings page.

TWITTER AND JOB HUNTING

There are mixed opinions about whether you should blatantly tweet that you are looking for a new job. Some have done so and gotten work that way. We feel that you *should* alert fellow tweeters that your status has changed. Why not? Nobody, of course, likes to disappoint a job hunter by out-and-out stating that they don't have a job open. But if you tweet that you are open to new challenges in the [Fill in the Blank] field, that's a lot different. No one has to tell you face to face or over the phone that they don't know of anything. They can just not respond to your tweet. Of course, the ones who may know of an opening will be happy to step forward with a simple tweet in return.

 Social Media Maven Plus Twitter Equals Great Job

Rayanne Langdon quickly and easily found a great job through Twitter.

Rayanne Langdon is a self-proclaimed "social media junkie" from way back. She started blogging at the age of 13. She was a chat-room fiend when that was all the rage. "I have simply always loved connecting with all types of people from any-place in the world through online means," she told us. "Lucky for me, this whole 'Information Superhighway' thing has started to make money for people! Even luckier, I've found a way to use it to make money for myself."

Not ready to end her education with a college degree, Rayanne enrolled in a graduate program in corporate communications and public relations. Soon after joining the program, she started a blog about her experiences learning about public relations (PR) and other interesting media-related things. It didn't take long for her to discover microblogging and, you guessed it, Twitter, the most popular microblogging site by far.

"I was one of the fortunate few in my class to have already spent a lot of time meeting interesting people on Web sites like Twitter," Rayanne said. "In January 2008, when it came time for me to find a work placement, some of the first people I reached out to were those in my Twitterati. I was looking for a

PR-related placement, and I immediately had responses from local agencies, and even one with offices in Boston and San Francisco. I guess there weren't a lot of students active on social media channels, and people like me were in demand," she mused.

She soon had a few interviews and received a couple of good job offers. She chose to intern at a local PR agency in the social media division. She speculates that the fact that she included her blog address, MySpace music site, and Twitter stream on her résumé, and the fact that she'd been blogging since middle school, helped her snag that job. "The company had already hired an intern and wasn't planning on bringing on another," she said. "But I guess they didn't want to let me go, so they figured out a way to make me a part of the team."

When it came time for Rayanne to move on from this internship, she remembered that she'd seen an interesting and very funny recruiting video from a company call FreshBooks. This company, just about four years old at the time, is an online invoicing, time-tracking, expense-tracking service for freelancers and small-business owners. "I remembered that I was following the company's Head of Magic (yes, that his real title)," said Rayanne. "I sent him a direct message asking if the company was still looking to hire a marketing coordinator. I had an interview a few days later, was asked to come in for a second interview, and was soon offered the position I was hoping for!" she said.

Now, it's clear to see that Rayanne has long been a confident social networker. But it's also a fact that were it not for her following the right people on Twitter, she never would have known about this opportunity, let alone had the access she needed to the person with the hiring power. All in all, this is a pretty respectable return on the investment of 140 characters!

WE FOUND OUR JOBS THROUGH TWITTER!

Going into this project, we certainly had our doubts about Twitter's effectiveness for job hunters, but now, count us among the tweeters of the world. Turn over a few stones, and you can find many accounts of people who have found work through Twitter and, as a corollary, who have hired people they've met through Twitter. Now, we agree that as of the present, these jobs tend to have a social networking or Web slant to them, but there are others that are more traditional. For example, any company of any size has people who handle public relations. And as Twitter grows, its usefulness as a tool for locating applicants and announcing new jobs will only grow with it.

WORDPRESS EXPERT Kim Woodbridge has found most of her freelance jobs through Twitter, and has even written an article about how to do this on her blog (see http://tinyurl.com/59aezv). The blog entry has led to even more jobs. "I've found that you have to be helpful and put a lot of time into Twitter before finding work from it," Kim said. "With my strategy, I've gone from searching for work to people seeking out my services."

CONSULTANT AND AUTHOR Ronald Lewis has Twitter to thank for his first book deal, as well as a number of new consulting engagements in his field of cloud computing and telecommunications. Simply by being an active member of the Twitter community, including sharing knowledge and also tweeting about his ongoing work and interests, he was approached by an editor to write *Stick It to the Man*. His consulting work came about as a result of similar tweeting.

COMMUNITY EVANGELIST Marina S. Martin got her job at Elastic Lab (www.elasticlab.com) through Twitter and continues to use Twitter to do her job. Marina explained to us that "Elastic Lab creates tens to hundreds of professional videos for the long-tail by hiring our nationwide network of filmmakers and crowd-sourcing their footage into the final videos. Twitter has been a fabulous way to find filmmakers and filmmaker communities across the country." Elastic Lab is so enamored with Twitter and its effectiveness as a recruiting tool that the company plans to hire freelance filmmakers on an ongoing basis for years to come, Marina said.

PUBLIC RELATIONS INTERN "I found a really great PR intern via Twitter," said John Sternal, vice president of marketing communications for Lease-Trader.com. "I think the service is a great way to get to know someone without the pressures (and expectations) of face-to-face interaction. But it also gave me a chance to see what kind of character she had before actually calling her in for an interview. As I grow my network of followers here in South Florida, I will definitely be monitoring Twitter to start grooming my short list for when I do need to hire a full-time employee. Then again, if my intern turns out to be spectacular, that won't be necessary because I won't let her get away."

VIRTUAL ASSISTANT "I hired a virtual assistant that I found through Twitter," said Tracy Gosson, who works for a marketing and business-development firm in Baltimore. At the time, Tracy was not even really sure what a virtual assistant was until she learned more about it on Twitter. "I also have to meet new potential contract partners, and through a few conversations, I am now working with a Web designer that I found on Twitter for a client project," she told us. Although when we spoke Tracy had only been using Twitter for three months, she's already found it tremendously helpful.

CONSULTANT Social media marketing expert Robb Hecht had long used Twitter successfully to network with people "he wanted to know and learn new things about." But, in the process, he struck gold in the form of recruiters seeking him out for paid consulting gigs. "Twitter Search is the culprit for this," Rob explained. "Twitter Search allows you to follow conversations that include keywords that you choose. So, while, for example, I was searching for the latest innovations in the Web 2.0 arena relevant to consumer product goods, I ran into recruiters passively who then would contact me and within say a week—I'd have an offer for consulting work. The key here, the client said, was that I connected my Twitter account to my LinkedIn profile—which allowed him to passively look at my background and then decide to approach me to see if I'd do any consulting work for their company."

SOCIAL MEDIA STRATEGIST Matt Batt, of Pipeline Media Relations, Inc., hired a social media strategist that he met through Twitter to conduct a day-long "boot camp" for his employees. He also has located two or three prospective client leads as a result of the connections he's made on Twitter after only a month!

Matt was the one who first told us about the chat sessions and groups that meet through Twitter. He himself meets Mondays from 7 to 10 p.m. Central Time with a group of public relations/marketing and media professionals who discuss challenges and strategies for working together. They follow him during these sessions after seeing his tweets and interactions. One client lead came from someone in Florida who is a "thought leader" in the beauty industry and was looking to increase her media exposure. She followed his tweets "and really liked my philosophies," he said. "In addition, I've probably connected with a dozen potential business partners (that is, agencies or companies that would complement our services)."

Social Media Campaign Strategist and Virtual Assistant Leslie Carothers, owner of The Kaleidoscope Partnership based out of Minneapolis, specializes in social Web conversations for the home industries. Here's Leslie's story in her own words:

> I own a business called The Kaleidoscope Partnership. I have owned it for seven years now and also write online and offline for two major industry publications, *Furniture Today and Furniture World*, on how retailers, manufacturers, and suppliers can use social Web conversations to connect and engage potential consumers.

> In January, I hired a virtual assistant through Twitter and have been very pleased with the quality and timeliness of her work for me. In addition, I will be signing a contract from a company to conduct a social Web media marketing campaign for them. We have never met, and the owner decided to trust me based simply on my "tweets." Interestingly, he lives in Spain, is a very successful businessman, and . . . is 18 years old.

> In addition, I have opened up viable business opportunities for both my clients for whom I am twittering: BiOH polyols—a division of Cargill—that sells a soy-based replacement for foam to the furniture, bedding, and auto industries and also www.yourfurniturelink.com—a Web site devoted to helping consumers quickly connect with manufacturers directly to order the furniture featured on this site.

Blogger Recently, writer Sarah Caron was tooling around Twitter and noticed that one of her Twitter contacts was scouting about for writers for a blog associated with a new online community, FamilyEden.net. "I sent her a note and got the gig," said Sarah. "I am the Family & Technology blogger." Ever the opportunist, on another occasion, Sarah used Twitter to contact an associate of hers who had taken on a new job at a prominent magazine. "I congratulated her, and she asked me privately for clips. No work from that yet, but I am definitely hoping," Sarah said.

Usability Specialist Jay Zipursky landed a job though Twitter in less than three weeks. Here's how:

> I was hired at The MathWorks (www.mathworks.com) as a usability specialist. A usability specialist is a role that uses a variety of methods to help design software interfaces that are easy to use, efficient, and satis-

fying for the end user. We do things like user research, graphical user interface design, and design evaluation and testing. After that initial exchange on Twitter, I chatted with my acquaintance via instant messenger to learn a bit more about the company and sent him my résumé. A couple days later [one week after the Twitter exchange], I talked to a couple of managers on the phone, and they decided to fly me out the next week for an interview. Since I had an engineering degree and several years' experience developing software before switching to usability, it turns out I was an excellent fit for one of their positions. I got a job offer shortly after. It was less than three weeks from Twitter to offer.

DIRECTOR OF NEW MEDIA Bob Wilson was hired by Moxley Carmichael www.moxleycarmichael.com, and if not for Twitter, it may never have happened.

"The tweetup was simply a few downtown Knoxville users of Twitter getting together for a few drinks and to meet each other in person," said Bob. "A few pockets of people knew each other, but in many cases the pockets did not cross over. We intentionally kept the size small to facilitate conversation, and that worked well. I had heard of other local events that were larger and did not work as well."

Entrepreneurs and Twitter

In researching an article we wrote for the online auction site Auctiva.com, we found many examples of entrepreneurs using Twitter to build their brands and drive traffic to their own Web sites, where they could complete sales. We've already discussed how consultants, for example, have found work through Twitter. Here are some other examples of how entrepreneurs can use Twitter:

- e-Commerce sellers tell their customers about new items they have for sale.
- Promoters such as David Mullings of Realvibez announce new products and clients.
- Anyone with a new Web site might want to let all his or her friends and past clients in on special discounts and deals.
- Growing companies that have a lot of people using their products tweet about outages, new services, special promotions, and the like.

Sarah Caron's Advice for Twitter Job Prospecting

Sarah Caron offers advice for job hunting with Twitter.

Pay attention to what your contacts are saying, and don't be afraid to just jump in the conversation. My editor at FamilyEden asked someone else to apply for the blogging gig, and I shot her a note asking if she was looking for any more writers. If I hadn't interjected myself, then I wouldn't have gotten this position. Also, there is such a wide world of social networking out there now that it helps to keep track of who the movers and shakers are. This particular editor was recently named to the most influential women in social media list.

Aside from actual jobs, many people have used Twitter as a tool to promote their work. Mike Michalowicz, author of *The Toilet Paper Entrepreneur*, is an example of the many people who have used Twitter to land media opportunities. Mike was able to get on a nationally syndicated radio show through a connection he made on Twitter—and has been on the show twice now because of the relationship he formed with the producer.

TWITTER TOOLS

We don't know if it's the name, the openness of the platform, or the growing number of users, but programmers sure seem to like developing great little programs for use with Twitter. We've listed just a few here. For the scoop on many more. see http://twitter.com/downloads.

Twitter search at http://search.twitter.com/ allows you to enter a search term—such as a company or a topic that interests you—to see what's being said on Twitter about it. Don't underestimate the power of this tool for finding information not only about employers but also about who may be conducting the latest medical research in an area that interests you. You can even do advanced searches on Twitter.

Twhirl is a desktop-based software program that makes using Twitter easier and staying on top of new tweets even simpler. You can download it at www.twhirl.org/. It runs on both Windows and Mac platforms.

TweetScan at www.tweetscan.com/index.php searches Twitter, identi.ca, and other sites and offers e-mail alerts, which are sent automatically should your search term appear.

Can't keep from Twittering even when you're doing other things on the Web? TwitBin at www.twitbin.com/ may be your savior. This little program is designed to work with your Firefox browser. It will let you monitor the latest postings from your Twitter connections and even send messages without leaving your browser screen. Note that the service is free, but it does run ads along the bottom of your screen.

Steps for Starting Out on Twitter

Miriam Salpeter, a career counselor who helps people use Web 2.0 tools to job hunt successfully, is a true Twitter expert. She was generous enough to share her tips for using Twitter. These were originally part of her blog post, "Use Twitter for Your Job Hunt." We highly recommend that you visit her at www.keppiecareers.com.

Miriam Salpeter owns KeppieCareers, an executive placement firm.

Brand yourself professionally. If you are planning to use Twitter for a job search, set up a designated profile and account. Choose a professional Twitter handle using your name or some combination of your name and profession that sounds good and is easy to remember, for example, JaneSmith or Marketing-ExpertJane.

Take time to create a professional profile that will attract your target market. If you don't have a Web site, link to your LinkedIn profile.

Before you follow anyone, start posting some tweets! Don't succumb to the temptation to share your lunch menu! Tweet about an article or an idea, or share a link of professional interest to your targeted followers. Do this for a few days. It may seem strange to be tweeting when no one is following, but you may be surprised to gain an audience before you even try. Once you have a great profile and a set of interesting tweets, start following people in your industry. Aim high! Follow stars—some will follow you back.

Continue to build your network by using Twitter Search and Twitter's Find People tool. Manually review profiles, and use Twubble to help you find new people to follow. Use directories such as Twellow and TwitDir. Grow your network slowly—you don't want to follow 1,000 people and have only 30 following you. That makes you look spammy, not professional.

Another tool to use to learn what is going on in your area of expertise is Monitter (hat tip to Steve Cornelius). Steve used it to look up information about a company where he was interviewing. It is also great to see what people are talking about and to find conversations to join on Twitter.

Give, give, give! Think about what you can do for others. Don't blatantly self-promote. Instead, help promote others. "Retweet" (pass along information someone else shared, giving them credit). You will earn followers and friends this way. Those who know (and like) you will become part of your network and will be willing to help you.

LOOKING AHEAD

No doubt you are now positively atwitter with all the possibilities of using Twitter to advance your career goals, learn new things, share your expertise, and have some fun, too. It's a very good thing that your creative juices are flowing because your next destination is MySpace. Much of the media attention that has fallen on social networking in the last few years has surrounded MySpace. You may have come to think of it as the domain of high school kids and rock stars, but that would be too shallow a definition for a site that blends creativity and work. If your profession leans toward the arts, including the art of merchandising, branding, or public relations, you may find that MySpace is your space, too.

CHAPTER 9

MySpace Can Be a Showcase for Your Skills

I n February 2005, less than two years after it was launched, MySpace (www.myspace.com/) was growing at a rate of 6 percent each week, according to the *Washington Post*. It was the hottest thing around since, well, MTV, at least if you happened to be a teen. It seemed that everyone was on the social networking site for hours at a time, checking out pictures of their friends, gossiping in chat rooms, uploading and embedding videos, and downloading music.

When News Corporation bought the company in July 2005 for $580 million dollars, MySpace had 18 million monthly visitors and was the fastest-growing social networking site. By buying MySpace, News Corporation instantly doubled its U.S. Web traffic. In a year, MySpace would be up to 54 million monthly visitors.

Fast-forward to spring 2008. Facebook had roared past MySpace by targeting a slightly older crowd and a much larger international base. Those "What's in?" and "What's out?" lists that newspapers like to print all agreed that Facebook was "in" and MySpace was "out." With more than 220 unique visitors per month, Facebook then and now remains atop the social networking heap, having doubled its base between 2007 and 2008 alone.

MYSPACE'S PLACE IN THE SOCIAL NETWORKING MIX

Facebook may have surpassed it in some ways, but don't feel bad for My-Space. It draws 125 million visitors per month and is still tops in the U.S. market, with 76 million visitors per month, compared with Facebook's 55 million. Not too shabby. And while Facebook may attract more visitors worldwide, nothing competes with MySpace when it comes to the venue it provides people in the arts.

There's no doubt that creative types and their fans have a home on My-Space. Yet this is a book about job hunting for *everyone*, not just musicians, filmmakers, and other artists. Where does MySpace (Figure 9-1) fit into the world of social networking at large? Should you even bother with it if you're not in a field considered to be the domain of only the creative?

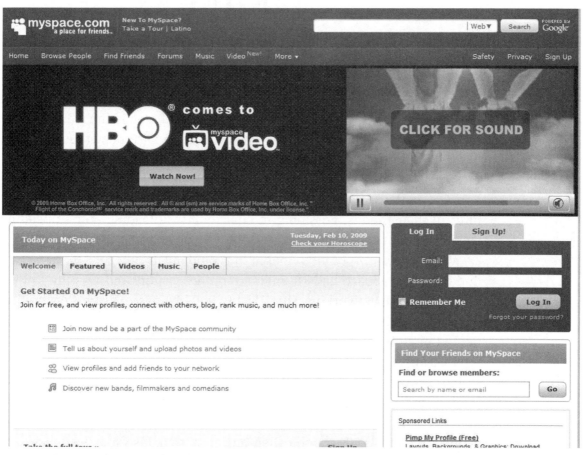

Figure 9-1: The MySpace homepage promises a colorful and dynamic environment in the world of social networking.

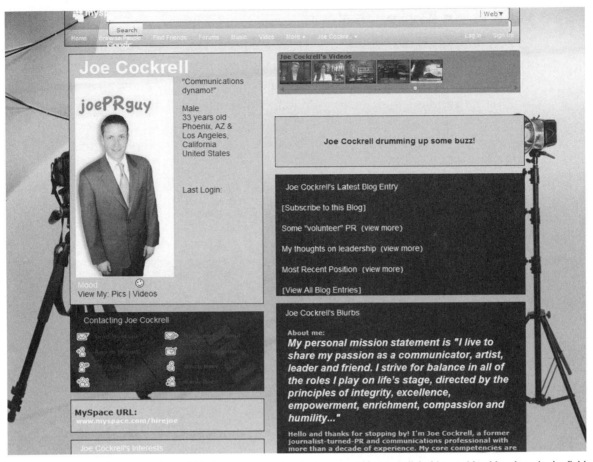

Figure 9-2: Through his MySpace page, Joe Cockrell was able to spotlight his considerable talents in the field of public relations. This page helped him to get his current job.

To be perfectly honest, we weren't so sure. Then we met "JoePRguy," otherwise known as Joe Cockrell. We learned about the $100,000 per year job as a communications director he got through a MySpace connection. Suddenly, dismissing MySpace seemed like it could be a big mistake. MySpace is too big, its audience is too large, and yes, the potential is too real not to be included in a discussion of social networking and job hunting.

Just take a look at Joe's MySpace site (Figure 9-2) for a model of what you can do to promote yourself as a business person on the site. We're getting a little ahead of ourselves, but there's nothing like inspiration to help you keep an open mind.

Who Is on MySpace Now?

Look around MySpace, and it quickly becomes obvious that the site is designed for teens and college kids. With giant banner ads for the latest music CDs, popular forums on campus life and games, and a people search page looking more like it belongs on "Match.com for teens," MySpace is your place if you're under age 25. While the company claims that it's for everyone, when it actually spells it out on its site, we learn that "everyone" means

- Friends who want to talk online

- Single people who want to meet other single people

- Matchmakers who want to connect their friends with other friends

- Families who want to keep in touch

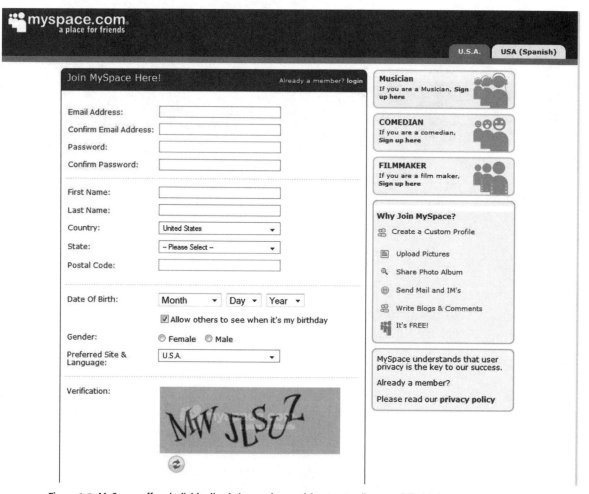

Figure 9-3: MySpace offers individualized sign-up for musicians, comedians, and filmmakers.

It's not until later that MySpace also says that it's for "business people and coworkers interested in networking."

Another way to assess who MySpace is for (as if looking at the site for a while doesn't tell you) is by considering its sign-up page (see Figure 9-3 on previous page). As you can see, musicians, comedians, and filmmakers have their own sign-up processes, their own doors into the site. While this is partly to ensure that MySpace is covered legally when musicians upload demos to the site, it's also to reach out to those who can provide its market with what they've come to expect from MySpace.

WORKING MYSPACE

We don't suggest that everyone should take the time to create a MySpace "presence." (*Presence* is the term that applies here rather than simply *page*— a lot more thought needs to go into creating a profile on the site than the word *page* would suggest.) Admittedly, some social networking experts suggest that job hunters stay away from MySpace entirely, implying that being there can do your career more harm than good. A profile on MySpace can portray you as being too frivolous, some suggest.

Well, we're not going to be that absolute about MySpace. People in the arts who are looking to promote themselves and sell more tickets, CDs, and even T-shirts in the process *need* to be on MySpace. Musicians, for example, can include playlists, note upcoming shows, share a blog with their fans, include a bio and contact information, and of course, performance videos.

But if we broaden the definition of creative work, it doesn't end with performance artists. There's also a home on MySpace for job hunters in such fields as PR, social media, blogging, and more. People in these fields should develop a presence that matches each site they occupy and the people likely to visit it to benefit from whatever that site might offer. There's creativity in many jobs, and a creative presence on MySpace just may give you the tools you'll need to spotlight how creative you actually are. Just remember that anyone, even that human resources person in the accounting firm you've applied to, may search MySpace to check you out. So, as with any site, be aware that you are operating in a very public forum. You don't want to screen yourself out because of something in a profile that seemed like a fun idea but actually works against your image or credibility.

Your MySpace Page

As soon as you sign up with MySpace, you'll be prompted through the steps you'll take as you create a profile and begin inviting friends and contacts to be a part of your new network. You've been through these processes before if you signed up for LinkedIn, for example. It's tempting to just jump right in; by now, this is nothing new to you. Before you go about creating your MySpace profile, however, be sure to look around at profiles for people in fields similar to your own. Perhaps more so than for any other site, your MySpace page must be compelling and complete. So you'll be adding more photos here; paying more attention to aesthetics, such as your page's background and how all the colors work with the site; and perhaps adding videos and even music. Overall, you'll be "talking" louder, "raising your hand" higher, and turning up the volume if you expect people to take you seriously here. While MySpace says that creating a profile is "fast, fun, and easy," if you're using the site for business purposes, you're wasting your time and effort if you don't tailor your profile to MySpace's audience and the employers who are most likely to be looking for people with your skills on the site.

You don't have to go it alone. If you have teens or young adults in your life, ask them to help. There are also many companies that provide MySpace layouts and templates, graphics, and backgrounds. We did an interesting Google search for "pimp your MySpace page," and it yielded more than 1 million hits! Perhaps a more dignified search would yield more business-like help, but there's no doubt that help is out there.

Let's take another look now at Figure 9-2, which shows the MySpace page for Joe Cockrell, who landed that great PR job thanks to his presence on the site. We think Joe's page is a great example of a profile for someone looking to connect with other business people.

While his page is on MySpace, in its own way, it's all business. The pictures, the copy, and the attitude all combine to portray Joe as someone who is successful, confident, connected, and hip. These are all traits that are important for people in his profession. If you were to look at some of the pictures he's posted to the site (Figure 9-4), you'd see that Joe has worked with Jay Leno, Tom Arnold, and Martin Sheen. In the world of public relations, those pictures speak volumes.

Now let's consider the page for the rock group New Method at http://www.myspace.com/newmethodband. Their approach is to treat their

TIP

Try MySpace Profile Editor, which simplifies the process of adding multimedia elements to your profile. In beta as we write this, this application promises to make the process of fashioning the right look for your MySpace profile much simpler than it is otherwise.

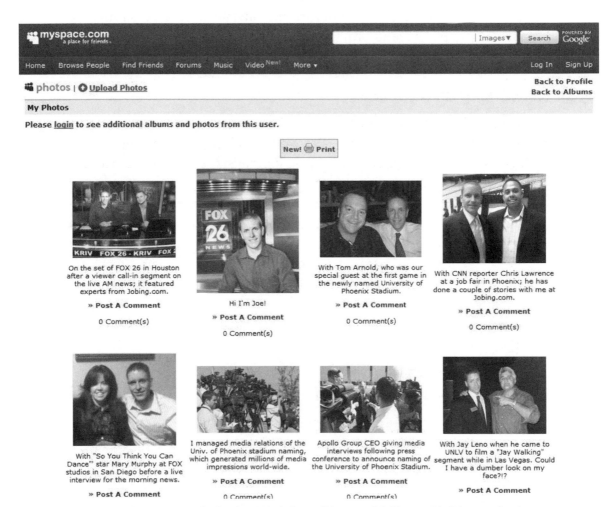

Figure 9-4: Joe Cockrell's photos, including well-known celebrities, provide living proof to the MySpace audience that he is exactly who he claims to be in the PR world.

page as a multimedia press kit. "Our page helps us get gigs with youth pastors because they can use it like a media kit by listening to our music, reading our bio, seeing pictures, and even reading about our general character in our blogs. It lets them know in a capsule form if we're what they're looking for to minister to their youth group," says band member Doug Meacham.

Whether they're music downloads, videos from performances, photos that show you're connected with the right people, or just a compelling blog, on MySpace you have to include compelling samples of your work that will grab other MySpace devotees. If you want your network to be strong and broad, you simply have to provide the content. Your competitors will be doing it, and people on MySpace expect nothing less.

Networking on MySpace

Self-managed singer and songwriter Laurier Tiernan networks through MySpace in a very systematic way. "Basically, I'm out to make friends with radio staff, record company staff, music journalists, and fellow musicians who perform music in similar genres," he said. "Usually I'll spend about an hour a day making friends in the aforementioned categories. For the first little while I was focusing on places I'd like to live, like California, England, or Japan (where I currently live), but occasionally I opened it up to the entire English-speaking world. Also, at a friend's suggestion, I spent a week focusing on Europe; to a certain degree of success, I'm still receiving 'random' friend requests from Italy, weeks later."

MYSPACE MYADS

On MySpace, you can let people come to you, which will definitely work, of course, if you're Bruce Springsteen or Will.i.am. If you happen not to be either one, you can target your potential audience with advertising. MySpace MyAds, shown in Figure 9-5, is new service that lets you create ads to target specific demographic groups. These ads are designed specifically for those who want to promote their businesses, whether music-related or not. The site steps you through the process of naming your campaign and then building or uploading an advertisement. Next, you indicate the markets you'd like to target, decide on a budget, and off you go. The site

Figure 9-5: The MyAds section on MySpace, where you can create advertisements to promote your work.

also provides real-time data that help you to monitor how well your ads are doing. You'll find lots more information at https://advertise.myspace.com/login.html.

MySpace Jobs

You can look for a job on MySpace through the MySpace Jobs area, shown in Figure 9-6. Through its relationship with job-posting aggregator Simply Hired, MySpace provides access to millions of job postings. You can search these by keyword or narrow them down by location. Of course, these are the same jobs available through other companies that have a relationship with Simply Hired, including LinkedIn. Aside from access to these jobs, MySpace also includes videos from CareerTV.com on career topics such as interviewing, creating a résumé, and even getting fired! The videos are definitely geared to MySpace's younger demographic.

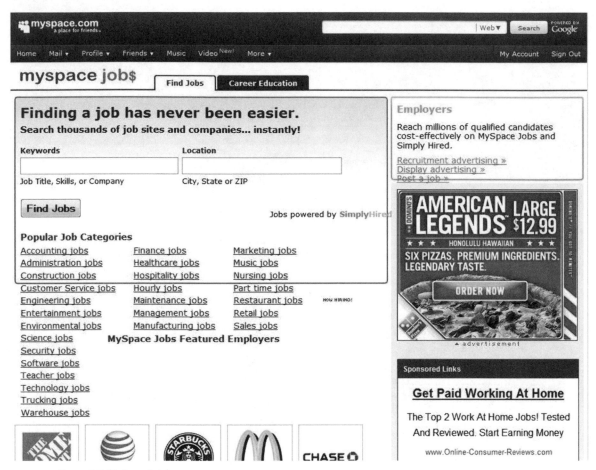

Figure 9-6: MySpace's jobs area.

WE FOUND OUR JOBS THROUGH MYSPACE!

Once again, performing artists and others in creative fields are the ones most likely to find work on MySpace. Here's a sampling of people who have told us about the jobs and gigs they've landed through the site.

Foreign Correspondent

Singer/songwriter Laurier Tiernan (www.myspace.com/lauriertiernan) decided last spring to take control of his career. First, he severed ties with the indie label he was signed to.

Laurier Tiernan found a whole new international writing career through MySpace. *(Photo taken by his wife, E. H. Tiernan.)*

I had just released my newest demo, and it had just got into regular rotation on the biggest FM radio station in Tokyo, so I decided to spend at least an hour a day on MySpace making friends with radio station staff from all over the English-speaking world. One day I found an Internet radio station called Westfield Radio (www.live365.com/stations/westfield1972), and I liked their introduction paragraph, so I e-mailed them to see if I could get some airplay. They were very friendly and supportive immediately, especially the owner, Ken Bailey. Ken puts out a weekly newsletter of music industry leads that he mails off to his friends, fans, and supporters who sign up. He also sends individual e-mails to specific people when he gets a lead that he thinks would be specifically suited to that person.

One day he sent me an e-mail saying that *Music Connection* magazine in Los Angeles was looking for concert reviewers, and he thought this might be a good side job for me. I wrote them a quick e-mail, and they sent me a quick but polite answer saying that they were not equipped to hire people from foreign countries at that time. However, some six months later I got another e-mail from the editor asking me if I would accept a position as a foreign correspondent. Of course I accepted enthusiastically, especially since my wife [photographer E. H. Tiernan] could get photo credits out of the deal.

Music Gigs

This is MySpace after all, and for recording artists, there may be no better route to self-promotion these days. New Method, the Christian pop/rock band (www.myspace.com/newmethodband) we mentioned earlier, has found several gigs through MySpace. Band member Doug Meacham says:

We often have youth pastors who are out on MySpace contacting us about coming to their church, youth event, or festival. We've booked around a half dozen gigs through MySpace in the last year. Advice that I could give to others trying to create a "presence" through MySpace is to target "friends" who fit within your target audience. For us, we've tried to target Christian music fans or church leaders with any promotion we do for our site. That helps us narrow our focus to make it more effective in promoting our music and getting gigs!

Christian rock band New Method relies heavily on their MySpace presence to attract new gigs.

Music Tours

Musician Kama Linden sings in the pop/rock genre and has gotten many bookings through MySpace (www.myspace.com/kamalinden). She's used the site to find fill-in gigs when she's already been scheduled to appear at local festivals. She's also gone so far as to arrange full tours in the United Kingdom and Australia. She's used the site to find agents, promoters and "song pluggers."

> I do searches by genre and by city, and sometimes it's like blowing on the dice and seeing what falls when you roll them. I have successfully found booking agents in almost all parts of the world. Plus, when you are friends with people like yourself and you do comments, you get more friends. Then you send out a bulletin when you need something like: Booking Agent—Please advise—and people respond!

Communications Director

Joe Cockrell landed a new six-figure PR job through MySpace.

> I was approached directly by the CEO of my new company, Inhouse Assist—a health care recruitment firm based in Glendale, AZ, because of a profile I created on MySpace (www.myspace.com/hireJoe). I posted a tweet (joePRguy) that led him to my MySpace page www.myspace.com/hirejoe.

If you look at that page you'll see I asked reporters and other PR professionals who are friends to post comments about my work. Even my photo album has pictures of me "on the job." The CEO said he loved it, and they were looking for somebody who thinks outside the box and knows social media. He e-mailed me, and we spoke over the course of a few weeks. Although I was not in an active job search at the time, my page was designed to showcase how to use social networking for career and employment. I eventually accepted the offer of director of communications for Inhouse Assist.

LOOKING AHEAD

By now you've seen clearly that social networking for business can be as varied and flexible as the number of jobs available. You may explore MySpace long enough to decide that you don't really think there's a place for you on this site. Or your exploration could lead you to new and interesting aspects for your creative outlets that hadn't occurred to you before. Not every social networking site is right for every person. That's why it's such a good thing that there are so many various sites from which to choose. Next, we'll turn your attention to Plaxo and then some of the smaller and lesser-known social networks that you may not have discovered on your own yet. The world of social networking is expanding so quickly that there's no doubt you'll find sites that are just right for you.

CHAPTER 10

Plaxo and Other Social Networks

Plaxo is not a toothpaste or pharmaceutical company from northern New Jersey. It's a trendsetter in the social networking field, with 30 million registered users and cable giant Comcast as its parent company. Many of the people we spoke with for this book were familiar with social networking pioneer Plaxo (www.plaxo.com/) and had even set up Plaxo profiles. Beyond that, they mostly stuck with LinkedIn for business networking. Facebook and, increasingly, Twitter were their online destinations for more social networking, although now you know that Facebook and Twitter also bring together companies and employees as well as friends and long-lost cousins. We can understand the allegiance people have to their familiar sites, but Plaxo, shown in Figure 10-1, is well worth a close second look, which is why we devote much of this chapter to it. By the end of our discussion, we're confident that you'll feel the same.

Beyond Plaxo, this chapter also covers the rising tide of smaller social networking sites that cater to specific regions or audiences. We can expect to have more of these smaller, more-targeted sites emerge as the whole trend of social networking for business purposes evolves. For now, some of these smaller sites include Ning, Ryze, and Xing. Part of your education in these smaller sites will include explaining just why they carry their unusual names.

Figure 10-1: Plaxo's homepage is colorful (trust us) and engaging.

PLAXO IS FOR PEOPLE

Plaxo may one day be called the granddad of Web 3.0 functionality. Here's why: As a company, Plaxo feels that the Internet's lifeblood is the people data. If you're on Plaxo, these data would include your profile, your network, and your address book. The company has led the charge for a new standard for "portable contacts." This means that you enter profile information once; then it becomes your Internet profile no matter where you want to build a presence online. Instead of repetitively completing a profile for each social network you'd like to use, portable contacts will allow your single profile to automatically follow you from one Web site to the next Web site. Wouldn't that be excellent?

Plaxo got its start in 2002, before social and business networking really took off, as a service for organizing your contacts via the Internet—an "Internet address book." Its core market is 30- to 50-year-old professionals. The average user is 43 years old. Like LinkedIn, Plaxo attracts top executives and high-level business people of all stripes. The most common titles in its database are "President," "CEO," and "Owner." "Because we've found our way to this demographic, we have very high quality networks," says the company's marketing director, John McCrea. Given its demographics, it's no surprise that the company's mantra is "How can we make this useful?" as opposed to "How can we make this fun?"

Swimming in the Lifestream

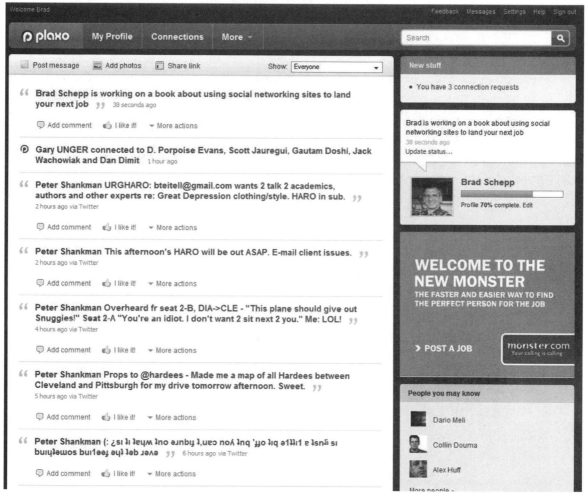

Figure 10-2: Plaxo offers you a handy dashboard to help you easily manage all your social networking efforts.

Immodestly, perhaps, Plaxo views its role in life as a "Web-wide lifestream aggregator." Through a handy dashboard that appears each time you view your profile (see Figure 10-2 on previous page), Plaxo provides a newsfeed from people you know. The company claims that it pioneered the concept of such an Internet-based lifestream aggregator in 2007. Fine, but what does that mean exactly?

People who use Plaxo are able to keep tabs on all their network members and what each one is up to all over the Web. Whether your contacts are posting to blogs, uploading pictures to Flickr and Picasa, sending tweets via Twitter, posting items on Facebook, or sharing videos on YouTube, their activities will show up on your Plaxo page. Plaxo gives you the dashboard necessary to keep track of your business contacts and friends.

Plaxo offers an interesting combination of features that you've seen in several other social networks. It's not as rigid as LinkedIn, but it's also not as loose as MySpace. It has something of a Twitter feel to it, with that lifestream pulsing every time you log on. As with Facebook, you can upload reviews, links, or polls to Plaxo. Your contacts don't even have to go to Plaxo very often to stay updated on what you're doing. They will still hear about your updates through the Plaxo Weekly Updates the company sends telling you about new connections you may want to know about and new postings your network members have uploaded.

Plaxo Premium

Plaxo is free, but there is also a premium version available that enables you to

- Eliminate duplicate contacts and calendar events
- Synch Plaxo up with Windows mobile phones
- Provide disaster recovery for your address book
- Add a customizable e-mail signature
- Send customizable and premium e-cards
- Receive round-the-clock VIP customer service

You can try Plaxo Premium for free for 30 days. If you find it useful, a subscription costs $49.95 per year. For more on the differences between the free and pay versions of Plaxo, see Figure 10-3.

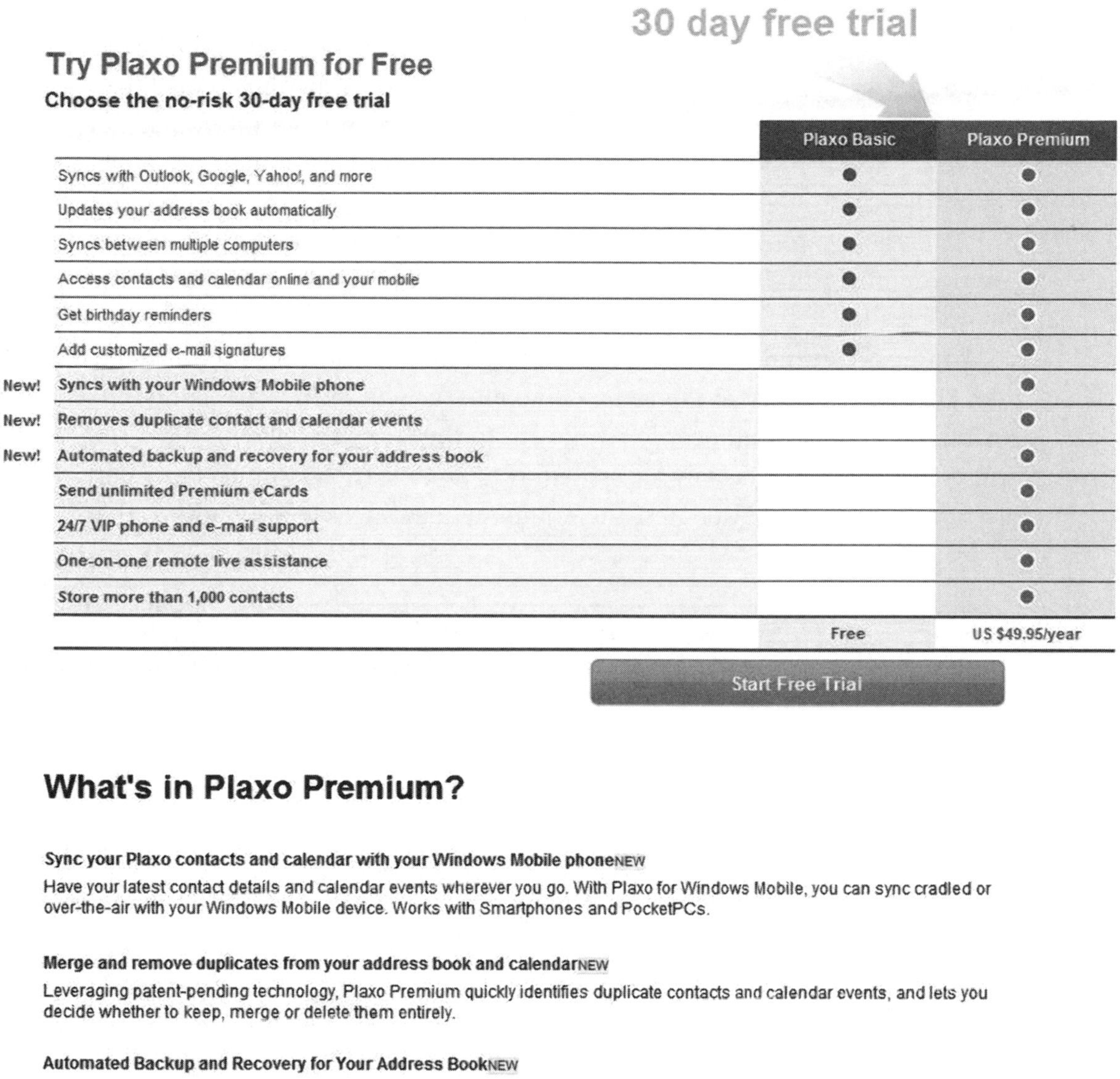

Try Plaxo Premium for Free

Choose the no-risk 30-day free trial

30 day free trial

	Plaxo Basic	Plaxo Premium
Syncs with Outlook, Google, Yahoo!, and more	●	●
Updates your address book automatically	●	●
Syncs between multiple computers	●	●
Access contacts and calendar online and your mobile	●	●
Get birthday reminders	●	●
Add customized e-mail signatures	●	●
New! Syncs with your Windows Mobile phone		●
New! Removes duplicate contact and calendar events		●
New! Automated backup and recovery for your address book		●
Send unlimited Premium eCards		●
24/7 VIP phone and e-mail support		●
One-on-one remote live assistance		●
Store more than 1,000 contacts		●
	Free	US $49.95/year

Start Free Trial

What's in Plaxo Premium?

Sync your Plaxo contacts and calendar with your Windows Mobile phoneNEW

Have your latest contact details and calendar events wherever you go. With Plaxo for Windows Mobile, you can sync cradled or over-the-air with your Windows Mobile device. Works with Smartphones and PocketPCs.

Merge and remove duplicates from your address book and calendarNEW

Leveraging patent-pending technology, Plaxo Premium quickly identifies duplicate contacts and calendar events, and lets you decide whether to keep, merge or delete them entirely.

Automated Backup and Recovery for Your Address BookNEW

Figure 10-3: Plaxo Premium is available for a 30-day free trial.

Building Your Internet Address Book

Like other social networking sites, Plaxo lets you easily import connections from your e-mail accounts, from Microsoft Outlook, or even from AIM. You've seen how this works before, but let's look at it once more, this time from Plaxo's vantage point. Let's say that you decide to send invitations to people you correspond with through Gmail. From the main Plaxo homepage, click on the Connections hyperlink at the top of the page, and you'll see the screen shown in Figure 10-4. From there, you could review the contact suggestions Plaxo presents. Another option on that same page (although not visible in Figure 10-4) is a hyperlink, Find friends in your e-mail. By clicking on that and entering an e-mail account and password for that account, you can search through the associated address book. By default, Plaxo shows you everyone in that address book, whether or not they are currently Plaxo members.

You also can build your list of connections by reviewing lists of Plaxo members who worked at the same companies as you during the same time period. Or you can find people who went to the same college you did. You don't even need to make any special effort to do this. In the Connections part of your Weekly Plaxo Updates, the company may include a hyperlink that

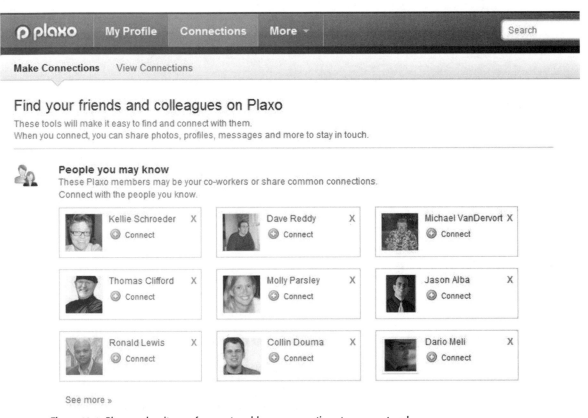

Figure 10-4: Plaxo makes it easy for you to add new connections to your network.

you can click on saying something like "Find classmates from Rutgers University-New Brunswick/Piscataway."

Once Plaxo presents you with a list of possible connections, you'll need to indicate whether that person is a friend, family member, or someone you know through business. Unlike LinkedIn, you don't have to reveal anything more than that (such as the company you worked at when you knew the person). Plaxo is much less rigorous in asking you to justify your connection to someone. This is a plus for causal networkers, a minus for those preferring a more restricted community.

Working with Your Network and Job Hunting with Plaxo

"We have always focused from the very beginning on helping you stay connected to the people you know and care about and reconnect with the ones you've lost touch with," says John McCrea, Plaxo's marketing director. "We haven't explicitly gone out after networking per se. We haven't focused on your finding people you don't already know." John explained that in the olden days before e-mail, when you left a job, you'd be sure to take a copy of your Rolodex with you. Then you'd have your contacts all in one place, at least for a while. Before too long, that information was no longer reliable as people moved on to other jobs or locations. Your contact information grew outdated. Now, through Plaxo, you can reconnect with those former associates, those people you may have lost touch with. While Plaxo is mainly about maintaining your current relationships rather than cultivating new ones, this doesn't mean that it can't be a great help to you in a job search. Once again, it boils down to networking. Starting your networking with your current contacts, whether you're on LinkedIn, Plaxo, or still clutching that Rolodex, is the first step you should take anyway.

As with any network you belong to, ensure that everyone in your Plaxo network knows that you're looking for a job. First, update your status, and let people know that you're open to new opportunities. Fill out your profile, paying special attention to the About Me and Professional Experience areas. Make sure that your network is fleshed out, that you have contact information for everyone, and that this information is current. Through Plaxo, you cultivate those relationships, making it more likely that you'll get a response when you reach out to your network. Regularly posting blog entries, links, and other items that give people insight into the kind of person you are and the type of employee you would be is definitely worth your time.

Consultant Terry Seamon is absolutely convinced that job hunters should include Plaxo as one of their tools. "I've seen a lot of people I've worked with from other companies there. Plaxo is a much simpler interface. I get a message when someone in my network makes a new connection. Right next to the announcement is a hyperlink to allow me to connect with that new person."

Because your connections on Plaxo are separated into three distinct groups—Family, Friends, and Business—you can easily customize your postings to the correct target audience. This is especially important when you are job hunting. In keeping with the dashboard analogy, you can post the pictures of your baby's first birthday to your Family and Friends contacts but not to your Business contacts. Then you can post your latest professional blog entry only to your Business connections. For your Business contacts, don't forget to include useful URLs, true professional insights, and other quality information that will support others in your field in their own jobs. This way, you make yourself attractive and valuable before you even broach the subject of a new job within your network. You prove yourself someone worthy to be "listened" to. Save the hilarious stories of your latest encounters with your unruly, not-quite-housebroken puppy for your family and friends. They're likely to love them. The beauty of Plaxo is that there's a place for both in one space.

◼ ◼ Ten Ways Job Hunters Can Use Plaxo

1. Use the company's Jobs section (see Figure 10-5) to review unique-to-Plaxo listings from recruiters and human resources (HR) managers and also search and browse the millions of listings from the Simply Hired job search engine. To reach this area, click on the Jobs link, which you'll see when you mouse over the More tab at the top of Plaxo pages.

2. Create a network that includes ex-coworkers, managers, influential neighbors and friends, and others in a position to help you.

3. Regularly send postings about new blog entries you've made, insightful articles or books you have read, and your take on important business news. You want to stay on people's radar screens in a way that showcases you in a positive light.

4. Scan the messages that others in your network have posted. You may just find a few diamonds there that will lead to something tangible such as an interview or at least a new company to track.

5. Invite important contacts to join Plaxo because the stronger the network becomes, the more valuable it will be to you.

6. Keep your status updated. This is important not just because you're seeking new opportunities but also because you want your contacts to know that you're active, vibrant, and ready should a good opportunity become available.

7. Plaxo is connected to more than 30 social networking sites; we've only mentioned a few here. Check out the others too, such as Yelp.

8. Check out the drop-down menu next to Plaxo's More tab to review other features that you may find useful, such as the Address Book, Calendar, Premium Tools, and Groups.

9. If you're running Windows, consider downloading Plaxo's Pulse Notifier for Windows applications so that when someone in your network posts something, you're immediately notified via an icon in your Windows Systems tray.

10. Keep your settings set so that you're receiving on-target business information and not sharing anything you wouldn't want a prospective client to see. Set your settings by clicking on the hyperlink at the top right of most Plaxo pages.

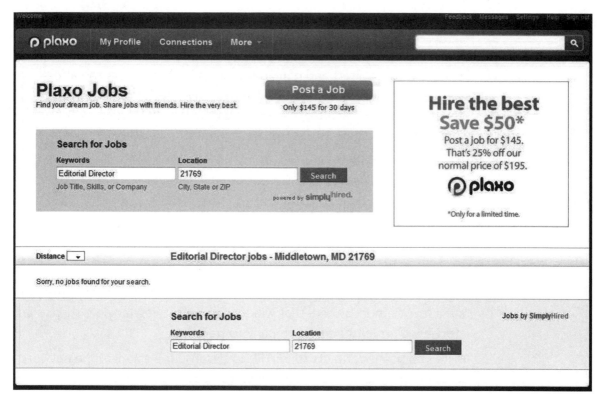

Figure 10-5: On Plaxo, you can search for job openings posted by Plaxo members, as well as those from the Simply Hired search engine.

PLAXO VERSUS LINKEDIN

As you know, LinkedIn also is great for building a business network, allowing you to cull contacts from e-mail address books and so on. So, for business networking, do you need to be on both Plaxo and LinkedIn? Well you don't *need* to be, and if it came down to using one service or the other, we'd opt for LinkedIn. However, with 30 million members, you're bound to find important contacts on Plaxo who are not on LinkedIn. Why miss a chance to connect with them?

Scott Testa, professor of marketing at St. Joseph's University in Philadelphia, advises that you use Plaxo to complement the rest of your networking and job-prospecting efforts. Certainly, when you're job hunting, you should use every tool at your disposal. So get on Plaxo, build a robust profile, and keep it up-to-date. Use the site to keep up with people when they move, change phone numbers, and so on.

Terry Seamon, an organizational trainer, uses Plaxo all the time, and although he feels that it "doesn't have the same suite of features as LinkedIn," it has his favorite feature: the ability to broadcast a message to his contacts via e-mail. "I can send out a quick message announcing my latest blog update or project," Terry said.

■ ■ In a LinkedIn World, Is Plaxo Irrelevant? Plaxo's Marketing Director Has the Answer

"I'm not trying to convince anyone that they need to come up with their own answer to the either/or question," says Plaxo Marketing Director John McCrea. "The Web is going social, and when we solve the interconnectivity issues, the number of people using the site will grow in leaps and bounds. LinkedIn is a great service, and it would be silly not to be on LinkedIn and also Plaxo. The thing that is fundamentally broken now is that there's no connectivity. When I connect with someone on LinkedIn, I end up getting access to their profile and their e-mail address. The magic for me is that when I take that e-mail address into Plaxo, if I get in touch with someone, I have full access to his business card, which includes his LinkedIn address and phone number. I can even get driving directions or pick up the phone to call him."

OTHER BUSINESS AND SOCIAL NETWORKING SITES

There are scores of social networking sites. So far, we've explored the most recognizable ones. They are all definitely worthy of a job hunter's time and effort. But what about the many other established social networking sites or even the new ones that seem to emerge every month? Let's explore some of the more prominent of those now. Then we'll close out by covering local networking sites and face-to-face opportunities for business networking.

The following sites each have their own flavor and appeal. As part of our descriptions, we'll include assessments from career and social networking expert Simon Stapleton, who writes the popular blog SimonStapleton.com.

▬ Ning (www.ning.com/)

Former Netscape Communications cofounder Marc Andreessen is one of Ning's founders, and for that reason alone, we felt that Ning, shown in Figure 10-6, was worth looking into. We encourage you to check it out, too.

Ning *hosts* networks; it is not a network itself. You can join the hundreds of thousands of networks already there or create your own. Creating your own network simply couldn't be easier. In fewer than two minutes, we had a bright, cheerful, fun social network of our own. Now, many of these networks, such as Quilt with Us or the Tyra Show, are not meant for helping you advance your career. But many others are.

Sign Up or Sign In / Popular Social Networks

Search networks

Create Your Own Social Network for Anything

Name Your Social Network

For example, Paris Cyclists

Pick a Web Address   .ning.com   **CREATE**

At least 6 letters. For example, pariscyclists.ning.com

Learn more about social networks on Ning

Ning Spotlight

Here are a few of the hundreds of thousands of social networks on Ning today...

7265 members

momlogic

Momlogic is the ultimate destination for Moms who want to know a little bit about a lot of things, but have very little time. *Created by Momlogic*

7185 members

PinoyCommunity.net

We are a site dedicated to bringing you—our Filipinos all over the world —the best of everything that is Filipino. *Created by Jun Osorio*

Figure 10-6: Ning provides a very simple way to create a colorful social network of your own.

Here are a few to get your gears going:

- Wirelessjobs.com
- OpenNetworkers.info
- Expertise for Hire
- Jobs in Social Media
- The Hospitality Career Network
- Indieproducer.net
- Classroom 2.0

There are many such niche networks on Ning, so your first step will be to see if your field of expertise or interest is already represented. Joining is as simple as providing your name and e-mail address, so there's really nothing to stop you. Your next step is to search the available networks using keywords that describe your field or even words such as "job postings." You're almost certain to find networks that interest you. If not, remember that you also can create your own network, and the help you need for doing is right on the site.

TIP

Simon Says

"What Ning is good at is content aggregation, and if your preferred job is in independent consulting or services where brand is important, then this is a good platform for showcasing your skills and experiences without needing to go down the blog route."

Ryze (http://ryze.com/)

In case there's any doubt what Ryze is about, you only need to look right under the company name on its Web site: *business networking.* Founded by Adrian Scott, a previous Napster investor and entrepreneur, Ryze, shown in Figure 10-7 appears similar to other social networks, but its simple, clean, and straightforward layout helps it to stand out from the crowd.

Like many of the other social networking sites discussed in this book, Ryze provides a home for people with common interests looking to network. The Ryze difference is its strict business emphasis. We like the fact too that by clicking on the Networks tab, you can see immediately which networks are most active and which have the greatest number of members.

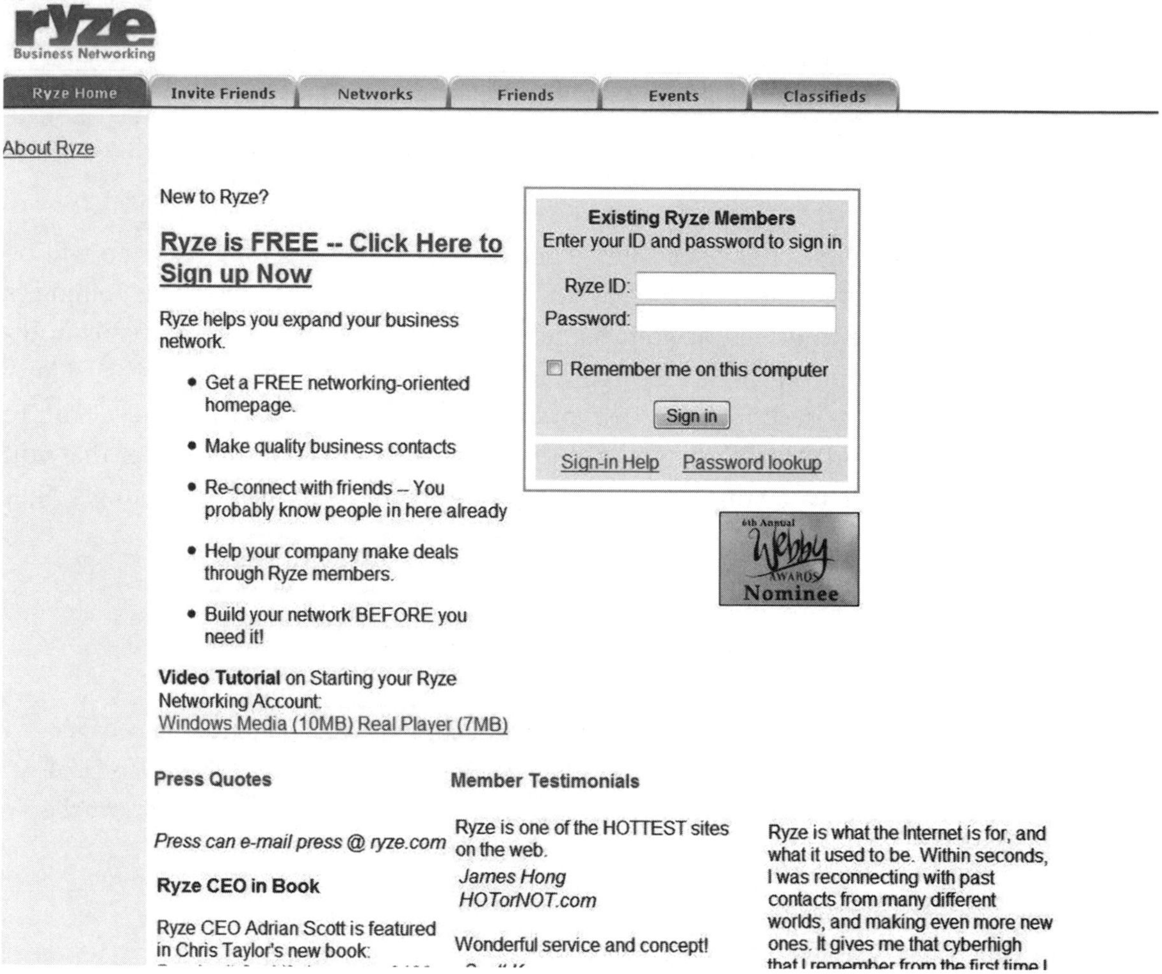

Business Networking

| Ryze Home | Invite Friends | Networks | Friends | Events | Classifieds |

About Ryze

New to Ryze?

Ryze is FREE -- Click Here to Sign up Now

Ryze helps you expand your business network.

- Get a FREE networking-oriented homepage.

- Make quality business contacts

- Re-connect with friends – You probably know people in here already

- Help your company make deals through Ryze members.

- Build your network BEFORE you need it!

Video Tutorial on Starting your Ryze Networking Account:
Windows Media (10MB) Real Player (7MB)

Existing Ryze Members
Enter your ID and password to sign in

Ryze ID:

Password:

☐ Remember me on this computer

Sign in

Sign-in Help   Password lookup

6th Annual
Webby
AWARDS
Nominee

Press Quotes

Press can e-mail press @ ryze.com

Ryze CEO in Book

Ryze CEO Adrian Scott is featured in Chris Taylor's new book:

Member Testimonials

Ryze is one of the HOTTEST sites on the web.
James Hong
HOTorNOT.com

Wonderful service and concept!

Ryze is what the Internet is for, and what it used to be. Within seconds, I was reconnecting with past contacts from many different worlds, and making even more new ones. It gives me that cyberhigh that I remember from the first time I

Figure 10-7: Ryze is a social network with a very strong sense of business.

Here are some examples of the networks with a home here:

- Small Business Think Tank

- Women in Networking

- Entrepreneurs

- Direct Selling

- China Business Forum

- Commercial Real Estate and Financial

- Human Resources: Recruiting, Hiring, and Staffing

Right now, there are more than 1,000 organizations hosting networks on the site. You'll want to take advantage of the Network Search feature as soon as you sign up. Also, as part of the sign-up process, Ryze steps you through filling out a form to create what it calls a "network-oriented homepage." Don't forget to include a photo on this network. The statistics directly from the company support how important this detail is. The average number of hits per page increases more than fourfold with the addition of a picture.

You may not have heard of Ryze, but don't let that keep you from trying it. People who use it are connecting with each other and finding new jobs and business opportunities as a result. It 500,000 members are spread throughout more 200 countries, so if you're looking to make international contacts, you shouldn't pass up this site.

TIP

Simon Says
"Ryze is much more of a bulletin board/forum and is easy to use and, in my opinion, is vastly underrated as a tool for job seeking. Ryze members have their tie off and top button open (maybe never had a tie on in the first place). What I like about it is its 'scroll-wheel-ability'—in other words you can scroll through a lot of information very easily. If you offer services in a niche, or you're looking for them, this is a great tool."

Xing (www.xing.com)

Xing, like Ryze, is for people who want to do business networking with others wherever they may be around the globe. It has more than 6 million members worldwide. Xing, shown in Figure 10-8, is a site with some LinkedIn-like features, so it should seem like familiar turf to you. For example, you can create a business profile for yourself on the site. There are also Groups, with more than 600 devoted to Jobs and Careers.

Help is easy to find, with FAQs, tours, and best practices to guide you. You can search for contacts by name, city, or industry. To get the most out of Xing, you'll want to sign up for the Premium service, which, for example, will give you the ability to search for members by a keyword of your choos-

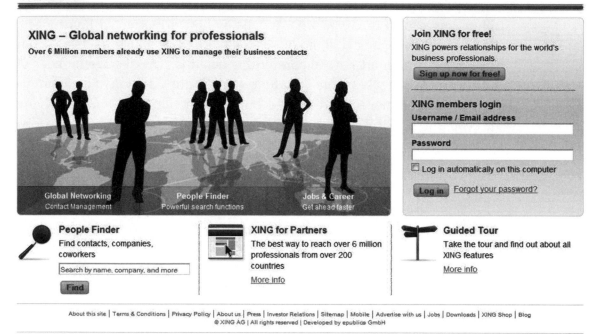

Figure 10-8: Xing brings a real international flare to social networking for business.

ing (see Figure 10-9 for details). Xing also has a marketplace for job seekers that includes job openings and the ability to use your network to find contacts at companies that interest you. You can sign up to try Xing's Premium membership ($6.50 per month) for 31 days a no charge.

How the Heck Do You Pronounce Xing?

What a great question! The answer is also quite interesting. According to Yee Wah Tsoi, junior manager of corporate communications, there really is no rule. "Our experience is that every linguistic and cultural area is pronouncing it differently," according to Yee. Here are just a few examples:

China: "Shing"   United State: "Crossing"
Spain: "Zing"   Australia: "Crossing"
Great Britain: "Sing"   Germany: "Ksing"

19,467 members online
+ Invite contacts 🖂 1 👤 0

Search [Search by name, company, and r] [Find]
Advanced Search | Powersearch | Address Book Comparison

👤 Start　　Search　　Messages　　Contacts　　Groups　　Events　　Marketplace　　BestOffers

My Start Page | My Profile | Settings | My Account

Benefits

Choose the best form of membership for you.
Here is a summary of benefits for each membership type.

Benefit	Premium Membership (Boost your career)	Basic Membership (Kickstart in Networking)
Invite people to join your network and accept contact invitations	✓	✓
Professional profile page: you decide who sees what information	✓	✓
No ads on your profile	✓	
Enter a status message on your profile (such as at a trade fair, not in the office)	✓	
Basic search: By first name, last name, city, university, interests, industry	✓	✓
Advanced Search: by company, position, wants, haves, etc.	✓	
Powersearch: Current and former colleagues, contacts who just had a birthday, and more ▾	✓	limited
See who just visited your profile	✓	
"What's new in my network" ticker: See all changes in your network	✓	limited
Send **private and secure messages** to members and contacts	✓	
Contacts: Efficiently manage your contacts	✓	✓
Organize and manage **public and private events** (basic members limited to 1 event/month with maximum 10 attendees)	✓	limited
Start or join a **XING group**, read and write articles	✓	✓
XING Marketplace: Read and create job postings (Make job offers available to Premium Members only; just 0.69 USD per click, including 10 free clicks worth a total of 6.90 USD per month)	✓	limited
Explore **XING BestOffers** and benefit from exclusive offers from our partners	✓	limited
Monthly cost	at € 4.95	Free

Figure 10-9: Details of Xing's Premium service.

"As you can see, the name Xing is quite striking," continued Yee. "It pays tribute to our international community with members from all over the world." And what exactly does it mean? "In Chinese, it means something like 'Can-do,'" explained Yee. "'It's possible' and 'You can reach your goal' are other choices, even 'Encounters.'" All of these sound good to us!

LOCAL AND FACE-TO-FACE NETWORKING

Networking is as old as humankind. Despite all the wonderful opportunities now available to reach out to like-minded people all over the world, eventually, it's to your advantage to push yourself away from your desk and go out among people. As we've mentioned, LinkedIn, for example, sponsors local networking events. There are also smaller business networking groups you can explore that cater to specific geographic regions, industries, or even ethnic groups!

The Web site Networking for Professionals (www.networkingforprofessionals.com/), shown in Figure 10-10, is a group that's quickly expanding from its New York City and tristate region roots to cities such as Atlanta and Los Angeles. Face-to-face business networking is the emphasis here.

The ICABA (which stands for Identifying, Connecting, Activating, the Black Accomplished), at www.icabaonline.com/, came into being in November 2008 in South Florida. It's specifically for black professionals and entrepreneurs who have reached a certain standing in their fields. The Web site's subheading is "Connecting the Accomplished." To join the ICABA, shown in Figure 10-11, you must be referred or invited by someone who is already a member.

A search on Google that combines "networking events" with your city or profession is bound to turn up some prospects for you. We found DC Tech Events this way, a group for "developers, tech professionals, and enthusiasts" at www.dctechevents.com/. It hosts breakfasts, presentations, trade shows,

Figure 10-10: Networking for Professionals is a New York–based group currently branching out to other U.S. cities. You'll find face-to-face networking opportunities here.

and a variety of other events sure to entice even the most agoraphobic among us to venture out and connect.

There are always the old-school standbys, such as the local Chamber of Commerce and the Rotary Club. Check your local newspaper's business section for notices about groups in your area that are scheduling events.

Figure 10-11: The homepage for the ICABA, a Web site for connecting successful and accomplished black professionals.

LOOKING AHEAD

Well, this time, that's all up to you! As we write this, social networking sites are blossoming with all the grandeur of spring, even though the calendar and our heating bills remind us that it's really the dead of winter. The world of social networking is here to stay, and as businesses and professionals learn to depend on them even more, the number of new sites and opportunities will continue to grow. The rate of that growth is clearly accelerating. This may be due to a multiplier effect, meaning that as more people join these groups, those people reach out to reel in even more members. And in the world of face-to-face networking, some events are so popular that they've had to turn people away.

We hope that you feel ready now to harness the power of social networking for job hunting and professional enrichment. We're confident that you'll find several online networking homes for yourself that will reward you with new contacts, new business, and new employment prospects. Give yourself some time to learn the lay of the land, and then get in there and make yourself known! You never know where the social networking journey will take you, but we wish you every continued success.

INDEX

ABOUT THE AUTHORS

Brad and Debra Schepp are the authors of 19 books that help nontechnical people make the best use of emergent technologies. Their areas of focus include e-commerce, telecommuting, and social media and social networking for business purposes. They were early pioneers in the fields of both green energy and telecommuting, publishing among the first books on those topics. The couple has focused on practical guides to help people best use these tools without over-hyping their potential. Among their best-selling titles is, *eBay PowerSeller Secrets* (McGraw-Hill, 2004), which through two editions has sold more than 35,000 copies. Their other most recent books include *Amazon Top Seller Secrets* and *How to Make Money with YouTube*. Brad and Deb are widely recognized as e-commerce experts not only through their books, but also through their columns for AuctionBytes and Auctiva (providers of leading e-commerce software). Brad and Deb have also conducted seminars about selling on eBay, and have been interviewed many times by national media including *LIFE Magazine*, *Good Housekeeping*, and *Entrepreneur* magazine. They have appeared on many radio shows, and on the television show *Retired and Wired* (even though they are only one of those things).